I0831815

THE EMERALD ECLIPSE

Book Two of The Crystal Halls

Thomas K. Carpenter

The Emerald Eclipse

Book Two of The Crystal Halls

Hardcover Version

by Thomas K. Carpenter

Published by Black Moon Books

Cover design by
G&S Cover Designs

Discover other titles by this author on:
www.thomaskcarpenter.com

ISBN-13: 978-1-958498-19-4

THE CRYSTAL HALLS
Shadows in Amber
The Emerald Eclipse
The Sapphire Stratagem
Chains of Obsidian
The Bloodstone Rebellion

The Hundred Halls Universe
SEASON ONE

THE HUNDRED HALLS
Trials of Magic
Web of Lies
Alchemy of Souls
Gathering of Shadows
City of Sorcery

THE RELUCTANT ASSASSIN
The Reluctant Assassin
The Sorcerous Spy
The Veiled Diplomat
Agent Unraveled
The Webs That Bind

GAMEMAKERS ONLINE
The Warped Forest
Gladiators of Warsong
Citadel of Broken Dreams
Enter the Daemonpits
Plane of Twilight

ANIMALIANS HALL
Wild Magic
Bane of the Hunter
Mark of the Phoenix
Arcane Mutations
Untamed Destiny

STONE SINGERS HALL
Song of Siren and Blood
House of Snake and Tome
Storm of Dragon and Stone
Sonata of Shadow and Thorn
Well of Demon and Bone

THE ORDER OF MERLIN
The Order of Merlin
Infernal Alliances
Tower of Horn and Blood

Other Series:

The Dashkova Memoirs
Revolutionary Magic
A Cauldron of Secrets
Birds of Prophecy
The Franklin Deception
Nightfell Games
The Queen of Dreams
Dragons of Siberia
Shadows of an Empire

The Kingmaker Saga
The Stone Tree
The Crystal Bard
The Ghost Tower
The Champion's Prophecy
The Shadow Labyrinth
The Autumn Empire

The Alexandrian Saga
Fires of Alexandria
Heirs of Alexandria
Legacy of Alexandria
Warmachines of Alexandria
Empire of Alexandria
Voyage of Alexandria
Goddess of Alexandria

THE EMERALD ECLIPSE

Foreword
"Or What Came Before"

Some readers asked me to add "The story so far" section to the beginning of my books much as they do for TV shows to remind you what you may have forgotten. I thought it was a great idea, so I'll be doing that going forward!

In the first book, Shadows in Amber, we meet Kuma Santos, son of Niran Santos, the head of Razor clan which is considered the largest and best run clan in the Undercity. He is anxious about his upcoming entrance to the Academy where he will have a chance to attune to a faez crystal. After a rough start, he manages to attune to an amber stone, which enhances his senses and starts his journey to becoming a great waku.

We also meet Pandora, a spy sent to the Undercity to infiltrate the clans. She manages to secure an invite to the Drops, the rival to Razor clan, and earns a sapphire stone which is considered one of the most powerful faez crystals available.

During the course of the year, Kuma and Pandora meet, finding themselves drawn to each other despite the forbidden nature of their relationship. The two clans aren't at war, but it's assumed that the peace could end at any moment. Making things more complicated is the rise of the Alliance, which is a grouping of smaller clans who've come together creating a three-way standoff in the Undercity. During a festival in the Terreno, Kuma and Pandora are forced into a duel which Kuma wins, sparing her life, despite the impact to his honor and his clan.

One

The grand emptiness above Kuma threatened to crush him. It was night in the city. The skyscrapers glittered like jewels, extending impossible distances above, as if they were crystals grown from the earth. He gaped at the sky from the comfort of the shadows.

"Too much for you, grounder?"

The guy speaking to Kuma wore an oversized puffy orange jacket with the tip of an automatic weapon sticking from the front. He wore a few pounds of silver around his neck, and his eyebrows had vertical lines shaved into them.

Kuma girded himself. Walking in the city was no different than being in Big Dave's Town or the Terreno. The only variation was that there was no protective layer of rock above his head. He had to remind himself that he wouldn't go flinging into the air, untethered from gravity if he stepped out of the archway.

"Been a while is all."

Two members of his clan came out behind him, stumbling into the street, laughing about some private joke.

"Little Bear," said Xylos, jutting his chin.

"Hey, Xylos. Adrena."

They both wore black clothes like him, but Adrenalynne wore a dark skullcap as well to hide the neon tattoos she'd gotten on the side of her shaved head. They glowed like miniature theater marquees. She could change the color or words by typing into her phone, a techno-enchantment she'd bought from a failed member of Cybermagics.

"What are we waiting for, Deacon?"

The guy in the puffy orange coat nodded towards the street. "For our ride to arrive."

As soon as he finished speaking, two black SUVs showed up. The three Razor clan members climbed into the back of the second. Deacon jumped into the passenger seat next to the driver and plugged his phone into the stereo. Moments later a thumping bass was followed by noises that sounded vaguely like screams and EDM beats.

Being in the back of the car was more comforting than standing outside. Kuma hoped that he wouldn't have to be in the open too much. He gestured to Adrenalynne in the silent speech of the Undercity, a place that rewarded silence with a longer life.

Can we trust them?

Adrenalynne rolled her eyes. She tapped on her tragus implant where her faez crystal was located. Kuma took the hint and tuned his amber to hear. When she spoke subvocally, the words barely coming out as a whisper, he heard her as if they were speaking normally.

"Does it matter? Your father sent us," said Adrenalynne.

"I thought you were in the city all the time?" he asked.

"Never run with the Black Crows before. They've given us intel, and we run goods through them sometimes, but never a joint mission."

Kuma frowned. "They don't look honorable."

"They're not, but if your father wants allies, they're one of the bigger gangs in the city. It's not like we have a lot of options right now."

The rebuke from Adrenalynne hurt, but he couldn't argue. The balance of power in the Undercity had shifted towards the upstart alliance clans in the northwest since they'd been finding unique stones like the black diamond that provided steelskin. If Razor couldn't find their own new stones, they could easily get overrun. The potential alliance with Black Crows was meant to provide much-needed manpower in exchange for faez crystals. His father had agreed to provide them with half a dozen ambers, an emerald, and an opal in exchange for their support. Kuma hated the idea that they were giving up stones to non-clan members, but his father had explained that these were extra. Nearly everyone that could have attuned to them had already been given a chance, and once they had the manpower, they'd be able to find new and more interesting stones. This job was meant as a gift to their new partnership.

Kuma caught Deacon watching them through the rearview mirror. The signal for "being watched" ended their conversation. Kuma spent the time staring out the window at the lights. It felt like the first time he'd used his amber, when the world was so overwhelming he was lost to the sensations. He was so busy focusing on the lights of the passing cars that when an enormous demon with a sword made of flame rose over a building, he exclaimed and shoved himself into the back seat.

Deacon immediately busted up laughing, slapping his leg and hitting the driver as he pointed above the nearby apartment buildings.

"I knew you'd never been in the city before," said Deacon, laughing as he looked over his shoulder.

Neither Xylos nor Adrenalynne had reacted to the appearance, and Kuma realized it was a trick.

"We're passing the second ward," said Deacon. "They make all sorts of crazy illusions near the Glitterdome. Fucking rich, man, seeing your face. You looked almost as bad as when you first stepped outside."

Kuma started to reach forward to grab Deacon by the throat, but

Adrenalynne stopped his hand. She shook her head covertly.

"It has been a long time," said Kuma, grinding his teeth. It'd been years. Since his mother was alive. They'd come up to the city during a rainy night on a whim when they'd been in Big Dave's Town. The storm had made it seem less expansive and they'd stayed under the awnings along the street, splashing through puddles and marveling at the cars speeding past.

A few times as they drove, Deacon rolled down the window and brandished his automatic weapon at groups of women on the sidewalk. He whistled and asked them if they wanted to suck on his metal dick.

Kuma was regretting asking to be involved with the raid. He'd wanted to show the clan that he could be useful. Since the duel last year when he'd offered to let Pandora yield rather than killing her, they'd treated him distantly. Second-year Academy waku usually didn't go on city jobs, but since he had two stones and the clan was stretched thin, they'd accepted his offer.

About a half hour after they left the Goblin's Romp, Deacon turned down the music. His dirty blond hair and gaunt pale skin made him seem like a ghoul as he grinned into the back seat.

"We near the eleventh. A warehouse we're gonna hit. It's got a small army of plastic badges on site, but that shouldn't be a problem for you wonderkin."

"It's waku," said Kuma. "What are plastic badges?"

"Rent-a-cops. Hired security. Good for keeping skater kids from pissing on your brick wall, but they won't stop us. 'Specially not with you three."

Adrenalynne leaned forward. "I thought we were hitting an unguarded warehouse."

Deacon sucked on his teeth with a bored look. "What would be the fun of that? We don't need waku for hitting a place like that, and our boss wanted to know this stone shit ain't no trick."

"Are you saying we're lying about our stones?" asked Kuma as he made himself Heavy. The SUV groaned as the shocks sunk down with the added three tons. The driver made an exclamation and glanced over his shoulder. Kuma switched back to his normal weight.

"Look," said Deacon. "I believe you and all that, but people be selling fakes for big jack. The boss gotta know what Razor is offering is real."

"But this isn't the job we agreed on," said Adrenalynne.

Deacon shot them a wink. "I'm sure you'll do fine."

The SUV pulled into a gravel lot behind a convenience store. Between the two vehicles, they had five Black Crows and the three Razor. The drivers would stay and monitor the streets and the police channels. One of the Black Crows was carrying a heavy duffle bag that sagged under its own weight.

"Once we start we got nine minutes to do the job before we'll have to shoot our way out."

"How do you know that?"

Deacon leaned away with a smirk. "You think we runnin' blind up here? We triggered the alarms a few weeks ago just to see how long it take."

Without waiting to see if they had further questions, Deacon headed the opposite way, behind the row of businesses. He reached a fire scaffold and started climbing. As more Black Crows went up, the entire structure rattled and a few lights came on in the apartment building.

"I don't like this," said Kuma.

"Neither do I," said Adrenalynne as she put her foot on the bottom rung. "But unless you're calling it, I think we gotta keep going forward."

Xylos shrugged as he went after Adrenalynne. "I've been on worse jobs."

After reaching the roof, they made their way until they reached the end of the apartment buildings. A gap of ten feet between them and the warehouse was blocked by a barbed wire fence at the top on the opposite side.

"You can see why we need you," said Deacon, gesturing at the fence. He scrunched up his face as he looked at them. "Which one of you is the emerald? You can make it over, right?"

Kuma sighed. "What do I do when I'm over there?"

Deacon handed him wire snips. "You'll understand once you've cut a hole in the fence." He shifted his mouth to the side. "Probably want to make sure it's not electrified first."

"You can jump that?" asked Xylos with an eyebrow raised.

"Yeah."

Kuma moved back a ways, checking his blades to make sure they were safely tucked away. He had a small pistol inside his jacket, but he was hoping he wouldn't have to use it. As he readied himself for the jump, he remembered the endless sky above him. The idea that he was about to make himself light as a puff of air brought a wave of fear that he would make the leap and rather than arc over the fence, soar up and outward, until he was swept into the clouds. Forever lost to the night sky.

"What are you waiting for?" yelled Deacon with his arms raised.

Spurred by the comment, Kuma sprinted forward, cycling himself to Lightness as he hit the edge of the roof. He slammed his foot down, propelling himself upward. In the caverns of the Undercity, jumps like this made him feel powerful, but crossing the gap that went down four stories to the street level had him feeling powerless. He cycled his feet as if that would help him move faster. The soles of his shoes barely drifted over the barbed wire fence. He landed softly, not a sound generated, waiting until after he'd hit to cycle to Heavy.

Using the back of his hand, he brushed the fence to find that it wasn't electrified. Then he used the snips to cut a hole through the fence. Once he was finished, he saw what the Black Crows had in the duffle bag.

It was a portable aluminum bridge. They threw him a rope, and once he had it, he pulled one end to his side and everyone crossed on their hands and knees.

Deacon slapped him on the back. "That was some fade-ass flying you did back there. Wasn't sure you'd ever come down."

"Me neither," said Kuma.

Deacon led them to an exit building at the center of the warehouse roof.

"Once we blow through this door, we're on a timer. Most of security is on the perimeter. That'll give us time to reach the goods."

One of the Black Crows pulled out a small charge of explosives, but Adrenalynne waved him off. She gripped the door handle and gave it a tug, using her topaz strength to snap the inner locks. The door swung open at the same time alarms blared into existence.

"Nice," said Deacon as he ran past Adrenalynne, headed into the stairwell.

Xylos shrugged and followed. Adrenalynne pushed Kuma forward, touching her tragus as a reminder to tune his amber. As soon as he did he grimaced at the clatter of the alarms. It sounded like a bell was being rung directly in his ear. About the time he was halfway down the stairs, the pulse of an automatic weapon sounded at the bottom. Kuma found the reason for the gunfire when he passed a dead security guard surrounded by a pool of blood.

It wasn't that his clan hadn't killed their fair share of people over the years, but it was usually a last resort when things went wrong, not a main facet to their jobs. Violence begets violence, his father had always instructed. The more of it you put out there, the more that comes back. The last thing they wanted to do was rouse the Invictus PD to investigate the clan. And once you've moved to strike, it left you vulnerable to counterattacks. Kuma was feeling mightily exposed as they ran across the packed warehouse.

The space was filled with shipping boxes and barrels, wrapped and stacked on pallets for easy transport. A worker on a fork truck dove off his vehicle, letting it crash into a steel girder when Deacon squeezed a round over his head.

They reached an inner building that had a G&T logo on the door. Deacon gestured towards Adrenalynne. She stepped forward and kicked the door open. The rest of the Black Crows and Xylos stayed on the outside, while Kuma and Adrenalynne followed Deacon into the building. He moved through the narrow, zigzagging hallways as if he knew the place. They passed shuttered offices that would probably be filled with workers during the day.

Deacon stopped at a door with no windows that had a security panel on the outside. When Adrenalynne moved up to open it, he waved her off and pulled a round puck from an inner pocket and set it next to the electronics. His arrogant demeanor turned reticent as he placed the puck near the security panel and pressed a button on the outside. A pair of crossed fingers told Kuma that they might have come all this way for nothing.

"How long is this gonna take?" asked Adrenalynne.

"A minute tops. It's the best cracker hardware money can't buy," said Deacon.

While they waited for the door to be opened, Kuma walked to the next corner to have eyes on the cross-hallway. The constant alarms had meant he'd kept his amber off, so he didn't hear the guard coming around the corner until he nearly ran into him.

Kuma kicked the barrel of the guard's gun, sending bullets into the concrete wall. He stepped past the length of the weapon, bringing a stiffened hand into the guard's throat, which made him drop the rifle. An open-hand slap to his forehead with a touch of Heavy knocked him out. Kuma slid the weapon back towards the other two, and Deacon mimed clapping.

"Impressive. So it's more than the stones."

Kuma straightened his jacket and came back to the door as the puck lit up green.

"Let's party," said Deacon, pushing into the room.

The interior was no bigger than a bank vault. The cooled interior was lined with smaller refrigerators. Each one glowed with inner lighting. Labels with strange names like "Lion Heart Basilisk" or "Purple People Eater" were affixed to the front.

Deacon yanked a duffle bag out of his puffy orange jacket. He searched for a particular name and opened the refrigerators, pulling out small boxes of vials and shoving them into the bag.

"Take some if you want," he said with a wink.

"What are these?"

"Special brews that you can't find anywhere else. The latest and greatest of alchemical genius, even better than what you can get in the D'Agastine labs with a fistful of cash. Time to blow!"

They followed Deacon out of the room to the sounds of gunfire.

The rest of the Black Crows were trading fire with the security team. Xylos had his hands on the shoulder of one of the Black Crows, healing a gunshot wound while the guy grimaced.

Deacon pulled three pucks from his jacket, winked at Kuma, and flung the first two across the smooth concrete. White gases emanated from the pucks, obfuscating their retreat path. He lobbed the third one a moment later and motioned to cover ears.

A concussive blow sent the white smoke swirling, giving them an opportunity to run across the warehouse to the stairwell. As they hurried up, Deacon said, "Six minutes, doing great."

The others ran across the aluminum bridge, shaking it thunderously. Sirens approached the warehouse from a distance. Kuma could see the red and blue lights bouncing off the nearby apartment buildings. When he crossed the bridge last, right behind Adrenalynne, a trio of police vehicles sped beneath. He thought they'd made it over without being spotted until the last car skidded to the side. Officers leapt out, immediately firing their weapons.

Reflexively ducking tipped the bridge off its anchors. Adrenalynne leapt at the last moment, grabbing the edge of the opposite building. But Kuma was only halfway across, and as he cycled to Lightness to make the jump, the bridge fell beneath him. Without a solid structure to push off, he fell four stories, maintaining his Lightness until he hit the ground.

The two officers who had fired on the bridge weren't paying attention to him as they'd probably assumed he would die from the fall. Additionally, Deacon and the others were firing on their position, ripping up the police car with automatic fire.

Presented with the side of the vehicle, Kuma ran for it, cycling to Heavy before impact. He knocked the police car sideways, throwing both officers onto their backs, and climbed over with Lightness then knocked them both out before they could gain their bearings.

Kuma sprinted around the apartment buildings wishing he was a topaz for speed, but no one from the security crew spotted him. He raced past a trio of kids outside the convenience store on their skateboards, practicing tricks in the parking lot. He leapt over one with Lightness on his way to the open door of the SUV where Deacon and the others were waiting.

They sped away as the door slammed shut. Everyone was checking their six to make sure they hadn't been spotted. It wasn't until they were headed into the third ward that everyone collectively relaxed. Deacon gave a top-of-the-lungs whoop and bounced back into the seat. He grinned into the back seat.

"That was some fade-ass shit back there. Thought you were a goner when the bridge fell, and damn that was impressive, watching you knock that pig wagon back."

Kuma grinned back despite himself. With his body flooded with adrenaline, he wanted to take off running for a few blocks, or leap on top of a building.

Xylos gave him the sign for good job, which was a fist tapped twice to the chest. Kuma could barely sit still enough to return the gesture.

As they drove through the city, he realized his earlier fear of the open skies had been washed away, and he found himself staring at the tops of the buildings, wondering what it would feel like to live in the sky. He was pretty sure that kind of life wasn't for him, but it was interesting to consider. He thought the city folk would probably have the same reluctance to live where he did.

When they returned to the Goblin's Romp, Kuma's leg was no longer bouncing and his shoulder started to ache from slamming it into the cop car. They climbed out along with Deacon, who gave them handshakes and shoulder bumps.

"Good heist, man. Good heist. I'm sure we be working together again after the boss hears about tonight."

"Next time it'll be in the shadows," said Adrenalynne grimly.

"I ain't afraid," said Deacon as he climbed back into the passenger seat.

The two SUVs sped away, leaving them standing outside the Goblin's Romp back entrance. Xylos jabbed his thumb towards the inside.

"I ain't ready to go back down. Anyone want to grab a few Pale Paws and a game of Runic Risk?"

"Count me in," said Adrenalynne as she punched Xylos in the arm, then pushed him towards the door. "Kuma?"

He sighed and stared at the glittering night sky. "I'll be along in a minute. Need to wind down."

Once he was alone, Kuma walked away from the safety of the brick wall until he had a good view of the Spire at the center of the city. Staring at the enormous tower, twice the height of the nearest building, made his neck hurt from craning it so far back. He lasted for a few minutes, until standing in the open made him feel like he was going to be attacked and he headed inside where he could relax with his clanmates after a successful job.

Two

The dig site sat at the bottom of a deep bowl, illuminated by glow lanterns hung on poles. The sound of water splashing from a stream that ran through the center was barely audible above the twin generators echoing through the cavern.

Pandora leaned on her elbows between Choo-Choo and Navos. She held up four fingers, signaling the number of Eights clan members she saw clustered around the hole, then pointed to a secondary dome of light at the far end of the cavern and held up two more fingers. Along with the four workers they assumed were deep in the hole by the number of oxygen lines running down, the excavation crew numbered ten. The three Drops clan members slid back down the rise.

"Fucking Eights," whispered Choo-Choo angrily. "This is our territory."

"We should go back and get more and show them the price of stealing our stones," said Navos, equally heated.

"By the time we get back, they'll be gone. It's the same as the others," said Pandora.

For the last few months, dig sites had been found inside their territory in the region that bordered the alliance clans to the north. They'd find abandoned holes with empty oxygen tanks and litter from their meals. The clans wouldn't stay longer than eight hours, which wasn't enough time for patrols to return to the Pajot for additional numbers. Talk of increasing the size and quantity of patrols had been shot down, since the Drops were already struggling to protect their own dig sites in the disputed region between them and Razor. The Drops had the largest population amongst the clans, but too many of their number were noncombatants, tied up farming the terraces for food and drugs.

"I hate this," said Choo-Choo. "We're getting picked apart at the edges and the only thing we're mining are ambers, the occasional topaz, and those null stones that only the mages can use."

"We can take them," said Pandora.

"You're kidding, right?" asked Choo-Choo.

"We have two sapphires and they won't know we're coming. They think they have the entrance covered, but didn't realize there was a separate entrance through the ceiling. If we don't start taking chances, they will pick us apart, and once one of the clans gets a stone superiority, it's game over for the rest."

Their silence was made from the bones of the clan's failures. After Shade's End, the incidents between the clans had been more frequent, and recently they'd heard that Demon Dogs had found more black diamonds. While some thought it was only rumor, designed to encourage mistakes, the clan leadership had taken it seriously. While they still trained at the Academy, half their time was spent on patrols or other important clan business.

"What about the peace?" asked Navos.

"Fuck the peace," said Choo-Choo, pounding his fist into an open palm. "I say yes, but I'm only an amber. You two are going to have to do the heavy lifting."

"We need all three of us," said Pandora. "And as far as the peace, these Eights are in Drops territory. We have the right to defend ourselves. No one would rule against us."

"Assuming we lived to tell the tale. It's six against three, and two of them have automatic rifles," said Navos.

Choo-Choo pulled out a pistol from his inside vest pocket. The cavern was warm and he had a patina of sweat across his chest.

"I have this, but once we get in a shooting war, we're outgunned."

"Guns aren't going to win this. Not at first anyway. We have to get close enough that they can't afford to use them or risk killing their own," said Pandora.

"Okay, theoretically, if we did this, do we take out the four or two first?" asked Choo-Choo, running a hand over his slick bald head.

"The four," said Pandora. "Once we take them out, we'll have numbers on the other two and their workers as hostage."

Navos screwed up his mouth as he glanced in the direction of the lights. "Are you sure we can do this? You're not trying to make up for the duel, are you?"

"Of course I'm trying to make up for that," said Pandora, looking away angrily. "No one trusts me. I worked so hard to be accepted and then he took that away when he offered yield."

"Would you have preferred he cut your throat?" asked Choo-Choo.

"I would have preferred to win," said Pandora. "He surprised me when he leapt through the stalactites, but I should have seen it coming."

"Was an epic duel," said Choo-Choo, nodding. "And I appreciate you not killing him before I could."

Pandora rolled her eyes. "Thanks, asshole." She tossed a pebble between their feet. "But this isn't just about me. We all know things are going sideways. Someone's backing the alliance clans, giving them money and more weapons and people, shifting the power in their favor. Razor's not sitting on their hands either."

"Would have never expected them to bring in a city gang," said Navos, shaking his head.

"Which means we need to start taking chances if we're going to survive," said Pandora.

"You know I'm in."

Choo-Choo leaned his head towards Navos, who knocked the swath of blond hair from his face before nodding with a single shoulder shrug.

"If you think we should."

Pandora crawled up to the edge. It was more than the Drops' future at stake—it was her own. Since the duel, she feared her mother's superiors no longer viewed her as useful, and if she ever turned into a liability, a simple leaked bit of information would leave her at the end of Duro's knife, or dropped into a deep, dark hole.

"What's the plan?" asked Navos as he knocked his bleach blond hair out of his eyes.

She reached out with her sapphire. The dig site was about eighty feet from their location, right at the edge of where she could feel with her stone.

"The weapon is new. I can't touch it."

"If you can't, then I certainly can't," said Navos.

"We have to get there fast or we're dead meat," said Choo-Choo.

"And there's the question of their stones. Any clues to what they have?" asked Pandora.

Choo-Choo extended a finger towards the Eights clan member standing on a ridge on the opposite side of the excavation hole.

"I'd bet Navos' sapphire she's an amber the way she's kinda spacey and distant. A strong one. A Hawk."

Pandora nodded. She'd thought the same thing but wanted confirmation from her friends.

"The guy with the gun might just be a soldado. Would be overkill to send six waku for one dig site," said Navos. "I can't imagine the Eights have that many waku to spare."

"Fair point," said Pandora. "You think you can take the guy with the gun with your pistol?"

"I thought you didn't want to get into a firefight."

"I don't, but we need him out of the way. I figure Navos and I can Pull ourselves down to their location and once they spot us, you can take out the gun. Once he's out, we should be able to clean up the rest, two sapphires against an amber and two others. If we're quick, then the two at the entrance won't have a choice but to flee."

"Not worried about survivors?" asked Choo-Choo.

"This is our territory, we have a right to defend it. You good?"

Navos screwed up his mouth. "Better plan than I could come up with."

Pandora gestured to their left. "You should come at him from a different angle in case Choo-Choo doesn't take him out. That way he can only get one of us before we get close enough for our sapphires."

Navos nodded and began moving along the ridge towards the location she'd suggested. Once he was away, Choo-Choo frowned at her.

"You're trying to protect me, keep me up here in case things go wrong."

"Now why would I do that?"

Choo-Choo stared at the ground. "For the same reason you keep bringing Vasy and my mami gifts."

"I like them."

"They like you." Choo-Choo cocked a grin. "You know my mami keeps asking if you're my girlfriend."

Pandora nodded towards Navos. "Not going to tell her?"

"Like all mothers, she wants kids."

"Not mine."

Choo-Choo tilted his head. "You never talk about her, or your dad."

"For good reason. Navos is in position. You ready?"

He held up the pistol. "You know I'm a terrible shot."

"Just don't hit me," she said as she crouched at the edge of the ridge and pulled out her twin blades.

Pandora gave Navos the signal as she leapt from the edge, using her sapphire to tug on the ceiling, propelling herself forward then Pushing as she neared the ground. The Hawk sensed them immediately, crying out an alarm, but it took the guy with the gun a moment to orient towards them. He hesitated between her and the rapidly approaching Navos, which was enough distraction. A single shot from Choo-Choo knocked the guy with the rifle over a pile of equipment, the weapon tumbling from his hands.

As she arced towards the excavation site, Pandora swiped out her hand, knocking over the glow lights and shattering all but one of the bulbs, leaving the area cast in shadows and dimness. Landing near the oxygen tanks, Pandora had to defend herself as the Eights with a long spear leapt after her. She tried to knock him back with a strong Push, but he jammed his metal spear into the ground, halting his movement.

Topaz.

And he was used to fighting sapphires.

He leaned down, clicked something on his boots, and approached with his weapon extended forward. It had more reach than her short blades. She tried to knock him back when he thrust with his spear, but his feet didn't move and he brought the bladed tip around, forcing her to bend backwards to avoid getting her throat slashed.

Before he could bring it back around, she Pulled herself backwards, out of his range. The purpose of his boots became clear. They anchored his feet to the ground, making her sapphire less useful. Pandora leapt back in, focusing on disrupting his spear rather than the warrior, but he was a topaz and his strength made him hard to counter.

She attacked the shaft of the spear, but gave up when she realized the entire thing was made of steel. Normally, an entirely metal weapon would be too heavy to wield effectively, but his topaz overcame the limitations. Their blows came fast and furious, her blades ringing sparks against his spear. She Pushed and Pulled on his arms, disrupting his attack, but he was too strong to nullify.

Pandora caught the approach of the other two Eights running furiously their way. If she didn't kill the Topaz soon, she'd be outnumbered. Distracted by their advance, the Topaz made a leaping advance, his spear thrusting towards her heart. She was too slow for the block.

A blast exploded in her ear and the Topaz went down hard with a hole in his chest. Choo-Choo nodded to her as he aimed at the approaching guards, firing at a steady clip and forcing them to dive to the ground.

To her left, Navos was wiping his blades on his pant legs. Two lifeless bodies were strewn near his feet. Without a way to counter his sapphire, they'd been easy targets.

Pandora was reaching out to the two guards on the cavern floor with her sapphire, checking if the weapon had been in the Undercity long enough to make it vulnerable, when she heard Choo-Choo yell to take cover. She barely dove to the ground before a figure appeared from behind the pile of equipment, spraying bullets in an arc.

The first waku that Choo-Choo had shot appeared to be unharmed. Before he could fire, the pistol flew out of Choo-Choo's hand and tumbled past the Eights Sapphire.

Pandora grabbed the spear from the fallen Topaz, and when the Sapphire turned to fire at Navos, who was sprinting behind a rocky outcropping, she threw the weapon. He never saw it coming. It hit him in the side and she was about to pump her fist in victory until she realized the spear had bounced off his flesh.

"Oh fuck," exclaimed Choo-Choo from her right.

He was both a Sapphire *and* a Black Diamond. With a gun. Pandora checked behind them, but it was too far to the ridge. They'd get mowed down before they reached its safety. With nowhere to go but forward, she leapt upward, using the ceiling to Pull herself high, then again towards the Sapphire.

The barrel of the rifle almost made it around when she landed, putting her shoulder into his chest. It felt like slamming into a brick wall. He fell from her overwhelming momentum, but she'd taken the brunt of the impact against his steelskin.

She abandoned her blades and fought for the rifle, but he kneed her in the gut. With her hands on the barrel, she lobbed it away, knowing that he couldn't touch it with his sapphire either.

The scramble had given the two guards a chance to advance again. When the one with the rifle lifted it to fire, she Pushed, knocking them down like bowling pins. But the distraction gave her opponent a chance to grab her around the neck. She couldn't Push him away, because he was Pulling her towards him. His strength was equal to hers.

His iron grip was crushing her larynx. Pandora pounded on his arms, but he'd locked them in place with the steelskin. Spots were rapidly forming in her vision. Choo-Choo tried to come to her rescue, but was knocked away with a Push.

A trio of gunshots had her worried that her friends had been hit, but she saw Navos running towards her with Choo-Choo's pistol in his hand. When the last Eights member tried to Push him away, Navos countered with a Pull. When he reached them, he fired two bullets into the side of the Eights member, but they deflected off his steelskin, one of the bullet fragments impacting into her hip.

The world started to fade away. She couldn't break his grip, and he was impervious to their weapons. As the spots in her vision were connecting, Navos leaned into view, forced the barrel of the pistol into the Eights' mouth, and pulled the trigger.

The explosion threw his head back, splattering warm dark blood on the ground. The Eights member vacantly stared at the ceiling.

"No steelskin in there," said Navos.

The stranglehold released, allowing Pandora to fall away, sucking in precious air. While she coughed painfully, the staccato of gunfire erupted over her head.

By the time she recovered, the workers in the hole had climbed out and there were no living Eights waku. Choo-Choo was busy binding the workers' hands and shaking them down for stones. He held up a small leather bag when he noticed Pandora had sat up.

Pandora grabbed a water bottle sitting near the hole and drained it in an attempt to soothe her throat. Her hand touched blood at her hip, but after pulling down the loose pants, she found the wound was superficial and would close on its own.

"How's the haul?"

Choo-Choo shrugged. "Dozens of stones, but no idea if they're useable. Some weird colors, but I think that's normal. Ol' Gaunt will have to figure it out."

Pandora rubbed her throat while she nodded. The Drops employed a Hall mage for interfacing with the magical world. Luscious Gaunt, in addition to his regular duties, had become their expert on the identification and use of faez crystals.

"What about the waku stones?"

"Navos grabbed them," said Choo-Choo, wagging his eyebrows. "Clan leadership will be beside themselves over the black diamond, even if there's nothing from the pit."

Behind them, Navos was pacing near the kneeling workers. Their hands and mouths were bound and they looked terrified. Navos had the pistol in his fist as he mumbled.

When she met his gaze, he said, "We can't let them go back, right?"

Pandora pulled herself to her feet tenderly. She was joined by Choo-

Choo as they approached Navos. His hands were covered in blood and his face had splatters across the jaw and forehead.

"Nav?" asked Choo-Choo.

The anguish in Navos' eyes was palpable.

"This was your first fight, wasn't it?" asked Pandora.

Navos swallowed and looked away. "It's never come around. I've always been on the patrols or guard duty when nothing happened. Until now."

"The first one is never easy."

"First?" he shot back. "I killed four. They almost killed me."

Choo-Choo approached Navos with his arms out. "You did great, Nav. But now it's over. You can relax."

Navos gestured wildly with the pistol in his hand. "But what about them?"

"Let us decide," said Choo-Choo, gently taking the gun from his grip and pulling Navos into an embrace. The taller Drops member sobbed as soon as his forehead tucked into Choo-Choo's shoulder.

Pandora crouched by the workers, who were watching her with wide eyes. Bending at the hip made the wound ache, but she wanted to get a good look at them. Two men and two women of various ages. She slipped her finger into the gag of the first woman and tugged it free.

"What's your name?"

She spoke in a language Pandora didn't understand. It could have been Scandinavian for all she knew. The woman had dark hair and a blotch of purple birthmark on her neck. She looked like a woman who'd led a hard life, and not by choice.

"You understand me?" asked Pandora.

The woman kept speaking in her language, forcing Pandora to sigh and return the gag. She moved to the next woman, who was a little younger. Her lips were cracked and she had a bruise around her eye.

"Can you understand me?"

"Yes," replied the woman in a heavy accent. "Please don't kill us. They make us go in deep places. Dig their stones. Beat us if we resist."

"Where did you come from?"

"I live in apartments in ninth ward, but couldn't pay rent because lose job. Someone told me about good work with good pay and when I show up, they take me into ground and make me dig. Live in shit room at Grotto."

"What or where is Grotto?"

"Big cave, lots of tents, stinks like smoke and shit. Keep us there. Will you let us go? Or will you kill us?" asked the woman.

Choo-Choo had his arm around Navos' shoulder, but he had heard the description. He shared a concerned look with Pandora. Letting them go was almost the same as killing them. Four workers without a way to defend themselves, and no way to find their way out. They could wander the endless cave systems for days.

But they couldn't take them back to the Pajot either. The Drops wouldn't accept them since they'd been working for the Eights and on their territory. Bringing them back might as well be a death sentence.

"What do you want?"

"Let us go. We find our way out," said the woman.

Pandora didn't think so, but she wasn't going to argue with the woman's delusion. She joined Choo-Choo, who had deposited Navos on the ridge, where he was wiping his face with a handkerchief and drinking water.

"What do you think?" she asked Choo-Choo.

"They're dead either way, but at least it's their choice."

"What if we took them to the Terreno? It's out of our way, but not terribly so."

Choo-Choo frowned. "Not a good look."

Pandora nodded. If it got back to the leadership that they'd let the workers live, it could come back to haunt her.

"Are you going to kill them?"

Choo-Choo paled, his lip snarling with distaste.

"And we know Navos can't."

She held out her hand and he gave her the pistol that he'd taken from Navos. After retrieving her blades, she cut the bindings from the workers and told them to remove their gags.

"Grab your travel supplies," she said, gesturing towards the bags in a pile. "Be ready to move."

The workers cautiously retrieved their gear, pulling out headlamps and fixing them to their foreheads. They glanced amongst themselves.

Pandora approached the woman she'd spoken with and grabbed her hand, placing the pistol against her palm, then gently squeezing her fingers over the grip.

"Head back through the tunnel where you came, but instead of going left towards the Grotto, try to go right occasionally. You might find your way to the Terreno, or you might not. Trade the gun for passage out. That's the best I can do."

The woman stared at the gun as if it were a live serpent. She held it awkwardly.

"Go. Before I change my mind. Good luck. May the shadows keep you safe."

Pandora watched as they stepped over the dead Eights on their way out, their lights bobbing in the darkness of the cavern. The woman she'd given the gun to spit on the guard who'd had the rifle, and one of the men grabbed the weapon, checking back when he had it in his hands. Pandora waved and they quickly hurried towards the tunnel.

"Was that a good idea?" asked Choo-Choo.

"Were you going to shoot them?"

He shrugged. "They'll die down here."

"At least they have a chance." She jutted her chin at Navos. "He ready to move?"

Choo-Choo nodded.

She wasn't sure when she'd assumed the leadership role in their little group, but the battle with the Eights had confirmed it. Pandora dug through the Eights' gear, making sure they hadn't missed anything valuable, and then shouldered the other rifle as they headed out of the cavern with a bag full of stones and the stink of death in their noses.

Three

The clan headquarters inside the Machi was a larger, multi-level building like the housing, with flat ceramic tile roofs and sliding paper doors. The central dining area was barely occupied, only a few tables with clan members. Kuma reached the back of the complex, where Carlos stood guard outside the chamber where his father was meeting with his Shadows.

"Where's Adrena?"

"Problems in Big Dave's Town."

A raised murmuring reached them through the walls. The interior was enchanted to keep their voices from penetrating, but sometimes the vibration could be heard.

The corners of Carlos' eyes creased. "Getting pretty heated in there." He gestured upward. "City okay?"

"Yeah," said Kuma vacantly.

"Been a while since you've been up top," said Carlos, nodding.

"A while. Forgotten how overwhelming it can be to be outside."

"You get used to it. Not completely, but it gets less terrifying over time."

"It bothered you?"

Carlos smirked. "It bothers everyone. Hard not to."

He rapped his knuckles on the wooden structure. The door slid opened slightly, revealing Instructor Kaz's chubby face.

"Where's Adrena?"

"Problems. Big Dave's Town."

The door opened wide enough for Kuma to enter. The conversation died as everyone's gaze fell upon him. His father and his Shadows were sitting around the ebony table with cups of tea. The room smelled like lavender.

Instructor Kaz jabbed a thumb in his direction. "Said there were problems in Big Dave's Town."

Niran frowned. "What happened?"

"Theft. Delilah was hit by one of the clans. They escaped into the western tunnels and disappeared in the Wastelands before anyone could catch them. Delilah was irate, complaining that her protection money wasn't getting her anything. Adrena and Xylos stayed behind to investigate and calm Delilah and the other business owners."

"I see," said Niran, his lips bunched. "Take a seat. We'll get to you in a moment after we finish our discussion."

Kuma found a chair against the back wall and placed his hands in his lap.

"The raid on Delilah's bar proves my point," said his uncle Brazio, gesturing towards Kuma. "We look weak and they're chipping away our edges. Soon they'll come for the meat. We need to strike first."

There was a head nod from Natsuo Torres, who was the business manager of the clan. He was the oldest member of Shadows, with deep valleys of wrinkles and round glasses that made him appear an inquisitive owl. He spent much of his time in the city, selling their illicitly acquired goods and making deals to keep the clan out of the eyes of the city police departments while keeping track of the finances. His silk suit would have fit in at the top corporations in the first ward.

The other two Shadows at the table, Instructor Kaz and Gabrielle Au, looked less swayed by the comment. The latter was the clan's resident mage, a woman of considerable power and beauty. Her blonde ponytail was pulled back tight enough to tug at her dark eyebrows. She was in charge of anything regarding the Halls or the use of magic within the clan. A bracelet around her wrist glittered with uncolored stones that increased the reach of her abilities.

"Strike who?" asked Niran as he stroked his stark-white goatee. "Hit the Drops and the Alliance finishes us. The same is true the opposite way and I'm not sure we can eliminate the Alliance with their new stones. Between the black diamonds and rumors of other powerful stones, their numbers, and their shadow backers, we might be outmatched."

"Might," said Brazio, pounding his fist on the table, rattling the tea-cups on their saucers. "We've no proof of these shadow backers. You have us jumping at shadows, but the longer we wait, the more powerful our foes become."

Natsuo adjusted his glasses by pushing on the bridge with a forefinger.

"Your brother has a point. The hit on the tunnels last week cost us hundreds of thousands of dollars and two soldados. They've never dared to attack our tunnels. If we don't hit back, then they'll continue to harvest our work."

News of the hit had Kuma sitting tall. He hadn't heard about it, which meant the leadership was keeping it quiet. The clan had built tunnels crisscrossing the Undercity and they used electric carts to move around illicit goods safely and quickly.

Niran quietly took a sip from his tea. "Who do you propose to hit?"

Natsuo adjusted the cuff of his sleeve. "I'm only telling you that our finances aren't looking good and these problems, the disruptions in Big Dave's Town and hits on our transport network, have created liabilities. Our city-generated income is down sixty-three percent this year. We're focusing far too much time on mining and not enough on income, unless we're planning on selling our excess stones."

"Excess stones?" asked Niran. "We've barely enough to cover our future waku. Our mines are the worst in the Undercity. The other clans have access to much richer sites, leaving us far behind. If we can't change this soon, we'll be overrun by their superior stones. Those black diamonds keep me up at night. We need our own source, which means we need to delve around the old Persphony mines. It's deep enough that we might find our own source of interesting stones."

Brazio drummed his fingers on the ebony table. "Or we can take the stones from our enemies. They might have better mines, but we have better warriors and the best and largest Academy. Let me hit one of the smaller clans. We'll get in and out before they know we're there."

"We've far too many problems already. Creating new ones will make our problems worse. If you hit the smaller clans, the rest of the Alliance will come down upon us," countered Niran.

"Not if there are no survivors. Like you said, we don't have enough waku or soldados for mining and protection and everything else. But we can get all three of those things with pinpoint raids. I'll choose targets we can overwhelm—the smaller clans. It'll get us stones, funds, and eliminate the need to mine, which will keep us protected. Like you said, we have too many problems. But let me take a select group north of the

Terreno where the Antimagus make their home. They're rich in stones, but weak of heart. They scrap like children with no sense of discipline."

The nods from the other Shadows had Kuma wondering if his father's position was less tenable than he'd previously thought. Despite his initial disagreements, his uncle's plan made sense. They had too many problems and not enough manpower to address them. Hitting a smaller clan could ease the pressure.

Niran didn't answer at first. He checked with each of his Shadows before addressing the group. "We're not breaking the peace. While I agree that plan sounds logical, the risks are too great. If even one person gets away and we're identified as the perpetrators, the rest of the clans will turn on us and wipe us from the Undercity."

"It's not my fault you tied our hands with that agreement," said Brazio angrily with fists presented on the table.

Kuma didn't need his amber to sense the shock from the other Shadows. This open challenge was new. His father glanced in his direction, a barely perceptible hesitation in his gaze before he turned to his brother.

"The agreement was the only thing keeping us from a collapse. The problems we have now are only a third of what we were dealing with a year ago. We squandered far too many waku and soldados on pointless battles for pride. The other clans bring in new members from outside their ranks, swelling their numbers and making it harder to compete.

While our system has benefited us for decades, the addition of the stones has raised the stakes. We must adapt and grow, or we'll become like the Vipers."

"I would put any one of our waku against three of the Alliance," said Brazio with a raised chin.

"I agree our warriors are the tops, but both you and Kuma were nearly bested."

Brazio scoffed. "Don't confuse duels and scraps, brother. I know it's been a long time since you've been in one, but they're not the same. There are no rules in a scrap. Surprise and superior tactics make a winning strategy."

Niran ran his palm across the smooth wood as he matched gazes with his brother, who eventually looked into his lap. The pulsing of Brazio's jaw was constant.

"What are your thoughts?" asked Niran to the rest of the Shadows.

Instructor Kaz cleared his throat. "I cannot speak to which strategy is better, but our Academy students are ready to scrap whether that's on patrol or if we fight a secret war."

"Gabrielle?"

The blonde mage had been fidgeting with her bracelet. "There are other options, Solrei. I have contacts within the Hall. A few mages on retainer would go a long way to bridging the gap in resources."

"We can't trust the mages. Look what nearly happened to the city because of their hubris, and once they were here they would see the value of what's happening in the Undercity. It would be a short-term fix, but cause more problems in the future."

"What about other resources?" asked Gabrielle, cagily referencing a previous private conversation.

"No. I appreciate your willingness to put yourself at risk, but that option is even less palatable."

Gabrielle inclined her head towards the table. "Understood."

"What about our competing ideas?"

She glanced between Niran and his brother. "They each have their merits. A strike on Antimagus could be very profitable and if undetected would shore up some of our gaps. On the other hand, I agree that if the attack failed, we'd be easily wiped out. It's a huge risk, but there's a bigger risk of doing nothing."

"I for one think your brother's plan should be strongly considered," said Natsuo.

"And why is that?"

"As the clan's accountant, of course, I think the quickest way to return our finances to the black would be in our best interest. But I'm also a proud member of this clan." He pulled back the sleeve of his jacket, revealing an ugly scar along his forearm. "I've been in my fair share of scraps in the past. I know the value of putting fear in your enemy. Razor clan has always stayed on top, not because of our tunnels, or because we keep tidy books, or the protection money from Big Dave's Town, but because our soldados, and now waku, are the best. When we showed up to a scrap, you could see them wanting to break and run even before the first blade clashed. That's part of our problem. They don't fear us anymore. A well-executed raid would remind them of who we are."

"Thank you, Natsuo, for your honest opinion," said Niran. He waved towards Kuma. "I think it appropriate we receive news of our joint raid with Black Crows. Kuma, would you repeat the events of this evening? Leave nothing out."

Kuma stood and bowed deeply before placing his hands behind his back. He spent the next ten minutes giving a moment-by-moment explanation of the raid on the alchemical warehouse. The four Shadows and his father nodded along with his tale.

"What did you think of this Deacon?" asked his father.

"At first I thought him undisciplined. He brandished his weapon at women on the street to get their attention and was sloppy in appearance. But, when it came time for the raid on the warehouse, it was clear that he'd come prepared. He knew the best route for entry, brought appropriate countermeasures for their security, and we came away with the goods without a single casualty."

The gleam in his father's eyes would normally have made Kuma proud, but he was in the room not as his son, but as a member of the clan. Kuma knew his report would have weight with their decision, and by the flat looks of the others, they knew the implications.

"A good raid," said Brazio, leaning away in his chair. "But it doesn't mean we can trust the Black Crows. Gangs in the city have no honor. They'll stab us in the back the first chance they get."

Natsuo adjusted his round glasses. "I concur. They're criminals in the basest sense of the word. We'd be putting our reputation at risk if we brought them into the conflicts of the Undercity. They're a much larger gang. If they can learn our ways, we might doom ourselves."

"I agree," said Niran, causing apprehension in the others. "That's why I believe it's not in our interest to simply ally, but eventually combine our clans."

"They're not a clan, they're a gang. There's a difference," said Brazio, leaning forward with his fists on the table.

Niran held up a hand. "I'm not suggesting we make this move right away. It will take time, but I've discussed it with their leadership. By combining, we can improve both fields of battle. The Black Crows are one of the largest gangs in the city. They'll increase our reach, numbers, and connections in the light, and our transport tunnels, access to stones, and training Academy provide substantial value to them."

"This will change us irrevocably," said Brazio angrily.

"Would you prefer extinction?"

Brazio held out his open hand, slowly closing it to a fist. "Let me raid Antimagus. We don't need an honorless gang to succeed in the shadows. Bringing the Black Crows in will be the same as killing us."

The wrinkles around his father's mouth deepened as he matched his brother's anger.

"Had I been able to negotiate a deal with Drops we might have been able to navigate the way forward without so much risk, but my talks were sabotaged by the duel and now neither side can extend a hand without losing the support of their membership."

A cold hand squeezed around Kuma's heart at the thought of the duel. He shrunk in his seat, but no one looked at him. They were focused on the conflict between the brothers.

"I did not sabotage those talks. I have my disagreements with you, but I would never defy the clan's direction."

"I'm not suggesting you did, only stating the fact of the matter. Someone incited the young Drops warrior. Probably someone from the Alliance side. It does them no good for our two clans to cooperate. But now, Daraja won't return my inquiries."

"Will you not consider my plan?" asked Brazio with a knitted brow.

Niran leaned back and ran his hand along the edge of the ebony table. "I will. But until that day, we'll continue my plan with the Black Crows. We'll take it slow, confirm their intent, and in the meantime, use their numbers to bolster our defenses and increase our mining operations."

Kaz cleared his throat. "You mentioned our Academy training as a resource for the Black Crows. Am I to understand we'll be accepting their members?"

Niran offered a warm smile. "You're correct. Part of the agreement involves the transfer of stones and a select number joining the Academy. A small number so they can integrate. Think of it as a test. If we can help shape their gang members into the type of warriors we expect from our youth, then we might be able to continue integration. If not, then I'll end the arrangement and strongly consider the warleaders' plan."

"An excellent path forward, Solrei," said Gabrielle, inclining her head. The others murmured their agreement with less enthusiasm, not meeting Niran's watchful gaze.

The idea that they'd be accepting members of the Black Crows into the Academy left Kuma uneasy, but he didn't have a chance to ponder it further because his father announced the end of the meeting. As Kuma stood along with the others, Niran gestured to him. "Please stay a moment."

The others filed out of the room. When the sliding door was shut Kuma took a spot next to his father when offered.

"What do you think of my plan?"

"Sounds reasonable."

His father's lips flattened. "Don't placate me, Kuma. I'm asking you as a member of this clan, and possibly a future leader, not as my son. What do you think? And about your uncle's plan?"

"They both seem reasonable. I do like the idea of hitting Antimagus. We've been on our back foot for so long that it's frustrating. I hear that from the other Academy members, but so many things can go wrong. An attack like that seems impulsive, not strategic.

"On the other hand, the Black Crows plan seems safer on the surface. We don't have to make a decision all at once, but there comes a point that we have to cross a line. That's when the decision will most matter."

"If you were in my spot, what would you choose?"

"I would have to think upon it."

Niran cocked a grin. "I'm not asking you to think about it, I'm asking you to decide. As your Solrei, tell me now, what does your gut tell you?"

"The first plan, however risky, is something I can understand. Then again, the Alliance clans are bringing in outside resources. What we'd be doing wouldn't be much different. As you've said many times, the Undercity is changing because of the stones. We can either adapt or be swept away."

With an eyebrow raised, Niran said, "You still haven't answered me."

Kuma inclined his head solemnly. "My apologies. It's a hard decision."

The comment brought a hint of a grin to his father's lips.

"The thing that worries me about the Black Crows is their intent.

Deacon, the guy that led the raid. He was extremely competent, but also sloppy, if that makes any sense. I don't know what to make of him, which worries me." Kuma shook his head. "It's not much to go on, but I don't trust him. Not with anything important, and if the rest of their gang is the same, then working with the Black Crows would only endanger us. If you're making me choose, I would pick the raid on Antimagus. It's risky but we can control the variables. Bringing the Black Crows behind our walls seems like the same hubris as the mages from the city when they wantonly summoned demons from the infernal realm, ignoring the dangers that those beings presented."

His father reached out and placed his hand on Kuma's shoulder. It wasn't the iron grip that he remembered, and the touch reminded Kuma of how much older his father was getting. While he was only in his early sixties, life in the Undercity, especially in his youth, had been hard.

"I share your concerns, which is why I wanted to have this conversation with you. There are few people in the clan I can truly trust anymore."

"You don't think your brother would...?"

"No," said Niran right away. "Get that thought out of your head. As disagreeable as he is, he would never break the rules of the clan. There may come a time when the clan votes him as their leader, but it won't be from bloodshed. That time may come sooner rather than later, if my plan doesn't work. And that's why I need you to keep an eye on things in the Academy. The Black Crows will be sending down a few of their members to join and hopefully attune to some stones. I want you to keep watch and report back to me how they're integrating."

"Why not Instructor Kaz?"

"Oh, he will report back regularly, but he won't see what you see, and despite his appearance of neutrality, I believe he's more inclined to my brother's plan. They're of a same age, and scrapped together, successfully I might add, and were of the first waku in Razor clan."

"Understood," said Kuma, inclining his head.

He'd forgotten that Brazio and Kaz were similar ages. His uncle appeared closer to his father's, even though he was fifteen years younger. The position of warleader had aged his uncle unlike Instructor Kazuki.

As Kuma stood, his father said, "Good job with the raid last night. The clan sees you."

"I wanted to prove my worth."

"I know, Little Bear. You have much to offer. It's why I'm trusting you with my request. It's also why I agreed for you to go on the raid."

"Why is that?"

"Because this Deacon will be one of the new members at the Academy."

Four

Pandora had been in most areas of the Pajot in her year as a member of the Drops except for the Overlook. The place the leadership of the clan lived and made their decisions was a series of caves that overlooked the wild canyons that gave the clan its name. The caves had been the early living spaces for the clan due to their defensive nature and then as they'd expanded into the caverns, the holes had been widened and blasted out until a sizable facility had been constructed.

Reaching the Overlook required climbing up a long, wide ladder. There were safety lines for those not sure about their climbing, but Pandora and her two companions made it without precautions.

The entrance was a set of enchanted iron doors, currently open, but capable of blocking out all but the most determined intruders. Electric light made Pandora squint, the artificial brightness harsh against her eyes.

They were led into a round room with maps and other information posted on the walls. Pandora's gaze immediately fell upon the map of the Undercity, marking the locations of the other clans, settlements, mining sites, and other interesting locales. It displayed far more territory than she'd known about. She was sure if she had time to study it, she could uncover valuable secrets about the Drops or other clans, but her inspection halted as soon as Duro turned to greet them.

The warleader of the Drops had a round face and black hair. At first glance he seemed amiable, until his dark brown eyes bore down as if he could sift through the contents of the soul. Even with her background, Pandora found herself averting her eyes towards the floor when he approached.

The heat of Duro's gaze warmed her cheeks. He gave a cursory glance to Choo-Choo and Navos, but returned to her.

"What's this about an attack on the Eights?"

That he knew about the events of their patrol and the anger in his voice had Pandora second-guessing herself. She counted the chairs in the room: eleven. Then the tattoos on his forearms: seventeen.

Choo-Choo held out two hands, palm up, one with the bag of raw stones, the other with the real prizes. Duro surged towards them, focusing on the colored stones. He squinted, picked up the smokey, dark stone and held it up to the light.

"Is this?"

"A black diamond."

The tension in his forehead smoothed away. "*You* three took down a Black Diamond and these other stones? Tell me."

Choo-Choo cleared his throat. "We found the Eights in our territory. They were mining stones. We thought about returning for more numbers, but Pandora convinced us they'd be gone before we got back."

Duro put a finger into her breastbone. "It was *your* plan to attack them?"

She inclined her head even more. "Yes, Shadowmaster Duro."

Duro placed his fingers under her chin, lifting it until they were staring into each other's eyes. She could feel his amber exposing her every secret.

"Explain. Every detail."

The debriefing went on for twenty minutes. At points, Choo-Choo and Navos added their parts. They left out Navos' breakdown after the fight and letting the workers go.

"You didn't know they had a Black Diamond when you attacked?"

"We probably wouldn't have tried to take them had we known," said Pandora. "They had more stones than we expected, but surprise, Choo-Choo's accurate shooting, and our sapphires carried the day."

Duro had been rubbing the black diamond between his forefinger and thumb.

"A nice trick putting the gun in his mouth and pulling the trigger. Good to know that steelskin doesn't extend past the outer skin."

The warleader paced before them for a long minute, occasionally stopping and examining the stone in his fist. Eventually he paused, forehead knitted with concern.

"What happened to the workers?"

Choo-Choo opened his mouth to give the answer they'd practiced on the journey to the Pajot, but now that she was standing before Duro, lying to him seemed like a bad idea.

"We let them go," said Pandora suddenly, catching glances from her friends.

"You let them go?" asked Duro suspiciously. "Why?"

"After questioning them, we realized they'd been held there against their will. The Eights had kidnapped them and brought them into the Undercity to work their mines."

Duro provided no clue to his thoughts. He stared at her as blankly as a canvas.

"Are we in trouble?" asked Pandora when the tension grew too thick.

"Trouble?" he repeated, chuckling. "Because you let some workers go after slaughtering six waku from the Eights?"

"They might tell others what happened."

"Good," he said. "Let them know that they tread on our territory at great risk." He shook his head. "Even if you'd given them hand jobs before you set them free I wouldn't care. You brought back a black diamond, something we've been trying to acquire since we learned about their existence."

"I just thought since the duel..."

"I don't care about the duel," said Duro sharply.

She cleared her throat. "At the Academy they call me a traitor."

"For what? Living? I was there, I saw you fight. You might have won, except for his clever final attack, coming through the stalactites like he did, catching you by surprise. You didn't choose to offer to yield."

"Yet they think I colluded with him."

Duro chuckled. "Kuma is like his father. He's clever. He did more by offering the yield than he would have accomplished by killing you. Razor clan does not accept outsiders, but we do. By letting you live, he put the idea that we cannot trust anyone but our own. It has made us more cautious about bringing in newcomers, though I for one disagree. I saw you fight. I know the truth of who you are, and this bounty proves my point." He put a hand on her shoulder. "I would have you fight at my side anytime. Any of you. You took a dangerous chance, scrapped well, and came away much ahead. If we have more like you, then we'll win this war."

Navos piped up. "Are we at war?"

"A shadow war. Eventually it will become the real thing, but for now, it will be at the edges."

When Duro turned to set the black diamond on the table with the other stones, Pandora risked a glance back to the map. She spotted markings near Big Dave's Town and other areas controlled by the Razor clan, suggesting that the Drops were already fighting this shadow war. She stared at her shoes when he turned back.

"You're to return to the Academy now, right?"

She nodded.

"Say nothing about the raid to your classmates. Not about the Eights, or the stones, and especially not the black diamond."

Pandora bowed, but Navos spoke up. "Wouldn't we want to let others know about our victory? The Eights will know and then the Alliance. Why not our clanmates?"

The ghost of smile rose to Duro's lips. "You want glory. You've earned it, but for now, you'll stay silent. That's all you need to know. Dismissed."

They bowed together and hurried out of the Overlook. When they were away from the ladder, Navos knocked his blond hair out of his eyes as he glanced back towards the lighted windows that looked over the canyon and the Pajot. He frowned.

"I don't understand why we can't say anything. The Alliance will know they lost. Why can't we?"

Pandora rolled the facts around her mind. "It's not the Alliance that he's worried about. It's Razor. He doesn't want them to know we have a black diamond."

"I don't understand," said Navos

Choo-Choo grunted. "He thinks we have a spy. Someone's passing information back to Razor. That's the only explanation."

"Seriously?" asked Navos.

"It would make sense," said Pandora. "Though it could just be caution. Shadow war and all."

"I saw the map," said Navos, nodding. "It looks like we've been hitting Razor already."

The next cavern was cut with terraces. Workers toiled amid the green plants beneath the artificial light. Pandora was busy pondering the information from the map when she saw Garrett on a separate path, waving her down.

"I'll catch up," she told her friends as they continued on the path.

She caught up to Garrett near a huge tank that held water for the terrace gardens. The outer shell was painted with a mural depicting a fight the Drops had with the infernal creatures during the Invasion. The scars of that day ran deep in the city.

Garrett looked different than the last time she'd seen him. Rather than the grungy work clothes, he wore baggy branded clothes that could only come from above. Silver chains hung around his neck and rings graced his fingers.

"You look like you're doing quite well," said Pandora.

He clucked his tongue and held out his hand as if he were turning a dial. "Killin' it at the Bogo."

"You hacked the pachinko machines?" she asked.

"No way. I just found my touch. Manager shits himself every time I come in. Tried to pay me to go somewhere else last time I was there."

"What's up?"

"Your friend wanted me to give you this," said Garrett, reaching into a pocket.

She accepted the item, finding a smooth black pebble in her fist. As soon as her eyes fell upon it, she had to steel herself from reacting. Garrett was staring at her curiously.

"What's it mean?"

"A bad joke." She looked up. "Where did she give this to you?"

"In the Terreno. She owns a shop there called the Rush. Sells stuff like blasting caps, climbing harnesses, and shit like that, though I don't understand the name."

Pandora chuckled. "The Rush. Like Gold Rush. When gold was found in the west it was the people selling shovels and packs that made all the money, not the ones digging in the ground."

"Who is she?"

"She's a fence, buys and sells stolen goods. The store is a front, though it's probably a pretty profitable one given how things are changing down here. Did she let you see her?"

"No. Wore a bulky cloak and a mask. What's wrong with her?"

Pandora assumed the story she used hadn't changed. "Unhappy customer threw acid on her. Tore her up pretty bad. Doesn't like anyone to see her face, or really anything."

"That's awful."

"It was." Pandora forced herself to smile. "Thanks, Garret. I have to get to the Academy."

"See ya around."

Away from the young maintenance worker, her lips broke into a scowl. She kept glancing at the black pebble as she made long strides towards her destination. Between the message and having to lie about her mother's condition, Pandora had to do everything she could to keep moving. Any thoughts she had about her past only brought the threats of the clicker, the endless brutal training that had made her who she was.

The past wasn't important, they'd told her. Thinking about it would only reveal truths better left hidden. Only the mission mattered. Only the way forward.

But the smooth black pebble was a message, telling her they weren't happy about her progress. They wanted intel and sabotage. The loss to Kuma at Shade's End hadn't helped. It'd made her look weak and undermined her position, and if she wasn't useful they would get rid of her.

A flash of tight spaces and choking black smoke had her frozen on the path, sweat beading on her forehead. Pandora stared at the terraces. Twenty-three workers. Five levels. Two water tanks. One stone.

She stared at the object on her palm. The urge to throw it across the cavern was strong.

"The map," she whispered to herself.

The information she'd seen on the map would be useful to them. It was the kind of intel she'd been sent to acquire. But she hadn't been allowed back at the Terreno since the duel. She needed to find a way to get there, even if she had to sneak out. The message was a reminder that they were running out of patience and she was nearly out of time.

Five

Kuma stood on the end of the seesaw with only a bucket of rocks on the other half. He rapidly cycled from heavy to light and back again. The long board oscillated, quivering up and down as he fought to maintain his position.

Instructor Kaz stood beneath the other end. If the bucket was disturbed too greatly, it would fall on his head. The wide-lipped Kaz had his arms crossed.

“Cycle faster. It’s sliding off the end.”

Kuma switched between the two modes of his emerald as fast as he could but it strained both his mind and body. Sweat poured from his forehead as he worked. Eventually he could no longer keep up the cycling and he dipped too low on the heavy side, flinging the bucket of rocks into the air. Before they could land on the instructor, he leapt with a spinning kick, knocking it away with his heel and returning to the ground as if nothing had happened. Kuma landed less gracefully than his instructor, then had to dodge a rock that had flown from the bucket.

"You think because you won a duel that you're hot shit? You don't need to train as hard?" asked the instructor as he approached.

The sudden switch in mood confused Kuma. Only five minutes before Kaz had praised his progress. Kuma straightened, sputtering out his answer.

"No, Instructor Kaz."

"Then why did you let the bucket fall?"

Kuma bowed. "I'll work harder."

Instructor Kaz put a finger to Kuma's temple. "Use your brain." Then he poked him hard in the sternum. "And your body. And most importantly learn to control those stones."

Kuma had kept the range of his amber no longer than the length of the seesaw, but when the instructor briefly glanced away, he expanded it, realizing the reason for the change in mood. Five figures stood at the entrance, smirking as they watched Kuma receive verbal abuse.

The overwhelming scents of pungent cologne informed Kuma that the Black Crows sent to the Academy had arrived. It made him feel a little better that the instructor hadn't suddenly decided he was an idiot, but that he was setting the expectations for the newcomers.

"Grab the bucket and come with me."

Kuma hurried to collect it, following behind. When he looked up, he was surprised to see Deacon, the leader of the warehouse raid, standing with the group. His clothes weren't as loud as they'd been in the city, but the silken tracksuit still stuck out compared to the training uniform that Kuma wore.

He didn't recognize the other four Black Crows—two men and two women—but they wore similar clothes and looked fit. They each had a duffle bag at their feet.

"Hey, Kuma. You must be Kazuki," said Deacon, holding out his arm as if he expected a handshake and a shoulder bump.

Instructor Kaz stopped short of the five Black Crows. "I thought they were sending their best?"

Deacon checked back with his mates, letting his hand drop and giving a shoulder shrug.

"We're the fuckin' cream, man."

Instructor Kaz brushed past them, striding quickly towards the Academy grounds. Deacon and the others looked confused.

"Grab your bags and follow," said Kuma as he hurried past.

Deacon jogged next to him with his duffle bag slung over his shoulder.

"What's goin' on? Why's he bein' a dick? I thought we were here to train."

The other Black Crows appeared equally agitated. A few of them were mumbling curses and one of them flipped Instructor Kaz off behind his back.

A host of answers floated into Kuma's mind, none of them helpful. He hadn't decided yet if he liked Deacon, but he reminded himself that it didn't matter. If his father's plan was going to work, the Black Crows had to prove they could integrate. It didn't help that Kaz was skeptical that it could work. He wouldn't actively sabotage things, but he wasn't going to give them special treatment either.

"He's testing you. Wants to see if you can follow directions."

"For real? I thought we were allies. He ain't my mate," said Deacon.

Kuma slowed his pace, putting his hand out. "You pulled some pretty slick stuff up there on the raid. It was impressive. But if you want to attune to a stone and be able to use it effectively, there's no better teacher than Instructor Kaz. At the beginning of last year, I wouldn't have been able to do anything I did that night. He taught me that. Just like he was working me pretty hard back there. I know our clans do things differently, but I promise you, if you do as he asks, you'll find a wealth of benefits."

Deacon rolled his eyes. "Fine. I'll play along. But if this is just a way to humiliate us because we're not your clan, then this whole thing's gonna go down faster than a turd."

"I promise you that he'll treat you the same shitty way he treated us."

Deacon chuckled. "Fine. I get it. He's a hard-ass and we're newbies."

"We should catch up."

The instructor led them to the Academy grounds. Going by their craned necks, the Black Crows seemed impressed by the structure. Instructor Helena was working with the first years on the obstacle course when they arrived. Kaz made a series of gestures and Helena gathered them up. The entire group headed to the common area in the main building at the top of the stairs. The Black Crows were examining everything with wide-eyed enthusiasm, which put a warmth of pride in Kuma's chest and made him hope that the Academy's strength would impress upon them to be on their best behavior.

The Razor students took their regular places while Instructor Kaz brought the Black Crows to the front of the room. Tick and Camina found Kuma at their table, settling next to him.

"What's this? Are we letting any street rat into the clan now?" asked Camina with a hard expression.

"Black Crows."

The name brought recognition to their faces since he'd told them about the night of the raid. Once everyone had settled, Instructor Kaz stepped forward.

"Good shadows to you all. Today we are going to be joined by members from outside our clan. These three men and two women are members of the Black Crows, a gang that runs a sizable region in the city. In exchange for support of Razor clan priorities, the Academy will be training their members, and some of them may even attune to some stones."

The news was met with shared glances and hard glares. The promise of stones was the prize that made students put up with long hours and hard training in hopes of becoming a famous waku like Brazio. Murmurs turned to comments until Instructor Kaz put his fingers to his lips and made an ear-piercing whistle, silencing them. Kuma saw that his father's choice wasn't being received well, at least within the younger set of the Academy. He hoped Deacon and his mates would overcome their doubts.

"I don't care if you agree or not," said Instructor Kaz. "It has been decided. It's up to you to support the decision as a member of the clan."

The Black Crows in their shiny new clothes looked like members of a band rather than warriors. They checked with each other nervously.

"These five new students will be joining the second years"— a ruckus from Yara and her crew was silenced when Instructor Kaz looked in her direction—"and will be testing for their stones within a couple of weeks. The only thing I ask of you all is to treat them like you would a member of the clan." He looked around the room as if he expected more comments. "Dismissed."

Instructor Kaz gathered the Black Crows around him, and after a brief conversation, which Kuma dared not eavesdrop upon, he sent them away with Instructor Helena.

The meeting ended with Kaz taking the second years, minus the Black Crows, to the sparring room. He set them in lines and had them working through basic fighting maneuvers, which didn't make sense to Kuma since these were skills they'd mastered years before they'd even come to the Academy.

When Instructor Helena returned with the five Black Crows in the training uniforms that everyone wore, they were placed in the lines with the rest of the class. The simple instructions were made clear as Deacon and his mates were placed in a third line. Kuma was on the end of the second row, so he was able to watch the Black Crows struggle with the punches and kicks. The only one that seemed remotely competent was Deacon, though his sour expression suggested that he was unhappy with the direction things were going.

Kaz put Helena in charge of the class, while he attended to the Black Crows, taking them each aside for personal instruction. By the end of the two hours, the newcomers were drenched in sweat and looked no better—and possibly worse—than they had when they first arrived.

"Instructor Helena, please take the other second years to the maze for some amber training. I'll work with our new students to help get them caught up."

As Helena led them from the room, Kuma caught Yara staring at the Black Crows. The plotting intent on her face left Kuma worried that she would try to interfere with them in an attempt to sabotage the integration. After all, she was Brazio's daughter, and while his father had assured him that his brother would follow the clan direction, Yara was much more an agent of chaos. She had no qualms about sticking her nose into places it didn't belong.

As they headed down the stairs, Camina muttered, "Are they serious about this? Tick could punch and kick better when he was six years old."

Tick was opening and closing his jaw, but he was able to control his compulsions long enough to scowl at Camina. "Is that supposed to be a knock on me?"

"My point is that how can we give them stones? They can barely hold their fists correctly and now they're going to be waku? I don't understand." When he looked to her, she held her hands up. "I know. Follow the clan direction, but it doesn't make sense."

"They seemed pretty good up top, or at least Deacon did. I don't recognize the others."

"How are they going to help us against Drops and the Alliance?"

"It'll take time," he countered.

"It'll take years," said Camina.

As they reached the entrance to the maze, Instructor Helena called out, "Shut your traps. Whatever complaints you had about the newcomers, it ends now. I want your complete focus, and I certainly won't allow their bad habits to infect the lot of you. You're only partially worthless, but I'd hate to give up that progress because of a group of know-nothing lighters."

The smirks and laughter from his classmates made Kuma realize that his father's plan wasn't going to be easily accepted by the rest of the clan. Which meant he needed to do everything possible to help the Black Crows acclimate.

Six

Pandora faced four first years with a metal-tipped staff in her hands. They held the curved blades favored by the clans, approaching her in an arc so she couldn't use her sapphire against them all without risking counterattack. Two of them had ambers, not that she cared.

"This isn't a dance party," said Instructor Irina. "If this was a real scrap, you'd have probably been overrun by her allies already."

The first years approached as a group. Pandora shifted towards the side of the circle to keep them from having a direct line, but the other students in the circle wouldn't budge. A few of the older students whispered, "Traitor."

A red rage filled Pandora. As the first attacker lunged in, she thrust the metal tip into his gut and then Pulled herself backwards in a sapphire-aided leap. The contact served as a starting gun, and they rushed her at once. Pandora held her staff horizontally and Pushed it forward, flying at their knees like a moving high jump. Two of them managed to leap it, while the other two were tripped onto their faces.

The two that managed to keep upright looked like the fox cornering a hen until she Pulled and the horizontal staff took them out from behind, slamming the backs of their heads against the concrete. Before the others could reach their feet, she brought the metal tip against their jaws, knocking them out cleanly: one, two.

With her opponents incapacitated on the fighting grounds, Pandora faced the instructor and bowed deeply with a snarl on her lips.

"My apologies that it took me so long."

The pleasure she felt from the comment lasted half a second until Instructor Irina leapt into the middle with a sapphire Push, striding towards Pandora and glowering over her. The instructor had height on her, and stared down as if she were a boxer at weigh-in trying to intimidate the competition.

"What did you say?"

The constant sniping and mistrust had left Pandora with a ball of unresolved anger. Receiving the black pebble from her mother hadn't helped. It'd made her feel like everyone was against her. She maintained the staring contest when she answered.

"I was apologizing that I allowed my opponents to think they had a chance. I should have taken them out in the first two seconds so they understood how important it is to listen to you, Instructor Irina. Better to be embarrassed today than dead in the dark."

Instructor Irina's jaw pulsed as she worked through her thoughts. Eventually she turned and called out in a stern tone.

"Clear the field and fetch me a staff."

As Instructor Irina paced away, Pandora caught looks of surprise from Choo-Choo and Navos. They offered shoulder shrugs and incredulous expressions.

After someone threw the instructor a metal-tipped staff, she spun around and faced Pandora with a scowl. She extended the staff towards her and addressed the class.

"This second year said something very important. Better to be embarrassed today than dead in the dark." She paused, letting her words sink in. "But I should also remind you that she lost to that Razor, an emerald, because she didn't see his line of attack. A lesson that I believe is even more important. Arrogance will lead you to an early grave."

Pandora sucked in a breath as she realized she was about to spar with one of the top waku in the Drops. The instructor was a three stone: amber, sapphire, and opal. The last one wouldn't be important for the fight, which meant it was mostly sapphire against sapphire.

Instructor Irina bowed. "May the shadows keep you safe."

"And the light weaken your enemies," said Pandora as she returned the gesture.

Instructor Irina leapt into the attack, her staff coming like a double bass drum. Pandora blocked most of the strikes, but at least three caught her around the arms and shoulder, until she could blast her opponent away with a heavy Push.

The impacts had left her limbs stinging. Instructor Irina smirked as she approached again; clearly she'd been toying with her. The leaping attack was bolstered with a feet-tangling Push, which Pandora countered with a twist, a combination of Push and Pull on opposite sides of the instructor's body, turning her before she landed.

The maneuver gave Pandora the time to roll back onto her feet, after getting knocked down, escaping to an open part of the circle. A few whistles went up from the other students, impressed that she'd lasted this long.

Instructor Irina growled under her breath as she spun the staff between her hands rapidly, blurring the weapon until it looked like she was surrounded by a silvery ring. As Pandora had learned over the last year, the head of the Drops Academy was a master at every weapon on the rack, and her stones made her second only to Duro as a warrior.

Before Irina could launch into another assault, Pandora threw her staff like a spear, using her Push to fling it at great speed. The weapon flew past as the instructor deflected it with her spinning staff, and before

Pandora could Pull it back, using the same maneuver she'd tricked the first years with, Irina used her own Push to throw the weapon outside of the circle.

Pandora had anticipated the response, closing the distance empty-handed and leaping through the air with a Push. Her foot flew towards the instructor's turned head. She was certain that she'd moved faster than Irina could counter, but the staff came around, deflecting her leg so she tumbled past, landing unceremoniously on the hard stone.

Instructor Irina swung the staff around, the tip coming for her when a strong male voice called out: "Hold!"

The staff halted an inch from Pandora's cheek. Instructor Irina looked perturbed until she looked up and her jaw loosened. With the tip hovering before her face, Pandora had to maneuver around to see Duro striding onto the training grounds. The keen gaze of Shadowmaster Duro fell upon them. Instructor Irina spun the staff away, leaving room for Pandora to return to her feet.

"I'm impressed, Irina. You've taught your students well when they can start to challenge you," said Duro with an incline of the head.

The instructor looked like she was searching for the insult, but returned the respectful gesture. She forced a smile that was anything but pleasant.

"We were having a bout of spirited competition today. Though this one has yet to learn the true art of scrapping. There is more to a fight than swinging a blade. One must keep the body in balance."

"Excellent. I'm sure we'll need this new cadre of waku sooner rather than later, but I hope they're in one piece when that day comes," he said.

Irina stiffened as her nostrils flared. "I assure you they will be ready."

"Good, because I need to borrow one of your students for a special project," said Duro.

Instructor Irina inclined her head as she turned towards the knot of fifth years that had been taunting Pandora earlier.

"They'd be honored to join you."

With heavy-lidded eyes, Duro smirked. "It's not them I want. I came for Pandora. She's shown she has a knack for scrapping and isn't afraid of taking chances. I need that kind of warrior for this task."

The request came as a surprise to the entire group, Pandora included. The instructor's shock was followed by another stiffening. The corner of her cheek twitched upward uncontrolled.

"Her? I beat her."

"She pushed you," said Duro. "I haven't seen you fight with that kind of conviction in a long time."

"She's only a second year."

"She's a warrior."

The glance in her direction was filled with simmering anger. Pandora had no doubt that the instructor knew about her raid on the Eights, but it hadn't swayed her opinion, unlike Duro.

"You're the warleader. I'm merely preparing them for the day you need them, but I worry you place too much faith in this one. I would hate to see her thread cut short when she still has much to learn."

The words were respectful, but the pulsing of her jaw and the anger in her gaze told of the simmering conflict between the two lieutenants. It was well-known that Irina wished to be the warleader of the Drops, but not a single member believed she was even close to his ability.

"I assure you I will take the same precautions you have," said Duro with a smirk. He jutted his head towards the dormitories. "Pack your bags, a few days' worth, including your old clothes. I'll stay and observe the progress of your fellow students' training."

Pandora bowed and ran towards the dorms as the shouts of effort continued behind her. At first she couldn't believe her good fortune, but she reminded herself that was why she'd taken the chance against the Eights. Instructor Irina would never acknowledge her gifts, but Duro, having seen the duel and the results of the raid, knew she had something to offer. And maybe it would give her a chance to return to the Terreno so she could check in with the Mod.

Back in her simple room, she threw her old clothes from before into her bag along with the other items for a few days' trip. By the time she returned, the class was moving through a series of maneuvers at great speed while Duro watched, a twitch on his lips. He raised an eyebrow at her return.

"Ready?"

She bowed again, but he waved her off as he turned to leave the Academy while she hurried to his side. "I don't want deference when we're in the city. I want you to listen and learn to anticipate what I want from you. Do you understand?"

"I...think so?"

"Fair enough. You don't know me and I don't know you, but I understand you're a quick learner."

She started to bow again, but held herself firm. "I will do my best."

Outside the Academy, Duro scooped up a black bag and threw it over his shoulder. She'd met him a few times, but had never spent more than a few minutes around him, so she was surprised by his arrogant swagger. But given his reputation as the most fearsome waku in the Undercity, she supposed it was warranted.

"May I ask what we'll be doing in the city?"

"You can ask, but I'm not telling you. Yet." He winked. "Do a good job and you might be invited on more trips like this, which come with certain perks."

"This is a test."

"Everything's a test," he replied. "A lesson I suggest you take to heart. If I were to show signs of slowing, or poor judgement, you can be sure Daraja would replace me as warleader. Probably with Irina. The same goes for her. She might be our clan leader, but only because she's shown brilliance in leadership. The Drops have prospered under her."

"I don't mean this disrespectfully, but in what way? As an Academy student I don't see much other than our training grounds, and the best gossip is about what we're having for dinner."

He chuckled. "This trip will be instructive for you then. Keep your eyes and ears open."

They left the Pajot not to the west, which was what she expected, but to the east towards Razor territory. She knew enough to keep her mouth shut. They moved without light. She relied on her sapphire, while he used his amber and the faint illumination from the fungi that made its home in the Undercity. He took them through strange caverns without clear paths, suggesting their route was an unusual one. At times, Duro paused, listening intently as his amber had a further range than her sapphire. Once he was sure they were safe, or whatever had been nearby had passed, he motioned for them to resume their journey.

During one section they skirted a deep canyon that looked like it'd been cut from the earth rather than created naturally. Her thoughts were confirmed when they passed old mining equipment that was covered in rust, hiding the maker's name.

It took them about three hours to reach their destination. She probably could have run it in less than forty minutes, but the unusual terrain and constant threat of danger slowed progress. When he reached the middle of an empty cavern, in an area that had scuff marks across the stone suggesting equipment had once been stored there, Duro switched on a small light then pulled a container the size of a matchbox out of a pocket and pressed a button.

Following his lead, she kept her mouth shut, wondering what the button had summoned, or who it had contacted. After a few minutes of waiting, he glanced up and gently pushed her out of the way. Moments later, a metal cage descended through the darkness, landing on the stone with a heavy thump. He threw the accordion door wide and gestured for her to enter, following her into the elevator. Duro pressed a button inside the cage and it lurched upward, bringing them slowly, inexorably towards the city.

Seven

The group of second years stood around the sparring room waiting for Instructor Kaz. Across the circle from Kuma, Deacon whispered in Yara's ear, their flirting grins bringing unexpected rage to his chest.

"I can't believe it," said Camina with her arms crossed.

"Me neither. I thought for sure she'd tried to sabotage the Black Crows, not sleep with them. She's probably doing that to annoy me."

Camina screwed up her face. "Not everything's about you, Little Bear. I'm talking about the stones."

Kuma ran a hand across his head. "We need allies that can fight."

"I should have had a chance at that topaz. Or Tick."

The smallest member of their trio looked up. He'd been examining a beetle crawling across his palm.

"I don't mind. If there's any stone that's a scrapping stone, it's topaz."

"Sometimes I wonder why you even joined the Academy," said Camina.

Across the circle, Deacon leaned back as Yara ran her hand along his tattooed neck. The topaz was prominently displayed in his ear unlike most waku, who hid them to disguise their abilities. Three of the Black Crows had stones: Deacon had both an amber and a topaz, while Syn had an amber and emerald and Laird wore an amber alone.

"It's wasted on them," said Camina. "They fight like children."

"We haven't seen them fight yet."

"I can tell," she said. "Sloppy punches and kicks. They have noodles for arms and legs. It's embarrassing."

Kuma didn't disagree, but he was trying to stay positive for the clan's sake. He wanted his father's plan to work, and for it to be successful, the Black Crows had to be integrated. He supposed he should be happy that Yara had taken a liking to Deacon, as she'd been his biggest concern, but it somehow felt off.

Deacon leaned into Yara's ear, and despite Kuma's attempt to overhear with his amber, he learned nothing. A moment later, the pair broke apart, laughing hysterically and glancing over at Kuma and his friends.

The crisp steps of Instructor Kaz had everyone gathering to attention, placing their feet wide and hands behind their backs. The three Black Crows matched the position but without the enthusiasm of the Razors. Kaz reviewed everyone from the center of the circle, a frown hoisted on his oversized lips, while Instructor Helena entered the room, but stayed at the back. The presence of the opal suggested that the day's lessons were going to be more intense than normal.

"Today we fight, and not the formal tournament style matches that exist in the light. I want to see you scrap as if your life depends on it. Because it will someday. Everyone grab a weapon from the rack. We'll pair up randomly. Matches go until I call it, your opponent yields, or is unconscious."

Under her breath, Camina muttered, "I hope I get matched with Deacon."

"He out-stones you."

"He doesn't know how to use it." She scowled. "And I'm sick of his cocky attitude. He acts like he owns the place, and he only just got here."

Kuma didn't disagree. The three remaining Black Crows were given leniency about the expectations and rules. Their disrespectful attitudes would have earned the rest of them a hundred arc runs.

As one of the last to the rack, he decided on a long spear as his weapon and returned to his place next to Camina, who had chosen curved blades.

Instructor Helena pulled two tiles out of a bag. "Tick versus Juliana."

Tick crouched to the ground and let the beetle crawl onto the hardwood floor before he stepped into the circle with his batons. Juliana had a short sword and buckler. The training weapons were dull, but could still do major damage with the right strike.

After the formal beginning to the match, the two combatants leapt into battle. Juliana was taller and stronger, but Tick, despite his twitchy demeanor, was a cagey fighter and managed to use his amber to great effect, anticipating her blows and dodging out of the way. The end of the fight came when he overextended with his batons. Juliana brought the buckler under his chin and stunned him, then used the flat of the blade against his temple to knock him down.

"Hold!"

The announcement was unnecessary as Tick lay groaning on the ground, while Juliana stood over him. Instructor Helena applied her healing energies into him and helped him limp from the circle.

As new tiles were pulled from the bag, Deacon said, "I don't get it. What's the point? This still ain't a real fight."

Instructor Kaz stared at the Black Crow member with heavy-lidded eyes. "Do you have a suggestion?"

"No, but my point is no one fights with just these antiquated weapons," he said, holding up the ball and chain he'd picked. "Where are the guns? Explosives. Fucking mage tricks. My one rule of fighting is never do it fair."

Instructor Kaz said nothing. He turned to Helena, who called out with a smirk and a shoulder shrug, "Camina versus Deacon."

After the pronouncement from Deacon, the rest of the Razors, minus Yara and her friends, called out encouragement to Camina as she stepped into the circle with her twin blades. The ball and chain hung by Deacon's side as he smirked at Camina.

After bowing and speaking the formal words, Instructor Kaz said, "Begin!"

"You got this," said Kuma to encourage Camina.

She stayed on the balls of her feet, swaying back and forth with the blades held before her. The ball and chain was a frightening weapon that could shatter an enchanted riot shield with enough topaz force. Most students didn't pick it, because they didn't want to hurt their fellow clan-mates, but that concern hadn't occurred to Deacon.

He twirled the ball in a lazy spin at his side, observing Camina with the intensity of a hyena. Behind him, Yara clapped her hands.

"Come on, babe. Show her what you got."

The setup couldn't have been worse for Camina. Her blades were suitable against most other weapons, but the ball and chain could break through the most strident defense, sometimes shattering thin blades. Her best bet was to entangle the chain and disarm him before trying to take him out.

Deacon head-faked, making Camina jump to the side in anticipation of a strike. It was one thing to get hit with a staff, or even have your arm sliced open wide, but the heavy ball would break bones. He chuckled at her skittishness, bringing a scowl to her lips. He did it a second time, but she lunged in, slicing his forearm with the blade. It wasn't as deep a cut as a real weapon would have inflicted, but beads of crimson formed along the cut, and he licked them off before refocusing on her.

Camina smirked, staying low and ready like a snake about to strike. Deacon spun the ball faster than necessary and Kuma sensed what he was about to do a moment before it happened. He loosed the weapon, letting it fly from his hand, catching her across the jaw. Before she could recover, Deacon caught her wrists and brought his forehead against her nose, shattering it.

His topaz had been active, but Kuma sensed the moment he reared his hand back that it vibrated to full power. He struck Camina in the chest, sending her flying backward to land unconscious on the wood floor with a bloody face.

As Instructor Helena rushed to Camina's side, Kuma stepped into the circle and slammed Deacon in the chest.

"What the fuck are you doing? You could have killed her."

"I thought we were learning to scrap," said Deacon, holding his hands wide in mock apology.

"Kuma! Get out of the circle," said Instructor Kaz as he joined Helena at Camina's side.

The furious rebuke left Kuma frustrated as he stepped back. Yara smirked at him from across the way. She kept eye contact as she kissed Deacon full on the lips upon his victorious return.

After a brief consultation with Kaz, Instructor Helena scooped up Camina in her arms. She moaned, unconscious.

"I'm taking her to Brazio. Her injuries are beyond me."

An emptiness filled Kuma as he watched Helena carry his friend from the room. The idea that he was supposed to support the Black Crows for his father's sake seemed like mist on hot stone. He barely heard when Tick tried to console him that she'd be alright.

Instructor Kaz stepped into the circle. "You'll feel much worse when your friends are dead on the battlefield because they weren't ready to scrap. As brutal as it was to witness, need I remind you that Camina is alive and will recover quickly. We have our opals to thank. Before the stones, injuries like that might have taken weeks or months.

"And if you think that Deacon fought too roughly, strike that thought from your mind. He fought to win, something you should all consider when your life is on the line. Use everything you have, leave nothing back. As Deacon said, never fight fair." He paused. "Since we don't have our opal on hand, we'll table the rest of the fights for a later date. Return your weapons to the rack. We'll work on our holds and throws. Everyone grab a partner."

Kuma returned to the rack, jostling until he was next to Deacon.

"You did that on purpose."

Deacon regarded him coolly. "I fight to win."

"We don't hurt our own."

"I did her a favor. I bet she trains harder after that and won't be surprised if someone tries that."

"Bullshit," said Kuma. "You tried to kill her."

Deacon set the head of the ball into the catch and turned back to Kuma. He placed a single finger against his chest.

"If you're not willing to kill, then maybe you're not a warrior I want at my side."

Deacon brushed past as Yara laughed, a cold, cutting sound that had Kuma fuming inside. Clearly Yara had told Deacon about the duel with Pandora. After returning his long spear, Kuma joined Tick on the far side of the room.

"She'll be fine. Your uncle is the best opal in the clan. Probably the Undercity."

Kuma blushed as he wasn't thinking about his friend, but the Crow and how much he wanted to hurt him. Even though he believed in his father's mission—that the way the clan was going to survive was to have allies—he wanted revenge for what Deacon had done to Camina. The idea that he would have to swallow his pride and work with Deacon was worse than any of Instructor Kaz's training.

Eight

The steel mesh elevator rumbled upward through the empty cavern, eventually slipping into a hole that had been drilled through the earth. Pandora knew about a lot of the entrances to the Undercity, but not this one.

"I didn't realize this was Drops territory."

"It's not," said Duro. "Call it neutral ground. The person that owns it owes me a few favors and lets me use his elevator in return. We're coming this way so no one knows we've left the Undercity. The other entrances are all guarded and watched."

When the elevator reached the top, they were in a simple room with an electric winch on the ceiling for lifting and lowering. Duro led them out of the cage and into a hallway. He paused briefly, pulling up his hood. She followed his example, enjoying the feel of her old clothes on her skin.

To her surprise, they exited into a store of some kind filled with teenagers playing games at tables and making entirely too much noise. The sights and colors were overwhelming and confusing. They passed a front counter filled with small shaped stones and other figurines. The pimple-faced worker behind it averted his eyes.

Relieved when they hit the outside, Pandora asked, "What kind of place was that?"

"You don't know?" he asked with a tilt of his head.

"No. I spent my time as a kid stealing from cars and running from the cops."

"Gaming store."

He headed the opposite direction. She glanced to the colorful mural on the brick wall, which included the name Freeport Games.

"Weird place for an entrance to the Undercity."

"If you met the owner, you'd understand. Assuming he let you live."

Pandora knew the city was the home of many strange and powerful beings, but she never imagined one might own a kids' store.

Duro bought tickets for the train at a nearby station. She'd figured their location as the ninth ward by their relation to the Spire at the center of the city. The top third of the massive tower was hidden by a flat, gray cloud layer. As she moved through the buildings, she was struck by how little she could feel with her sapphire. Unlike the Undercity, the aboveground portion wasn't awash in faez.

"October?" she asked as they rumbled along the tracks, sitting across from a family of four that were clearly tourists by their Hall branded shirts. The youngest boy, no older than seven, was playing with a plastic dragon that made roaring noises when he pressed a button on the back.

Duro screwed up his face before it smoothed to laughter. "November."

The parents across the aisle appeared incredulous that she hadn't known the month, but she'd been in the Undercity so long and without a calendar, she hadn't known.

They left the train in the seventh ward near the Canal District. As they headed towards the southern part of the ward, she worried where Duro might be taking her until he veered towards the west and into an apartment building that overlooked the ring road that separated the inner wards from the outer ones.

He banged on a third-floor door near the back of the building. A muffled question reverberated through the wood.

"I got everything but the eggs," said Duro.

The door opened a moment later, revealing two members of Drops that she only vaguely recognized. Neither had the face tattoos that many of the waku preferred. On a table in the back, automatic weapons, explosives, and other weapons were piled together.

Duro pushed past and said over his shoulder, "Phillip and Dane. This is Pandora."

"Is she gonna be the key?"

"I hope so, or this is gonna be a big waste of time," said Duro, heading into the kitchen and rummaging around the refrigerator until he had a beer bottle in hand. "You want one?"

"Don't we have a job to do?"

He smiled over his shoulder. "Not until after dark. Time enough for a drink. Only one if you're worried," he said with a wink.

Duro tossed the bottle to her then threw himself onto the big leather couch. He cracked his beer and chugged half of it before letting loose a gut-rumbling belch.

"How are sales?"

The two Drops members, soldados she assumed, made gestures that equated to a lack of enthusiasm.

"Too many people want them, not enough have the money to pay. We had some wayhos try to snatch Dane's bag last week. It didn't end well for him. Then there's the PD. They seem to show up whenever we try to get settled. Trying to clean up this fucked-up town. Good luck," said Phillip, chuckling.

A short time later, Dane and Phillip left the apartment on errands. Pandora didn't bother asking. It didn't matter. She had a job to do and that was the only thing.

Duro finished his beer and grabbed another. "You got a family?"

The question caught her off guard. She leaned forward, dangling the beer from her fingertips. "Old man took about fifty bullets in a shootout with a rival gang. They rolled up on him when he was picking me up from school."

Duro nodded knowingly. "Sorry."

"He was a good dad. Planned on taking us somewhere else once he had enough money, but you know how it is. Never seems enough when there's more to be had."

"Mine died in a scrap with the Vipers," said Duro, lifting his beer bottle in respect. "What about your mom?"

The mention had her squeezing her bottle hard enough it would have broken had she been a topaz. The sound of the clicker echoed in her mind.

"She showed up after he died. Been gone pretty much since I'd been born. Took me away from Chicago for a while but we came back later."

"You don't like her."

"Like isn't the right word. Mothers are mothers. You have to have one." Pandora took a drink. "She has her own demons to fight. One that makes my problems seem simple."

"Where'd she take you?"

"Back home. Spent time with my grandfather and the rest of the extended family. It was a much different life. Even harder than Chicago, or the Undercity." She tapped her fingernails on the bottle. The urge to count was strong, but Duro was staring right at her. Right through her as if he could read her soul. Pandora swallowed.

"Must have been tough. You fight like you have something to prove."

Pandora set the empty bottle on the table. "What about you?"

"Mama lives in the Pajot. Knits clothes for the youngins," said Duro with a wistful smile. "She lived a hard life. Founded the Drops back when it was just a bunch of holes in the ground, little food, danger at every turn. But she carved out a home for us. We owe her generation to keep things going, whatever it takes. I will kill whoever to keep her safe."

Pandora was no stranger to the hardness in his gaze. She lifted her bottle towards him.

"To mothers."

"To mothers."

She watched the sun set from the window. The cloud cover had broken up, splashing pinks and oranges across the horizon. As the light faded, the city came alive with neon signs, car headlights, and the illusionary battles near the second ward. The rebuilt Glitterdome sparkled with fireworks announcing the start of a big show.

"Were you here for it?"

"Of course."

"Doesn't look any different from before," she said.

"The scars run deep. The Halls aren't the same place as they were before. They can't use magic like they used to because of whatever it was that fixed it. Still dangerous, but you know, not the same." He checked his watch. "Time to go."

Duro led them on foot into the second ward through the pedestrian tunnels that went under the ring road. Gang tags littered the concrete walls. Pandora spotted a graffiti crow with crimson eyes permanently displayed at the center of the wall. He acknowledged the tag with the gesture for "Warning, stay alert."

They entered a basement through a back door. Dane and Phillip were waiting with big, bulky bags. The concrete wall had been broken out, leaving an entrance to the sewer tunnels. The smell wasn't heavy, but still made her nose wrinkle. She took their nonverbal gestures of communication as a warning to be silent. The four of them trudged through the tunnels until they reached another broken-out wall. Whatever they were here to do, it was long in the making. Stepping through the hole put them in a small room with a heavy steel door on the opposite side. The two soldados placed little black boxes at two corners of the room before motioning to Duro.

"Good, we can talk now."

"What is this place?"

"One of the main warehouses for the Black Crows. They keep a lot of important things here, some of which we wish to acquire for ourselves," said Duro.

"You said I'm the key?"

"Reach out with your sapphire."

She did as he asked, finding the door awash with faez. It was covered in enchantments. She also felt a faint vibration.

"Do you feel that?"

Duro nodded. "Whatever it is, it doesn't matter for what we're doing."

"And the door? Is it safe?" she asked.

"Nothing on that door is reactive as long as we don't touch it. It's meant to hold it closed, keep people from getting in this way, and the enchantments are only sensitive to physical contact. The door was put in years ago when they smuggled their equipment into the building, and then they boarded it back up and forgot about it."

"Can't blow through it?"

"It'll set off the enchantments," he said.

She nodded. "But those same enchantments make it vulnerable to my sapphire."

"Exactly. If we're going to get in there, you're gonna have to pull it off the wall."

"Won't that make noise?"

"You saw the fireworks over the Glitterdome? There's a big concert there, lots of heavy metal bands, some who specialize in flashy and loud illusionary shows. It'll be banging over there all night. If they detect anything, they'll think it's the concert."

"And you think I can just yank this door off its hinges?"

"That's the idea. I've seen you use your sapphire. You're stronger than any of the others we have in the Drops."

Pandora faced her challenge. She wasn't so sure, but then again, she'd never tried to tear a door off its hinges. She reached out with her sapphire, feeling the contours of the magic. There was a marked difference between the steel barrier and the frame around it. Pandora pushed and tugged, trying to get a better idea of what she needed to do. She appreciated the compliment from Duro, but didn't think she had the strength to rip it out without preparation.

Once she'd examined her task, she Pulled with the sapphire. It felt like yanking on the faez-imbued ground. She tried two more times before turning to Duro.

"Are you sure about this? It feels like I'm trying to throw the earth."

Duro said nothing and gestured towards the door. Pandora tried again. She put her entire being into the Pull, but found herself sliding towards the door rather than yanking it away. As she was looking around for something to grab ahold of, Duro approached from behind.

"May I?"

"Thank you. Just try not to squeeze my guts out."

With Duro's strong arms around her waist, she Pulled again. The door rattled in its frame.

"Keep going," he said.

She kept up the Pull. The harder she yanked, the more Duro had to dig his hands into her hips to keep her from sliding. If it weren't for his topaz, they both would have been shifting forward. At the point she thought her efforts were going nowhere, the frame connections started to crack. Encouraged by the change, she dug deeper. The welds snapped, and Duro yanked her backwards as the doors fell over, slamming onto the concrete and sending up a dust plume.

A massive headache piled into her mind the moment she released, leaving her bent over. Duro let her recover, handing her water as the other two started putting on their gear and checking their automatic weapons. They gave her a formfitting mask, which slipped over her face comfortably. She retrieved the curved blades from her bag while Duro pulled out a pair of batons.

"The target is on the far side of the lower level. There might be guards, or not. We'll have to find out as we go. If we have to fight, end it quickly and quietly. We don't want to get into a prolonged fight. There are probably twenty or thirty gang members in the building at any one time, though they rarely come into the basement."

Duro slipped on his mask and they entered the building by stepping over the fallen door. A low level of faez allowed her to see with her sapphire, while the two soldados used military-grade night vision goggles. She hadn't expected to be able to use her sapphire, but maybe faez had bubbled up from below, infusing the area.

The interior of the lower level had surprisingly high ceilings. They crept forward towards heavy equipment. Duro paused briefly at the mining gear. There were huge drill bits that looked both new and worn, lying on wooden pallets. On the far side of the basement a huge set of double doors blocked their view. She could feel the vibration coming from that direction. Duro looked like he wanted to investigate, but he went past the equipment towards a door on the far wall.

The door was locked, but Duro grabbed the handle, braced himself, and yanked, snapping the bolt. He gave them the "Hold" gesture and went into the room. Pandora investigated a set of wide steps that went up to the ground floor. Faint conversation reached her ears. It sounded like someone might be heading down. She motioned to Dane, but he spread his hands. Duro was still inside the room.

She saw boots appear around the corner. A group was headed into the basement. She checked the open door to find Duro nowhere to be found. He'd gone into one of the many rooms in the hallway. She motioned for the two soldados, and they slipped past the door, holding it closed because the bolt had been snapped off. Her heart thundered in her ears as she heard many voices headed down the stairs, including one she hadn't expected. Dane and Phillip cocked their weapons, preparing for a fight that would leave them massively outnumbered.

Nine

Kuma was summoned from the obstacle course training grounds to find Deacon chatting with Brazio like old friends at the gate of the Academy. His uncle had bags under his eyes, but seemed in a good mood.

"Little Bear," he greeted, offering a half-hug.

"Uncle."

Kuma made a point of not standing near Deacon. Camina had needed to be sent to an above ground hospital to be fixed with more complex magics.

"You two are going on a little trip."

"We are?"

Brazio bunched up his lips. "His bosses want to see how things are progressing with the training. They want to know we're not yanking their chains. You'll head through the tunnels using one of the carts. Don't worry, the passage is secure. Gabrielle has made some modifications to the entry points. We won't be surprised again."

"Why me?"

"They know you from the raid and you're a clan leader's son."

Kuma thought about pointing out that Yara was available, but it appeared it'd already been decided.

"Understood."

"Grab your things. You'll only be gone a day, but look sharp." Brazio held out a small bag. "Give this to Gregor. He's the head of Black Crows."

The leather bag jingled with small stones, barely any weight. Kuma returned to his quarters, putting on the dark slacks, white shirt, crimson vest, and black jacket that marked their clan. In the privacy of his room, he checked the contents of the bag, finding five ambers and two topaz. While the ambers were common everywhere, and they had extras of topaz, he hated the idea that they were giving some away.

He found Deacon at the rendezvous point, wearing the tracksuit he'd worn when he'd arrived in the Machi. They were led into a room where a half dozen electric carts waited.

Kuma thought Deacon might protest being blindfolded but he

accepted the loss of sight without comment. If he thought he might be able to figure out the pathways, he would be disappointed as there were direction-confusing enchantments at certain points that Gabrielle had placed to keep people from detecting the route without sight.

The cart sped through the tunnels, illuminated by the headlamps on the front, which made the passage seem faster than it was. Kuma sat next to Deacon trying not to sink into the misfortune that had placed them back together.

"I'm real sorry about Camina," said Deacon, his muffled voice coming through the black bag on his head.

"If you were sorry you wouldn't have done it."

"I ain't used to holdin' back. You all have honor down here. You treat each other like family. But in the city, if you show weakness, you get your head taken off. I'm just not used to how you do things."

Kuma's amber annoyingly told him that Deacon was being honest.

"You could have killed her."

"I only wanted to prove myself. You know I come into your world, your Academy, and everyone only sees the outsider. We dress different, talk different, and you treat us different. The best way of proving yourself is to put someone else down. But I went too far. I see that now."

The rest of the journey was made in silence. The electric cart arrived in their hideout in Big Dave's Town. The place seemed subdued when they strolled into the open. The buzzing of the neon Devil's

Lipstick sign seemed overly loud as there was no one in the streets, and Razor soldados stood on every corner with automatic weapons slung over their shoulders, giving nods of recognition as they passed.

"Always like this?"

"Usually way busier. No wonder the businesses are unhappy. They're safe from theft and customers," said Kuma.

The climb up the ramp was long and exhausting. Halfway up, Deacon pointed to a gash in the stone.

"Was this from...?"

"Yeah."

Deacon checked behind them. "Much damage to the town?"

"Not as much as you'd expect. They came through the streets, killing anyone they saw, but didn't touch the buildings. The bar at the top was a different story. Wasn't big enough for some of the larger demons, so they knocked down the walls and ceilings to get out. Were you in the city?"

He nodded. "We hunkered down in the tenth ward. Not a lot of casualties and when the fighting was over, we were able to afford some of the buildings in the second ward, take over territory that had been run by other gangs that took too big of a hit."

Outside the Goblin's Romp, a black SUV with tinted windows was waiting for them. Kuma steeled his guts and made the short walk into the open air before climbing into the back seat. His heart was racing, but he managed to keep a calm façade. Deacon knew the driver and hopped in the passenger seat. They started talking about what had been happening since he'd gone underground, leaving Kuma to stare at the fireworks exploding over the Glitterdome.

The journey was short, only one ward away to the second. The front of the building looked like a fortress. Deacon led them through a security room where their identities were confirmed by video feed before they were let into the main area.

A heavy-set man in a silk suit with greasy black hair and a mustache needing a trim greeted them with open arms upon arrival. Deep pockmarks made his cheeks gaunt. He grabbed Deacon around the neck and hugged him to his side.

"Deacon, you slimy cunt, it's good to see your pale ass again. I hope you behaved yourself. Ol' Deacon here can be a bit prickly." The exchange seemed like the equivalent to grabbing an unwilling dog, mussing with their fur, and presenting them to a guest. "You must be Kuma Santos."

Kuma bent deeply at the waist and then extended his hand. "I am. May the shadows keep you safe."

"Gregor Anderson if you didn't already know," he said as he kept his arm around Deacon's neck, shaking him slightly. Deacon looked uncomfortable but said nothing. "You hear that, Deacon? I like that greeting. May the shadows keep you safe. We need something like that. Maybe it should be, listen to me or I'll pull your fucking guts out, or something like that."

He pushed Deacon away. The fellow trainee straightened his jacket and tried to keep a neutral face, but Kuma could see his simmering anger.

Gregor led them into a formal conference room with a big mahogany table at the center. He poured himself a coffee from a machine on the wall, gesturing towards it as he was sipping from the cup.

"There's water in the fridge down there, or whiskey if that's your thing, but you don't look the type," said Gregor as he took a seat.

Kuma took one a few seats away, leaving a space for Deacon between them. Gregor stared at them as if he were deciding which steak to eat, the twenty-eight-ounce sirloin or the fifteen-ounce fillet.

"Lemme see it," he said, holding out his hand.

Deacon knocked the hair away from his ear, revealing the twin stones set into his tragus.

"Topaz and amber. The topaz is the strength one, right? Show me something, Deacon. Make me proud."

Deacon rose from the table and checked around the room. He found a crowbar leaning in the corner. Kuma had a pretty good idea why it'd been there. Deacon presented the crowbar on his flat palms, bowed slightly, and then strained with effort as he bent the metal bar into a U shape.

"Outstanding," said Gregor, clapping his hands. "Not only is our Deacon upgraded, but he's learned respect. Something I would never have thought possible. It's like teaching a hyena to eat at a table like a real human." He winked at Kuma. "Maybe this arrangement is having benefits I didn't anticipate, though you could have dressed better, Deacon. Look how sharp Kuma is. So, how's the training?"

Deacon returned to his seat. His lips were squeezed white and Kuma sensed boiling emotions inside with the amber.

"Good. There's a lot we don't know, but Instructor Kaz has tailored our training to our skill sets." He looked up, even though it was clear that eye contact with Gregor was painful. "Maybe in the future we can send younger students so they can learn the full component of skills. Or incorporate some training like Razor's into our new recruits."

Gregor smoothed his greasy mustache and stared at Deacon with dead eyes.

"What did I say about thinking, Deacon? Not too much, or you'll get yourself in trouble." He winked at Kuma, showing off how he could beat his dog. "But it's a good thought. I'll consider it. What about you, Kuma? What kind of stones do you have?"

Under normal circumstances, Kuma wouldn't have divulged the information, but after the duel at Shade's End and his time training with Deacon, there was no reason to keep it hidden.

"Amber and emerald."

"Emerald," said Gregor as if he were tasting the word. "That's the one that makes you heavy?"

"Or light."

"Care to give a demonstration?"

Kuma inclined his head. "Of course." He stepped behind the big chair and cycling to Light, leapt onto the back, balancing on the wobbly seat as if he were a feather. Kuma pulled the curved blades from his inside pockets, twirled them around his hands while he stayed balanced, and then shoved them back into their sheaths. He dropped to the ground, cycling back to Heavy, which made his landing thud loudly.

"That was a cooler trick, Deacon. You need to work on your showmanship. You good with those knives?"

"Not as good as many others like my uncle, but getting better," said Kuma.

"So you have something else for me?"

Kuma reached into his pocket, producing the small leather bag. He slid it to Gregor, who peeked in, pulled out an amber, and held it up to the light.

"It won't make me dizzy, will it?"

"Eventually," said Kuma.

"How bad was it for you?"

"My attunement was longer and more brutal than most. But in the end, I managed."

"They said mine was average," said Deacon. "The topaz was much easier than the amber."

"A fucking wonder," said Gregor, shaking his head. "All the power the mages have except condensed down to this little stone. Right under our feet this whole time and none of that fancy Hall bullshit to get in the way. It gives me great pleasure to know that they're getting knocked down a peg or two, not only because of the stones, but their weakened magic. Of course, I'd like some of the fancier stones. Amber is good and all, and these topaz will be a boon, but we need more of the others. What's the strongest stone you think?"

"Some think it's the sapphire, while others believe the black diamond might be strongest."

"Black diamond? I ain't heard of it."

"It's very rare, only a few have been found and none by Razor. The user can turn their skin to what amounts to impregnable steel."

"Like a fucking tank."

"Almost, but it's not perfect. My uncle beat one in a duel last year. Cooked her alive with his opal."

Gregor finished his coffee, setting the cup down with a rattle. "My understanding is you beat a sapphire in a duel."

"I did."

"So the stones aren't enough."

"It takes training to use them. Even an amber can beat a sapphire if their opponent doesn't know how to use their stone."

"Did your opponent?"

The memory of Pandora brought warmth to his middle. "She was good. Really good. But I'd been training against our sapphires, and I knew how to counter her, and when an opportunity was presented, I took it and won."

Gregor leaned over. "But you didn't kill her. Why was that?"

It was a question he'd been asked dozens of times since, and he had a practiced answer.

"I owed her a debt. She stopped a rival clan from killing me. This was before she became a Drops."

Gregor drummed his fingers on the table as he considered the explanation.

"If it were me, I would have cut her throat. Never leave an enemy alive." He wagged his eyebrows towards the ceiling. "You know how we got this place?"

"I know it was after the Invasion."

"Used to be owned by the Joker Sixes. Big gang, lots of money and power. Had local commissioners in their pocket, bribes to the cops, that sort of thing. But the invasion hit them hard, and they were weak and scattered. While the demo crews were tearing down the old Glitterdome, we moved in like a scythe cutting down wheat. We hit them hard and fast and left no one alive."

Kuma nodded respectfully, but said nothing while Gregor stared at him.

"If we're going to ally with Razor in the Undercity, eventually we're going to take down the Drops. They're your biggest rivals and the ones nipping at your heels. I hope when the time comes you'll cut that bitch's throat and every other Drops that gets in the way. No man, woman, or child standing."

The thought of killing children made him sick, but it wasn't his place to offer disagreement.

"No one left standing."

"Good," said Gregor, his jaw pulsing. "I don't do half measures."

The head of the Black Crows grabbed the bag of stones and moved towards the door.

"I'm gonna put this away until I've decided who to give them to. When I get back, the three of us are gonna head into third. There's a nice club there where we can have a good time, no questions asked," said Gregor with a wink.

The heavy-set leader of the Black Crows left the room. Kuma watched through the window as he headed down a set of stairs.

"He's interesting," said Kuma with an eyebrow raised.

"Don't. Just don't," replied Deacon with rage in his eyes.

Kuma moved to the refrigerator to grab a bottle of water when the sound of gunfire from below had him rushing out the door along with Deacon. They were joined by a dozen men and women with guns rushing down to the lower level, as Gregor came stumbling up, sweat dripping off his nose as he fired downward.

"They're in the fucking storage rooms! Kill 'em!"

Without a gun, Kuma wasn't about to rush into the basement and get caught up in friendly fire. He stood at the top as the Black Crows spread out, firing at unseen assailants. Return fire pinged across the heavy machinery, but it seemed much less than what the Black Crows were laying down, suggesting that they wouldn't last long outnumbered.

Behind them, Gregor was screaming into his phone, bringing other members from rooms deeper in the facility. He looked like he was about to have a heart attack by the way his cheeks were bright crimson.

Kuma happened to glance back down the stairs the moment he saw the line of Black Crows firing their weapons get flung backwards as if an invisible hand had punched them.

"A sapphire," said Deacon breathlessly. He ran back into the room, grabbing the crowbar and bending it back as Kuma pulled out his curved blades.

He crept down, reaching halfway when a figure in all-black with a mask blurred past the bottom of the stairs. The staccato crunch of batons hitting bones was followed by screams of agony. There was more than one waku in the basement. Kuma leapt down with Light behind a big metal box where multiple gang members were either unconscious or moaning, tuning his amber to a low level and scouting the wide space.

Kuma barely sensed the figure approach in time. He'd fought other waku dozens of times during training at the Academy, but none of it prepared him for the speed and power of his opponent. The black-clad figure struck like a cobra with the strength of an elephant. After two narrow blocks, he leapt backwards with Lightness to avoid getting his skull crushed in. The figure looked like he was going to continue his attack until gunfire sprayed across the ceiling, forcing him to retreat.

The basement level was surprisingly open, with high ceilings, and was filled with heavy machinery. He saw two others with automatics slung over their shoulders, one of them moving as if they'd been hit, and a third following behind with her hands up. Kuma could tell it was a woman by the slender hips and a familiarity that was unmistakable. When he reached for a fallen automatic weapon, she knocked it away with a sapphire Push.

The four invaders disappeared around the corner as Deacon appeared at his side with his crowbar. Gregor came halfway down the steps with a pistol in his fist, shouting, "They stole my fucking property! Get it back! Kill those motherfuckers and get it back!"

The head of the Black Crows threw the pistol towards Kuma. He caught it and shoved it into his back waistband. Then he ran to where they'd fled, slowing at the corners in case they were waiting with their weapons. Deacon was right behind with a rifle he'd scooped up along the way. After checking to make sure it was clear, he ran down the hallway towards a massive hole in the wall that had been ripped out.

"Shadows below."

He followed the sounds of the injured gunman, hurrying but at the same time being cautious. They followed through holes in walls, smashed open at some previous time, until they reached the streets.

They had a good head start. Deacon ran ahead, using his topaz to move faster, while Kuma was able to boost his speed using cycled Lightness. They ran under the ring road, catching sight of a dangling rope being yanked up the side of an apartment building in the second.

"Fuck, we can't follow that," said Deacon, looking up.

Kuma spotted a couple of windowsills spaced close enough and put his blades away. "I can."

He made himself Light, leaping up and catching the sill. He cycled Heavy briefly as he stood and then back to Light for the next jump. In a matter of a few seconds, he'd scaled the side of the building and landed on the roof.

With his amber, he spotted lines of blood leading away from the edge. He was reaching for his blades when he heard footsteps and looked up to see Duro's round face and his twin batons moving at him in a blur. There would be no one to save him now. Kuma barely got his weapons up in time. Two blocks. Three blocks. He couldn't keep it up forever.

Kuma leapt to the top of a metal HVAC system with Lightness as Duro sped after him. Reaching back into his waistband, he started to pull the pistol out. Duro was flying through the air with batons ready to smash his face. The pistol was going to be a hair late.

Right before the batons came down, an invisible hand Pushed him off the HVAC and the edge of the building. He fired just wide of Duro's chest. Kuma saw the masked form of Pandora standing to the side with her hand out as he flew over the edge. Kuma fell from the roof, using Lightness to land gently, then cycled Heavy to compensate.

Duro looked over the edge of the apartment building and then disappeared. Deacon had been starting to climb the wall, but leapt back down when Kuma landed.

"Who the fuck was that?" asked Deacon.

A torrent of answers raged in Kuma's head. "That was Duro Hernandez. The warleader of Drops."

"I can't believe you leapt off that building. Even after seeing you do it before, I thought you were dead."

"Yeah, I thought I was dead too."

But he wasn't because of Pandora. There was no other explanation. She'd saved him by pushing him off the edge. But had she done it to save Duro, or for him?

The sounds of distant sirens had Deacon nodding his head back the other direction.

"We should go."

Kuma checked up the building once more and considered following once again, but decided he'd pushed his luck enough. The idea that the Drops had hit their allies complicated things. While it wasn't a direct violation of the peace agreement, it was sure to cause waves within both leadership teams. The case for hitting the Drops would grow even stronger, and might not be avoidable given Gregor's anger.

As they jogged back the way they'd come, Deacon asked, "How'd he move that fast? I didn't think you could do that with a topaz."

"Duro might have been the best scrapper in the Undercity before the stones, and now with them, he's a singular force. He uses them in ways few others can."

"Could your uncle beat him?"

"Probably, but no matter the outcome, it'd be a hellacious fight."

"I'd like to be there for that."

Kuma nodded, even as he wasn't so sure he agreed. If those two were fighting, then the whole Undercity would be at war.

Ten

"Hold fucking still," Duro told Dane as he pressed his hands against the gunshot wound.

Pandora threw her gear down and paced around the kitchen. Her hands were shaking. Three bottle caps on the counter. Seven gas grates on the stove. She counted until her heart slowed enough she could breathe, but then she found Duro staring at her with bloody hands.

The moment she'd Pushed Kuma off the building was a beacon in her head. It'd happened in the blink of an eye. When Duro had been flying towards him with the batons, she'd reacted, not even seeing the gun until the last moment. A whole host of questions ran through her mind. She should have let Duro kill him, but she couldn't and now she didn't want to think of all the reasons why.

The warleader of Drops was staring at her and she feared that saving Kuma had exposed her. He'd probably kill her as a traitor. She would run but knew there was no way she could escape him.

"That Push," said Duro, approaching. "You saved me. I didn't know he had a gun until it was coming around. Would have hit me point-blank in the chest and I would have gone over the side, not a damn thing you could have done to stop it."

"It happened so fast. I didn't know if you were going to reach him in time," said Pandora breathlessly.

He walked past and reached into the refrigerator, pulling out a fistful of beers.

She'd chugged half before she even realized it, letting out an awful belch. Pandora leaned against the counter, relief coming in waves, not from the fight in the basement but from Duro's interpretation of her Push.

"Bad fucking luck they were there," said Duro as he leaned against the counter and crossed his arms. "Worse that I'd taken my mask off. Damn thing got in my eyes when I was carrying Dane up the rope and so I yanked it off."

Pandora had been so intent on her own mistakes, she hadn't thought about the implications of Duro being spotted.

"Will it break the peace?"

"Technically, no. Nothing that happens in the light matters, and this was a hit on Black Crows, not Razor. Kuma shouldn't have gotten involved."

"I thought they were allies."

"They are, but that's not part of the peace deal either. Outside groups are fair game." Duro slammed his bottle on the counter, smashing it. Glass and foamy beer went everywhere. "Fuck. Black Crows are going to want blood, and they'll push Razor to take it."

"Did you get what you were looking for?" she asked.

Duro grabbed a wastebasket and swept the whole mess of glass and beer into the container, wiping the liquid on his shirt when he was finished. He grabbed his black bag, unzipped it, and pulled out a small steel box that held alchemical elixirs. He opened it up, revealing a cushioned interior and six vials. The burning black circle of an eclipse was shown on the round glass.

"What is it?"

Duro held up a vial of dark liquid that seemed to glow of its own accord.

"It's called Eclipse. What we know is that it helps with attunement. Instead of a thirty percent rate, less with the rarer stones, it's more like seventy or eighty percent."

"The black diamond," said Pandora, suddenly understanding.

Duro nodded. "The randomness of attunement makes building the best waku difficult. But if we can guarantee our best warriors have the best stones, we gain a huge advantage."

"But that means Razor already has it."

Duro chuckled. "As far as we know, they're not aware of the existence of Eclipse. The Black Crows have kept that from their allies. It might be because they only have a small supply of the elixirs, or they're not sure if they can trust each other yet."

"Where did it come from?"

"G&T Industries. The owner is some rich kid from Alchemists that used to make party drugs, but now he's an up-and-coming player in the elixir market."

"How did he even know about the stones?"

Duro shrugged. "No idea."

Pandora took another drink, letting the implications settle on her mind.

"If he can make more, then the whole balance of power could change."

"As far as we understand, he only made a small batch of Eclipse. I was hoping to get the entire cache, but there were only two boxes. My sources say there were supposed to be ten that Black Crows liberated."

"Can we get the formula and make our own?"

"Not possible. There are no written formulas to steal," said Duro.

"Are you going to take the black diamond?"

He swirled his beer, taking a sip before grimacing. "I already failed attunement. We didn't know about Eclipse at the time."

"Then who?"

Duro looked out the window at the fireworks exploding over the Glitterdome.

"Grab your gear. We should get out of the city." He kicked the couch where Dane and Phillip were seated. "You too. This place isn't safe. They tracked us close to here. Who knows how much blood you lost along the way. We'll have to consider this hideaway busted until we know otherwise. Switch clothes before you go."

Pandora pulled the clothes out of her bag and quickly changed, catching a glance from the others when she was in her underthings, but no one made a comment.

Duro led her out of the apartment. He paused at corners and kept checking the sky. Once they were out of the building they jogged a few blocks north before hailing a taxi. When they headed west around the ring road, she asked, "Not returning through Freeport Games?"

"We were already spotted." He chewed on his lower lip. "What's with the scars? You fall into a barrel of glass?"

Pandora reached towards her back. "I'd forgotten about them."

"And?"

"Your guess was close to the truth."

He stared at her keenly. "Fair enough."

Memories tried to bubble up, but she pushed them down, resorting to counting the primes she could find along the route. There were worse things than a gang war, she reminded herself.

The taxi dropped them off southwest of the statue of Invictus. She caught sight of it a few times through the gaps in the buildings.

"Not entering at the Lazona?"

"I have an errand in the Terreno. Swinging by there before we return home," said Duro.

He led them into a fashion boutique store called Canyons. A group of ladies in cardigans and wide-brimmed hats were drinking tea and having the attendants show off the latest winter gear. The well-dressed employee with meticulous makeup behind the counter nodded at them as they passed. Duro pulled a keycard out of a pocket and swiped them into the back area. He keyed them through a second door, revealing an elevator.

"This goes to the Undercity?"

"No, but it shaves off a few hundred steps," said Duro as he held the bag of elixirs to his chest.

When the door opened, it led to a series of rooms and a stairwell that went down. As she glanced backwards at the elevator, he said, "It's one of Daraja's shops. She's been investing our profits into legitimate businesses and diversifying our risk."

"I thought the Drops hated the light?"

"It'd been my mama's dream to live and work in the city. Moving belowground had been a last resort. While some never want to leave"—he touched his face, signifying the tattoos that many wore—"others would like the option should they choose."

"I had no idea."

"I hope you'll keep it that way. Daraja's been doing a lot of things that wouldn't be acceptable to the rest of the clan, but she's doing them with their best interests in mind. There's far too many of them that live on rage and grievance."

"But not you."

Duro paused on a landing. She saw darkness in his gaze. "I will do what is necessary to protect them. Even if it means losing myself."

The journey to the Terreno passed in silence. Duro had been a mystical figure to her before, someone her clanmates spoke of with reverence and fear. Having spent the last day with him, she saw him for what he was: a warrior. He'd given himself completely and utterly to the cause. The clan didn't know how lucky they were. She also hoped they would never be on opposite sides, because he fought every battle with the intensity of a caged lion.

"I'll meet you at the Poinsettia in five hours." He handed her a wad of cash. "Enjoy yourself. You earned it."

Pandora stared at the money her hand. After everything he'd said, she felt bad taking it. He furrowed his brow.

"You deserve more than that. You did well today. When the time comes, I'll ask that you get a chance at another stone."

He left her in shock. She'd been afraid that she'd given away her feelings for Kuma during the fight, but thankfully, Duro's interpretation had been the exact opposite.

"What am I doing here?" she muttered to herself, shoving the cash into her pocket.

She found the Rush on the opposite side of the Terreno. There were few people in the area. She spotted a couple of drunken Voyna stumbling out of the Bogo pachinko parlor, and a group of No Land negotiating with a couple of prostitutes, one male and one female, at the edge of an alley. They looked so immature, even though she was certain they were only a year or two younger.

Pandora almost knocked before she remembered it was a place of business. The sign outside had been made in the shape of a pickaxe and wagon. She wondered if the Mod had gotten it from some old-timey western store and repurposed it for the shop. She went in, finding a lighted interior filled with modern mining kit, including blue bottles of oxygen, hard hats, headlamps, and a wall full of climbing equipment. She was about to call out until she noticed a splotch of blood on the floor.

Eleven

Kuma returned to the Machi and headed straight for the main building, finding his father and uncle eating together in the private room. Steaming bowls filled with noodles, a plate of fried chicken, and a half-full bottle of soju sat on the table. The haste with which he'd arrived had them both sitting up straight.

"Kuma?"

He spent the next fifteen minutes explaining what had happened with the Black Crows and their reaction afterwards. He told them about how Gregor had been frothing at the mouth, yelling and kicking over trashcans and smashing bottles against the wall. Niran stared into the distance when he was finished, while his Uncle Brazio poured him a glass of soju and slid it over.

"Have a seat."

Even though both men were family, under the circumstances, it didn't feel that way to Kuma. He felt the anger radiating from his father, smoldering beneath the surface like a dormant forest fire waiting for the right breeze to catch flame again. The veins on Niran's forehead looked like pulsing rivers. It was also surprising that his uncle was the calm one.

"You're sure it was Duro?"

"Positive. He'd lost his mask. Nearly smashed my brains in with his batons."

"You're lucky to have survived that. Few can say that much," said his uncle.

"I nearly put a hole in his chest. The sapphire knocked me off the roof before I could pull the trigger."

"Duro's stronger than a bullet. I've seen him take five or six at point-blank range, kill the shooter, and then heal himself in the aftermath. He's a hard man to kill," said Brazio.

His father pounded his fist on the table, rattling the ceramics. "Shadows below."

"Niran," said Brazio.

"I know. We have to respond."

"Gregor said as much."

Niran growled under his breath. "I'm not responding because of that greasy fuck. I'm responding because the clan will demand it once they hear what happened."

Hearing his father disparage his ally surprised Kuma. Brazio chuckled under his breath.

"Careful, brother, you're going to pierce the illusion of stable leadership for your son."

"He's aware of the contradictions." Niran looked up, the wrinkles in his tanned face deeper than normal. "But the Black Crows are useful to us. What did Duro take?"

"I don't know," said Kuma. "He never said, but whatever it was, it was extremely valuable. You'd have thought someone had killed his kids by Gregor's reaction."

"He doesn't have kids thankfully," said Brazio. "What are we gonna do?"

"Do you have a suggestion? And stop looking so smug. If Kuma hadn't seen Duro's face, I would have thought it was you trying to trigger a war."

"If I wanted to do that, brother, I could have done it long ago. Hitting the Black Crows doesn't help us, and even as much as I want to take the blade to the Drops, I wouldn't do it that haphazardly."

"I know," said Niran, frowning. "How do we hit them without breaking the peace? It should be obvious that it's us without revealing our hand."

"We could hit their businesses in the light. Or have Black Crows do it," said Brazio. "That would piss Daraja off, but there'd be little she could do about it."

"A possibility."

"What about the Lazona?" asked Kuma.

"What about it?" asked his father.

"The elevator. If the Drops want to have a stronger economic base like we have with Big Dave's Town, that easy passage into the Undercity is important for their long-term prospects. I can't imagine they have guards along the entire construction project, especially as difficult and ambitious as it is."

Niran raised an eyebrow. "Intriguing, but risky."

"We could herd some critters into their area," said Brazio. "It's worked in the past."

"No," said Niran. "It's an indiscriminate attack. Only their workers or families would get hurt."

"They won't extend us the same courtesy," said Brazio.

"Our principles have guided us this far," said Niran.

"The only principle that matters in war is winning."

Niran shook his head. "Do we have a good list of Daraja's businesses?"

"Fairly complete. There are probably some that have escaped our notice."

"Work with Black Crows on hitting them. As long as it's their people, we're in the clear," said Niran.

"But that won't make our people happy. There has to be some retribution. Duro almost killed your son," said Brazio.

"We'll do something, but I need to think on it. Thank you, Kuma. You can return to the Academy. Let nothing of what we've discussed slip your lips."

Kuma left the two brothers conversing quietly. When he returned to the Academy, the evening meal was in full swing. He joined his friends at their table, catching a head nod from Deacon, who was sitting with Yara.

"Did you really fight Duro?" asked Tick, a little too loudly, bringing stares from the others.

Kuma sensed a great interest in his answer and since it was clear Deacon had been telling stories, he thought it was okay to divulge.

"Fight? I'm not sure I'd call it that. Did my best to stay alive."

Camina leaned forward. She was back from the above ground hospital, looking like nothing had happened. "Deacon said you nearly blew a hole in his chest, but got thrown off the building."

"I had the drop on him," said Kuma, pride welling in his chest as he caught the many stares from around the room. With everything that had happened, he hadn't considered how others might view him after the fight. He'd always been in the shadow of his father, but now he was making a name for himself. Kuma felt buoyant.

The normally stoic Camina grinned with wild abandon. "First the duel on Shade's End and now Duro. Soon the Drops will be whispering your name in fear."

"I don't know about that. I can't imagine Choo-Choo feeling anything but rage."

"Put a target on your back," said Tick as he scooped up some broth with his spoon.

"For sure," said Camina.

Kuma leaned back in his chair. They were right. The duel and now the fight with Duro would make him a target whenever the war started. He was finally getting out from under his father's name, but realized that infamy came with new problems.

Twelve

The blood was fresh. Pandora pulled a blade from her duffle bag, edging towards the counter in the back of the store looking for signs of her mother. The equipment was a mix of old and new, which made it hard to feel with her sapphire. The click of a gun made her freeze.

"Oh, it's you."

The disappointment felt like hot ash across her skin. Pandora turned to find a hooded figure pointing a large handgun in her direction. The weapon dropped to their side and they pulled away their hood, revealing a person who'd been mangled and put back together more than once.

"Hello, Mother."

"Don't say that here."

The woman standing at the back of the shop had one real eye while the other was a faintly glowing amber globe in her socket. Scar tissue radiated down her neck, and the right side of her mouth was pulled into a permanent grimace. The half of her head that had the missing eye was shaved to the skin, revealing lines of knotted tissue where her skull had nearly been torn in half.

"You have a new eye."

Her mother threw the gun into a drawer, slamming it shut while the scowl never left her lips.

"What are you doing here?"

Pandora gestured behind her. "There's blood on the floor."

"Fuck," said her mother, a quick glance to the back room betraying some foul deed. She grabbed a rag and threw it to Pandora. "Make yourself useful."

The blood left a stain on the wood, but she soaked up the liquid, handing it to her mother, who dropped it in a metal trash bin. Pandora caught the flash of her mother's left hand beneath the cloak. It looked like steel and bone and gold.

"A new arm too."

Her mother pulled her left arm to her chest, sucking the artificial hand out of sight.

"I wasn't presentable last time."

"I don't care what you look like," said Pandora.

"And I don't want your pity."

"But you want my obedience. I got the message."

Her mother looked up from her desk, a mixture of anger and devastation.

"You're running out of time to be useful."

Pandora ran her fingertips across the front of the desk. "They asked me to infiltrate the clans. I did that. They wanted me to get a stone. I've done that. I have their trust too. What else do they want?"

"War. Between Razor and the Drops. Once they've destroyed each other's strength they'll be easy to eliminate."

"That might be happening already," said Pandora.

She gave a brief explanation of the earlier raid on the Black Crows. Her mother gave no hint of her impression, and not for the first time did Pandora wish she hadn't failed attunement to an amber. Being able to read people would help her navigate the treacherous waters ahead.

"Aren't you going to say anything?"

"What are *you* doing to bring this about? All I heard was a successful mission for the Drops. You should have let the boy kill the warleader. There would have been no peace then."

Pandora listed about. She couldn't tell if she wanted to please her mother, or the demands of her spying. At least there was no clicker on the desk, threatening the horrors of the past. A benefit of surprising her mother.

"It's not that simple."

"Then make it so."

Pandora pulled her hand into a fist, not in anger, but to exert control over her life. She stared into the curled fingers, the white knuckles, and tried not to imagine what it would have been like to have a mother like Choo-Choo's.

"I'm working on it," she said absently.

Her mother disappeared into the back, returning with a small satchel in her artificial hand. The pale bone fingers flexed as she held the bag out, revealing gilded tendons and steel interiors. Pandora couldn't take her eyes off the arm.

"It was a gift."

"That's not a gift."

Her mother touched the strange eye with her good hand. "This allows me to see things others can't, and this hand is stronger than one of your topaz. I'm better now, more useful."

"You don't need to be useful to me. You just need to be my mother."

"Silence, girl. You'll get us both killed."

The strange eye strengthened in its amber glow then reduced as she turned her head slightly.

"No one's about. You're lucky." She shook the bag. "Take it."

Pandora held out her hand, but hesitated over the strap. "What's in it?"

"An acceleration to war. Place this near the processing building. Give yourself enough time to get away from the blast radius."

"The processing building? It's nothing but old men and women and kids in there."

"Their rage will be unquenchable. After what you told me about the raid, they'll have no choice but to believe it was Razor." Her mother grunted. "Take it, girl."

"Girl? Do I have no name anymore?"

"Stop playing games, *Pandora.* Does that make you feel better?"

A knot welled up in her throat. She felt sick as she squeezed her hand around the strap, taking the load from her mother.

"Go on, get out of here. I wasn't expecting you. There are others stirring outside. Leave before they pass."

Like an automaton, Pandora turned and shuffled towards the door with visions of the Pajot whirling through her mind. The harvest building was a place of laughter. Choo-Choo's mom, Triana, worked there sometimes along with Vasy. She wouldn't be surprised if Duro's mother spent time there as well. Hitting it would trigger a war with no chance of ending until one side was eliminated.

She made it to the door near a wall of blue oxygen bottles, chained and locked into place. Pandora stared at a patch of rust around the neck of the nearest bottle, smelled the dust in the air, felt the warmth of the Terreno pressing against her flesh.

"No."

Pandora turned back, striding quickly to the desk and setting the bag of explosives on top where her mother had been reviewing inventory sheets.

"I'm not doing that."

The tilt of her mother's head, the pulsing of her eye, they made Pandora want to curl into a ball.

"This isn't a choice. Take the bag and leave," she said as she reached towards a drawer. Pandora knew what was inside. Just the threat brought visions of the box and the sharp feet that flayed skin.

"I will find another way. But I won't do that."

"This is your human weakness speaking. When they let you leave, you promised that it was gone, that you'd buried it along with your father. Don't be backsliding now. It won't end well."

The drawer slid open slowly, the wood on wood sending Pandora's heart rate into the stratosphere. Using her good hand, her mother scooped up the clicker. Pandora could see nothing but the way her mother's thumb caressed the brass dome, threatening the reminder.

"Go on, Pan. Take the bag and leave. Do your duty. The rewards will come later and you can forget about these people. They don't love you. The only reason they took you in was because you were useful to them."

"Like you?" asked Pandora, nostrils flaring.

"Come now, Pan. You know I love you unconditionally. But you and I are a part of something greater than us. We have to push aside our own wants and needs."

"I'm not taking the explosives."

Click. Click.

The sound was a thunderclap in her ears. Sweat rolled down her spine. Pandora swallowed, bared her teeth in a grimace. Horrors in the darkness assaulted the edges of her mind.

"No. Not that way. I'll find my own. But not that."

She turned. Taking the first step towards the door felt like stepping out of an airplane without a parachute. Every fiber of her being was screaming not to go.

"Pan. Pandora. Don't you dare leave without this bag."

The second step was easier than the first, and before she knew it she was outside, leaning against the wooden building, hyperventilating on the fresh air as if she'd been underwater for ten minutes.

She assumed her mother could see her through the wall, but didn't care. There were a lot of things she would do, but not that. Pandora stumbled away from the shop, wandering aimlessly while trying to calm the beating of her heart. She found herself outside the Onyx.

As she pushed inside, she couldn't help but hope that Kuma would be there with his friends in one of the booths, laughing with the redheaded hostess, drinking a bottle of champagne. In her mind, she'd walk over to the booth and sit down with them, ignoring the animosity between their clans. A pleasing fiction that helped the quivers of her hands finally stop.

But when she went inside, the place was nearly empty. An older man with long gray hair and a scar bisecting his cheek was drunkenly singing a ballad on the stage while one of the hostesses was clapping and whistling for him. The little lights from the chandelier cast glittering shadows across the carpet.

"Pandora?"

The soft voice had her heart jumping. She found Leesa sitting in a booth by herself, sipping from a glass. Pandora joined the hostess. Her mane of red hair was swooped on top of her head, revealing her slender neck.

"What are you doing here?" asked Leesa, forehead hunched.

"Passing through."

Leesa held out her drink. "You look like you could use this."

Pandora was about to say no, but Leesa shook it at her. She took the glass and downed the clear alcohol, which burned the whole way down. Leesa leaned over the edge of the seat and waved two fingers at the bartender.

"Seen a ghost?"

Pandora stared into the empty glass. "Something like that." She looked up. "Pretty empty."

"Hasn't been the same since Shade's End," said Leesa with a raised eyebrow.

"No, it hasn't."

"Have you?" she asked.

"No. Not sure we will again."

Leesa smiled wistfully. "The shadows are like that. Make you see things that aren't really there, or hide the dangers you wish weren't actually about to leap out."

While they listened to the old man on the stage sing a song about love and loss, she heard a familiar voice. Pandora ducked down as Garret, the kid from the maintenance shop, came out of the back room with one of the other hostesses, a beautiful woman with thick black hair and ruby red lips. He gave her a kiss on the cheek and stuffed a couple of bills in her hand as he headed out of the Onyx.

"He come here often?" asked Pandora.

"Whenever he's in town, which is a couple times a month. Elani keeps him busy."

"Yeah, she does," said Pandora, staring after the young man. Questions about where he was getting the money for a hostess club as a maintenance worker were lost when the bartender brought two glasses. Leesa thanked him and he returned to the bar. She held out her glass, which

Pandora reluctantly clinked against.

"To hope."

"Hope?" asked Pandora. "Wasn't what I was expecting you to say."

"Why not? Why shouldn't I hope?" asked Leesa.

Pandora thought about the bag of explosives that her mother had wanted to give her, the brass clicker in her hand, and the strange eye and arm that hadn't been there before.

"I'm finding it hard to these days."

"I'm surprised. You went from waitress to waku in a few months, fought a duel that's still being talked about, and are hanging around with the most famous of all the waku. If anyone's a symbol of hope in this dark place, it's you."

"You know I'm here with Duro?"

Leesa cocked a grin. "It's my job to know these things."

"What else do you know?" asked Pandora harshly.

Leesa held her hands back. "Nothing important. I deal in people. My job is to make people forget about their troubles for a short time, help them believe they have a friend in this unforgiving place. So it's important for me to know who hangs out with who." She winked. "I saw you two enter the Terreno when I came in for my shift. Nothing more."

"Do you ever miss the light?"

Leesa glanced upward. "I go up now and then to satisfy my curiosity, but honestly, I like it here. I make good money, great money. And I enjoy the job. It feels good to make people happy, even if it's fleeting."

"I wish I could say the same." Pandora took a drink, being careful not to chug the second glass. "I'm surprised you're not asking me to buy you a bottle."

"It's my job to read people, and I can say without a doubt that asking that question is the last thing you want to hear. You want to forget about something that you recently learned and you're unhappy about."

"Does it ruin the mystique, you telling me how you're manipulating me?" asked Pandora.

"I don't know," said Leesa. "Does it?"

"Not really."

"See. We want to believe in the illusions that life presents us, even when we know they're not real, because the alternative is much worse."

"That no one cares?"

"No," said Leesa. "That they do care, but we're not worthy of their feelings."

Pandora sat in the booth with Leesa for a few hours. Neither said another word and occasionally they shared a creasing of the eyes. She had two more drinks during that period, but never felt more sober in her life. When she realized she needed to be leaving, she tried to pay, but Leesa wouldn't accept it. They hugged briefly, and Pandora couldn't figure out if the redhead was actually her friend or was playing the part of the hostess.

Outside the Onyx, the glittering lights of the Terreno and the noisy clinking of pachinko balls felt distant. Pandora wandered around, avoiding others until she spotted a fruit and vegetable vendor. She took the money that Duro had given her and bought as many bags of food as she could carry.

When it was time, she found Duro at the Poinsettia. He was sitting at the bar drinking a beer and eating gyoza. He raised an eyebrow at her overstuffed bags.

"Hungry?"

"For Triana."

The corners of his lips curled slightly as he pushed away his plate and empty beer, tossing a few bills on the counter. "Let me help carry them."

She handed them over and the two of them headed back to the Pajot in comfortable silence.

Thirteen

The vibration of jackhammers deep in the earth reached Xylos from his perch. He stood in a cubby against the wall, hidden from all except the most observant. Botan stood by the hole occasionally monitoring the oxygen lines, an automatic weapon held tightly against his chest.

Xylos kept his amber on alert. They were near the wastelands, the deep canyons and caverns that held dangers more fearsome than the other clans. Their location was near an ancient underground lake, bringing cooler air than normally existed. The mine was in a spot that had many exits, making setting up defensive measures more difficult.

He checked the handheld monitor for the sensors placed around the area. The meters were dark. Xylos lifted his walkie-talkie.

"How's the walkabout?"

A crackle was followed by Kuma's voice. "Nothing out here. Quiet as a tomb. We're headed past the lake and swinging by your location in a few."

"Let's keep it that way. Going to grab a drink."

Botan motioned to his hidden location that he'd heard his request and was acknowledging it. As a stone-less soldado, his senses were entirely ordinary, but the wide cavern made it easy to keep watch on the sight lines, and besides, Kuma and Deacon were almost back. Their regular patrols made sure no person or critter larger than a cave cricket was getting near the mine.

"I'm falling asleep," said Botan with a wry grin. "This guard duty is as boring as your sex life."

"Grab an energy drink," said Xylos as he reached into a bag for a water bottle. "I ain't getting my guts ripped out because you fell asleep."

"What does it matter? I don't have an amber. You can hear much better than I can. I could take a nap and it wouldn't matter," said Botan.

As Xylos dug the bottle out of the bag, a gold necklace with a pendant slipped out of his shirt, dangling around his neck.

"Nice," said Botan, wagging his eyebrows. "I bet you got that hitting one of the Drops city stores."

Xylos tucked it away. "Shut up, Botan. We're not supposed to talk about that."

"Fuck, man. Everyone knows. It's not like it's a secret that we've been hitting the Drops' businesses. Even they know, but they can't do a damn thing about it." He held out his hand and made a fist. "Squeezing their necks until they run out of oxygen."

"Another reason to stay alert. We're not far from their territory."

"They wouldn't dare," said Botan with a shrug. "It's one thing to scrap in the light where it doesn't matter, but if they attack us, it'd break the peace and the alliance would have to help us eliminate them."

Xylos put a hand on the younger clan member's shoulder. "Botan. With all due respect, you've never been in a scrap. Until you've gotten your blades wet, or fired even a single bullet in anger or fear, you should shut the fuck up."

"At least I wasn't hiding in a grease trap when the Invasion happened," said Botan.

"That isn't the insult you think it is, my young friend. When the shadows wake, you do what you can to survive."

Further conversation was cut short when one of the sensors gave them a warning beep. Xylos immediately expanded his amber, listening for signs of intruders at the various entry spots. He put his hand on his walkie-talkie while he listened for secondary warnings.

"It's the western—"

"Shut up," whispered Xylos as he pulled out a single blade, keeping his other hand on the radio.

Another beep from the western sensors sent his heart rate soaring. A third had Xylos toggling the radio.

"Might have something incoming. Would appreciate it if you high-tailed it back."

"Will do. On our way," replied Kuma's voice.

Xylos could believe that three beeps might have been caused by a roaming tunnel rat looking for food, but a fourth indicated something larger was headed their direction.

"Get them out of the hole," said Xylos as he crept forward to get out of the dome of light to where his amber vision would help him scout the western entrance. Keeping the blade in his left hand, he pulled a pistol with his right and shifted over until he was against the wall of the cavern. The stone sweated and a fuzzy green fungus grew in patches. Xylos leaned over, trying to get a good view of the archway that led to their cavern.

Behind him, Botan called into the hole for the miners to climb up the scaffolding. Xylos wanted to check on Kuma's progress, hoping it was soon because he was getting a bad feeling. The beeping from the monitor back at the hole was growing more insistent. Straining ahead with his amber, he tried to figure out what was triggering the sensors.

He saw something along the ground, moving between the rocks. Its low profile made it hard to discern if it was a threat or a wandering critter in search of food.

Xylos checked back to see Botan edging towards a perpendicular exit with his rifle pointed forward. The angle made it hard to tell if anything was coming from that direction, and he had his own issues to worry about. His amber revealed that something was ahead in the rocks.

The cocking of a gun had Xylos looking back again. Botan was half-way across the cave, aiming his weapon into the darkness. Xylos wanted to yell for him to get back but he didn't want to give away his position.

The scratching of claws on stone had Xylos returning his attention ahead of him. He saw something move, and lifted his pistol. A squat creature lunged out of the shadows and Xylos squeezed the trigger, the report echoing in his ears. He hit the creature solidly and ran forward to find it was a dead tunnel rat. A big one. Probably fifty pounds, but not the threat he'd expected.

Xylos exhaled and called back to Botan. "All clear here, man. It was a fucking tunnel rat."

When he checked back he couldn't see his clanmate. Botan was nowhere in sight. Xylos bounded across the rocks, reaching the last place he'd seen him. The exit that Botan had been approaching came alive with movement, shadows exploding with fast-moving creatures. Xylos unloaded his clip as the shadows threatened to overwhelm him.

Fourteen

Kuma was a few hundred meters from the dig site when he heard a single shot. They'd been moving quickly, but carefully, as not to put themselves in danger, but as soon as they heard it, they increased their speed. Kuma bounded over obstacles using his emerald for Lightness, scaring up a nest of cave crickets, while Deacon poured the topaz into his pumping legs. He wasn't quite the blur that Duro could achieve, but he'd learned to move quickly.

They reached the cavern as more shots were fired. Kuma leapt over the metal scaffolding of the mine as shapes moved out of the shadows towards a lone Xylos. He'd thrown the gun to the side and was yelling at the top of his lungs with his blades held wide.

The first creature that met him looked like a four-legged slinky made of gnarled pink flesh with toothy maws at the end of each appendage. Tumblers. He'd only seen a dead one once, dragged back to the Machi by some soldados that had found it on a patrol. Tumblers lived in the deepest canyons of the Wastelands in places the clans feared to tread.

In a time like this, Kuma wished he was a sapphire to push the faez-rich creatures back en masse. A tumbler came after him, rotating mouths snapping eagerly. He dodged to the side and sliced off a limb with his curved blade, then leapt with Lightness as two more converged on his location. He landed hard, tipping off balance as the rocky ledge cracked beneath his feet, slipping to the ground. A tumbler came rolling towards him, but Deacon appeared with his blade, killing it before the toothy maws could reach him.

The three of them fought off the tumblers, killing all eight, leaving the rocks littered with bloody appendages still twitching. The miners had climbed out of the hole and were clutching pickaxes, ready to defend themselves.

"What in the dark are they doing up here?" asked Kuma, breathing heavily as he wiped the sweat from his brow.

"What are they?" asked Deacon, eyes wide.

"Tumblers," said Kuma. "They normally don't come up this high. They tend to stay in the deep earth where it's brutally hot."

Xylos was searching ahead using his headlamp. "I can't find Botan."

Kuma checked around them. "What do you mean? Where is he?"

"I was investigating something on the far side that ended up being a tunnel rat. He was standing almost right here when I fired my weapon, and by the time I checked back, he was gone. There's still thirty feet before the tunnel leading out. No way he moved that fast in the few seconds I wasn't paying attention." He checked his arm, which was soaked in blood. "Shit, I think I got bit. I'll deal with it after we find Botan."

A sickening feeling invaded Kuma's stomach as he searched the nearby area, seeing no signs of the soldado. He checked back to Xylos to see him looking unsteady on his feet. Kuma grabbed his arm, examining the wound to find it flayed down to the bone.

"Shadows below, it got you good. You need to fix that."

"Yeah, I guess I do," said Xylos, blinking heavily.

Mina, the lead miner, approached Kuma, her face covered in dust and dirt. The whites of her eyes looked bright against the grime.

"What do we do? We were close to a new vein. We think some interesting stones are down there, but the ground isn't stable. If we leave now, it could collapse before we come back," said Mina.

"Stay at the mine, keep your weapons. Take Xylos back so he can heal himself. Deacon and I are going to find Botan. Once we do, we'll resume the mining."

Mina returned to the mine with Xylos. The older waku looked drunken by his steps and Kuma wondered if he was poisoned. Little was known about the tumblers except that they sometimes gathered in groups of fifty or sixty at the bottoms of the deep canyons, feeding on anything that mistakenly wandered into their midst.

Using his amber exposed Kuma to the grotesque and bloody interiors of the tumblers as they looked for signs of Botan.

"Where did he go?" asked Deacon.

"It had to be this passage. But I don't understand. Tumblers don't come this high up and they don't make frontal assaults on people. They tend to go for the smaller critters, or tunnel rats, and scurry away when they see people."

"Should we really leave them back there?" asked Deacon, checking over his shoulder. "Xylos didn't look so good."

"We have to find Botan."

Checking where he was stepping, he saw lots of scrape marks from the tumblers. A clear line could be drawn where they'd passed, but he saw no signs of Botan's boots. It wasn't until they were about sixty feet from the last location he'd been seen that Deacon pointed to a rock where half a bloody handprint remained.

"What in the actual fuck?" asked Deacon. "Dude, I do not like this."

"If we assumed that was Botan's handprint, the question remains how did he get here? Something other than tumblers is going on here. They would have eaten him where he lay."

Kuma checked all around. His senses were overwhelmed with the metallic scent of blood, his own body odor, and the fear of something coming out of the darkness. He calmed himself, pinching his nose between forefinger and thumb, breathing deliberately until his pulse was no longer ringing in his ears.

When he reexamined the ground, sweeping the area before them, he spotted a drop of blood on a rock further up the tunnel. He carefully followed, making sure to check the stone before placing his boot down. The passage led towards the canyons. Kuma found blood droplets for another fifty feet, but they grew more distant each time. Then he found a sneaker print. It was a partial—the shoe had clearly slipped off the hard rock and hit dust, leaving an impact.

"This wasn't random," said Kuma, pointing to the print. "Someone drove the tumblers to us, using the distraction to snatch Botan."

"How? Those fucking things didn't seem like the herding type."

"No idea, and that worries me."

"But where's Botan?" asked Deacon.

"The line suggested they took him towards the canyons. It's a couple hundred meters that way. You can go back with Xylos if you're worried we're too far."

"No, man. I'm staying with you," Deacon said, checking around them. "We have to find him."

Following the trail wasn't easy, but using the assumption that they'd taken him to the canyon helped them stay on course and find a dwindling blood trail.

"Do you think this was Drops?"

"If it was, they took him away from their territory rather than towards it."

"How can you tell? It all looks like the same fucking cave to me," said Deacon, scowling.

"Benefit of growing up underground, I guess."

As they neared the drop-off, the air grew warmer and the middle distance was sheer blackness rather than the glinting of rocks from their headlamps. The closer they got to the edge, the more Kuma was certain they wouldn't find Botan. He also had an itchy feeling between his shoulder blades that someone was watching, but they'd hidden themselves well. He couldn't detect them with his amber.

The edge of the canyon dropped off severely. Kuma scooted forward, careful not to place his weight on unstable rocks. He scanned the area, seeing no sign of Botan or anything else.

"Haven't found a spot of blood for a while," said Deacon. "I don't think he's here."

Kuma kept searching, but the trail of blood had disappeared. He wanted to keep going, but Deacon reminded him that the others were left unprotected, so they turned around. When they got back, they found Xylos sitting uneasily on the rocks with Mina holding him up. The other miners were spread out holding pickaxes, which would only protect them against the simplest of critters. Mina looked relieved when they returned.

"You okay, Xylos?"

"I think I'm poisoned. I tried to get rid of it with the opal, but I don't feel so good. It's like I have the worst hangover."

Kuma checked his arm. The wound looked better since Xylos had closed it, but it was uneven.

"Gonna have a good scar."

"Women love scars," said Xylos hazily.

"What do we do about the mine?" asked Mina.

Kuma checked Xylos' unfocused eyes. His skin was pasty and damp. Almost greenish.

"I don't want to leave it, but Xylos isn't doing good."

"If someone else comes along, they'll be able to finish what we started in a short amount of time," said Mina.

"What kind of stones were you finding?"

Mina shrugged. "It's always hard to tell, but we'd found a vein of faez crystals that were increasing in quality the further we dug in. We had to shore up the ceiling so it wouldn't fall on us. But from what we could gather by studying the earlier stones, it might be a vein of sapphires. Good ones. The last time I found a vein like this we managed to get six high-quality emeralds."

Kuma checked back to Xylos, who was leaning over, moaning softly and holding his stomach. Deacon had to hold him up.

"We're gonna have to carry him as it is."

"You'll have to carry him. You're the topaz," said Kuma.

The idea of leading the group back to the Machi with only him as defense seemed dangerous. But he also hated the idea of leaving the stones for someone else to take, especially if they were sapphires. The stones would immediately improve the standing of their waku.

"Deacon. I want you to take Xylos back. I'm going to stay and finish mining."

"But you don't know anything about how to extract the faez crystals," said Xylos

"Then teach me."

"No. I'll stay with you," said Xylos

"I can't let you do that," said Kuma. "Deacon can carry Xylos, but the rest of you need to take the guns. It's your best shot of getting back. Whoever took Botan is still out there."

"Are you sure about this?" asked Deacon as he grabbed Xylos and threw him over his shoulder while he kept the automatic rifle in his other hand.

"No, but we need the sapphires."

"I said I *thought* there were sapphires," said Mina. "Sometimes the mine dries up and you dig for hours to find nothing."

"A chance I'm willing to take. Now tell me what I'm doing."

Mina looked unsure of how to begin, or thought he was being foolish. Eventually she collected herself.

"About forty feet down, there's a side shaft. You'll see the lamps. Take one of the small picks. You'll have to use this special light to see the crystals. They glow when exposed to the illumination. The vein isn't so much a vein but a constellation of stars—they can be hard to find and easy to lose. Chip around the stone. You can't hurt them, but you can dislodge them and they'll fall onto the ground beneath you and be hard to find. When you have a chunk ready to fall, hold the basket beneath until you break it free."

"How do I know if it's good crystal?"

Mina handed him a small eyepiece. "This will help you see their crystalline matrix. The good ones have parallel lines while the bad ones look partially fractured. But in the end, grab it all and bring it back to the Machi for testing."

"Anything else?"

Mina's mouth shifted to the side. "Don't do this. You're more likely to get yourself killed, especially with another clan on the loose. Or asphyxiate yourself accidentally. The stones aren't *that* important."

"But they are. Our future depends on them."

Deacon led the group out of the caves towards the Machi. The Black Crow looked genuinely concerned. He said nothing but gave a head nod on the way out.

Kuma turned the lamps off, plunging himself in darkness. He

switched on the oxygen bottles and climbed into the mine without hooking up to the safety harnesses. The lights deep below guided him through the natural hole that had been widened at certain points. The stone beneath the city of Invictus was porous with multiple layers of caverns. Some of the deeper layers, especially those with faez crystals, were assumed to have been entry points from the infernal realm.

He reached the location Mina had told him about. The side passage went perpendicular into the darkness. This section had clearly been excavated, the excess rock dumped into the deep hole beneath, using baskets to transport.

Switching on his headlamp, he crawled across the stone, taking a pickaxe with him. He reached the end of the tunnel and using the penlight found the crystals imbedded in the stone they'd been digging around. The idea that he'd pop down and quickly grab the stones was quickly dismissed by the thickness of the surrounding rock and the way the shelf had to be supported by steel rods to keep the entire thing from collapsing. He could see why they'd been taking their time. He was a little unsure about continuing the dig and considered leaving, but decided against it. The needs of the clan were too great.

Kuma situated himself cross-legged with a basket in his lap and started picking away. Chips flew, stinging his face and making him wish he'd grabbed goggles from the others to protect his eyes. He worked quickly and steadily. While the miners had better technique, the years of honing his muscles at the Academy meant he could strike the rock harder and more consistently.

He was drenched in sweat by the time he broke the first crystal free. Using the eyepiece, he examined the matrix, finding a bluish tint and crystalline structures that went crossways. It probably wasn't viable but he'd let someone else worry about that later.

He threw the chunk in the basket and continued breaking the rest of the crystals free, feeling more confident about not bringing the entire tunnel down on his head. There was a line of eight crystals barely peeking out of the stone along a two-foot section. He checked them with the eyepiece, finding nearly all of them had parallel lines and a bright blue coloring. The excitement of the find made his head swim. He'd be bringing back a boon that could change the course of the arms race. Rather than break them apart individually, Kuma tried to bring the whole piece down. He wanted to get them out of the rock and back to the Machi.

Time passed quickly. The sweat on his skin collected dirt and dust, leaving him grimy. He wished he'd brought a water bottle down. His mouth had grit in it that kept crunching against his teeth. It wasn't until he grew dizzy that he realized something was wrong.

Pausing mid-strike, he listened with his amber. At first he heard nothing, and then he realized that the nothing was the problem. The tube running down the scaffolding was no longer feeding him oxygen. A beep from a meter hanging off a rod brought him crawling out of the hole to find the CO_2 levels were rising.

When the scaffolding rattled, he realized someone was up top. He couldn't see anyone coming down, but the tunnel didn't go straight up, making it hard to see. He grabbed his blades that he'd left at the flat section, crouching to the side when a heavy rock at least a hundred pounds came crashing down the scaffolding, snapping poles and bouncing into the darkness below. More rocks came down, tumbling fast and hard, making it impossible to climb out.

Some of the rocks started getting stuck about twenty feet above him at the narrowest point of the shaft. The realization that he was being trapped underground settled into his bones. He started breathing fast and shallow, but forced himself to calm, or use up the remaining oxygen. The crash of rocks continued for about ten minutes and then it stopped, leaving dust motes floating in the air in the lamplight.

When he was sure nothing would fall on his head, he climbed up using the remaining pole that hadn't been shattered, or the opposing walls. He reached the blockage, finding it completely covering the hole. There was at least five feet of stone between him and the opposite side.

Kuma rested his head against the warm stone. He was trapped. Permanently. The rest of the clan had headed back to the Machi. Whoever had taken Botan had circled back, turned off his oxygen, and blocked his exit. Either they hadn't cared about the stones, or hadn't known about what lay beneath the ground.

He had two options. Try to open up the tunnel with his pickaxe so the blockage would fall away, or descend further in hopes of finding an alternate route. It was more likely that it would lead nowhere, or be too narrow for him to pass, but the longer he waited the less oxygen he had to work with. The beeping had increased in frequency. He checked the meter to find he was rapidly running out of time.

Kuma climbed back into the tunnel, finding the supporting rods had shifted. The huge rocks being dropped down the shaft had shaken some loose. He figured he had another half hour of work to free the sapphires, which was more than the air he probably had to work with, especially if he was pushing himself.

He hated leaving the sapphires, but if he were dead, then it wouldn't matter. On the other hand, if they tried to come back later, the entire tunnel would likely be collapsed from the digging. If he wanted to bring back a sapphire, it had to be now.

The end section had a crack in it. He thought if he worked it quickly, he might be able to free two sapphires. Kuma slammed the pickaxe into the crack, widening it while keeping an eye on the metal supports. The impacts shook them, sending dust upon his head while the beeping forced him to work faster. Once the piece broke free, Kuma grabbed the rock, shoved it into his pack, and prepared to climb down the shaft.

With a headlamp affixed to his forehead, and the pickaxe shoved in the back of his pants, Kuma moved downward, using the opposite walls to maintain at least three points of contact. He shimmied down about fifty feet before he reached the waste stone they'd been dumping. Fear that there was nowhere to go rose up in his throat until he had to force himself to push away the panic.

When he leaned down, he found a perpendicular passage heading into the darkness. It wasn't tall. He'd have to crawl on his belly to make it through.

As he maneuvered himself flat, crawling forward on his belly, the ground shook and a rock fell on the back of his calf. The impact felt like getting kicked by Instructor Kaz. Kuma grimaced and continued forward, the beeping from the oxygen monitor growing fainter. He'd thought about bringing it, but if the oxygen ran out there was nothing he could do about it. It would only be one more thing weighing him down.

Shimmying forward grew more difficult as the passage narrowed. His hips got caught on the rocks and he had to wiggle to free himself. The headlamp revealed a cluster of unusual pale insects clustered around a crack in the ground. Not wanting to get poisoned on top of being trapped, he tore a part of his shirt off, wrapped it around his hand, and smashed the colony before continuing.

The heat was unbearable. Sweat rolled into his eyes. The only saving grace was it made his limbs slicker to pull himself forward. Kuma kept thinking the passage would end and he'd be stuck, but he found more room. As it started angling upward, he grew hopeful. He was sure he'd crawled a hundred feet already.

As the passage turned vertical he found himself stymied by narrows too slender for his muscled body. Pulling the pickaxe out, he worked the stone while protecting his eyes from the dust and chips falling on his head. He'd knocked half the protrusion free when a wave of dizziness hit him, forcing him to lean against the wall and catch his breath.

The weight of the rock above him pushed down. He had to work to control his breathing. The last thing he wanted was to hyperventilate.

"Breathe," he told himself, using the exercises from being an emerald to calm.

But when he returned to the rock, the same dizziness remained. He worried he was running out of air. All the training with Kaz about holding their breath for minutes at a time wouldn't matter once the oxygen ran out. He needed to break the rock free quickly.

Kuma returned the pickaxe to the back of his pants and grabbed the point of the protrusion with both hands. Then he made himself Heavy with his emerald at the same time he pulled down. He stayed Heavy for twenty seconds without breaking it free. After cycling Light, he tried again, this time hearing a faint crack for his efforts, but not enough, as he had to return to Light. On the third try, he put everything he had into it, including the fear that he'd never get out. He'd never made himself Heavy for that long and feared he might rip his arms out of their sockets, but then the rock snapped and he fell a few feet, jamming his knees out to catch himself.

With the protrusion out of the way, he pulled himself upward, hating that he hadn't tasted fresh air yet. Fearing that meant the passage would go nowhere. But as he climbed higher, he saw more of the little insects, the cave crickets and centipedes that were common.

When his headlamp revealed a flat top to the passage, his heart sunk into his gut. He was trapped.

But the top was odd, too flat, where stone should have been uneven.

He kept going until he reached it, finding the exit covered by a layer of carpet fungus. He punched his fist through, exposing fresh air, and dropping a bunch of crickets and other insects on his face.

After knocking them off and wiping his face clear, Kuma switched off the headlamp and carefully climbed through the fungus and into a cavern. As if the earth had given birth, he lay on the soft fungi catching his breath, feeling the cool air against his face. The sound of water trickling through rocks made him realize he was near the underground lake, which wasn't too far from the cavern.

With his amber, Kuma confirmed he was alone before climbing to his feet and exposing himself. He stayed in the darkness, relying on the faint illumination from the fungus. His legs ached and his arms were exhausted from fighting through the earth, but he was relieved to have made it out.

After an hour of cautious travel, Kuma made it back to the outer guard posts of the Machi, where he confirmed that the others had made it back. As he was headed over a wooden bridge towards his father's house, he ran into Yara, who looked like she'd come from training.

"What the fuck happened to you?"

A pithy answer died in his throat when he remembered that her friend Botan was missing, and likely dead. He wiped his mouth with the back of his hand, which only made her suspicious.

"What?" she asked, lips snarling in anger.

"I'm sorry, Yara."

He proceeded to explain what had happened. Yara stared over his shoulder with the heat of a fiery furnace on her face. When he was finished, Yara gave him a brief nod before heading towards the Academy.

Fifteen

Pandora shoved the last cricket-and-cream-cheese stuffed mushroom into her mouth, the delicious flavors exploding on her tongue. Triana was making homemade tortillas with her handpress on the other side of the counter while going on about the gossip she heard during the night's harvest.

"Lara thinks her idiot child is going to be the next Duro, rattling her gums all night long while the rest of us are trying to work. We do twice what she does because she's always standing with one hand on her hip, saying nothing at all. That oscuraweed don't pick itself, you know."

"Triana...I'm sorry, I have to get back to the Academy."

"I know, Pan," said Triana, looking up from the press. "But it's nice to see you when you get a chance. Being Duro's protégé has come with some nice perks."

Pandora took her plate, washed it off in the sink, and set it in the drying rack. When she turned around, Triana had her arms open.

"Stop by anytime. You're always welcome."

"Thank you."

A host of words got caught in her throat, so Pandora smiled instead of finishing her thought as they hugged. She grabbed her shoulder bag and headed to the front, right as Vasilisa came through the door.

"Pan! Hey, guess what I hit the bullseye three times in a row and Nikolai said I'm the best in class even with only one hand and I know I'm going to—"

"Vasy!"

The shout came from Triana in the kitchen.

"What?" Vasy yelled back.

"Pan has to get back to the Academy. She's on very important business for Duro."

Vasy scrunched up her face. "Then why is she here?"

Pandora grinned. "I wanted to stop by and say hey and hear about your training, but I have to go. I'll have to get the rest next time." She put her hand on the girl's shoulder. "You're getting taller."

"Almost fourteen," said Vasilisa brightly.

Before Pandora could move, Vasilisa threw her arms around her midsection, squeezing her tight.

"I'm glad my brother didn't kill you in training," she said.

"Me too," said Pandora, squeezing her back.

Pandora stepped through the door and instead of climbing down the ladder, leapt outward, using a well-timed Push to halt her descent. An unfamiliar warmth filled her as if she'd been sitting next to a crackling fire, leaving her grinning despite herself.

The journey back to the Academy took her through the main areas of the Pajot. The terraces were filled with workers as they normally were during all hours. To outsiders, the Drops appeared fearsome and crude with their face tattoos and brutal ways, but she'd learned they were industrious and organized as well. The terraces were in constant rotation so there was always work to do: seeding the ground, pulling weeds, harvesting, or preparing the soil for new planting. They'd turned their corner of the Undercity into a bountiful garden. An oasis, even. One of the older ladies with a tattoo of a bird of paradise on her neck gave Pandora a wave, which she returned.

Nearing the processing building—where they cleaned and wrapped the food from the terraces for storage or distribution amongst the clan members and processed the oscuraweed to be turned into drugs that would be sold in the city—she spotted Garret in a silk tracksuit with gold chains around his neck hurrying down the path as if his pants were on fire. He was looking every which way, but she stepped behind a water tank when he glanced back. She'd avoided his gaze for reasons she didn't quite understand at first.

It didn't take an amber to see he was agitated about something. Pandora strode after, preparing to confront him about his behavior until she made the connection. The Mod. Her mother.

Pandora went straight for the processing building, sending out her sapphire radar in all directions looking for the satchel full of explosives. As she circled the building made of corrugated steel and repurposed wooden pallets, she could hear the laughter inside.

She found the satchel on the back side near the generator, which was humming along providing power to the building operations. Carefully unzipping it revealed two bricks of explosives connected to a simple timer. Pandora gave the wiring a quick once-over, confirming there were no dummy leads or quick-fails, before yanking the triggers out of the explosives. The setup wasn't meant to be found. She switched the timer to the off position, zipped it back up, and slung the satchel over her shoulder.

With long strides, she caught up to Garret in the cavern before the maintenance shop. He froze when he saw her approach with the satchel. Pandora grabbed him by the shoulder and shoved him against the rocky wall.

"Are you fucking insane?"

His eyes were bloodshot and his lips had a pallor. "I...I had no choice."

"There's always a choice," she said, slamming him against the wall, using her sapphire to hold him tight.

Tears flowed down his cheeks in streaks. "You don't understand, I have to."

"I understand more than you think," she said, shoving him again. An unrelenting anger rose up in her at the thought of what that explosion would have done.

"You would have killed old men and women, and children."

Visions of Triana and Vasilisa were front and center in her mind. She shook him again because it was the only thing keeping her from grabbing her blades and cutting his throat. Only as she stared at him did she see the devastation in his expression. His cheeks were haunted and gaunt. Garret looked like he'd barely been eating.

"What are you going to do?" he asked in a timid voice.

"I'm deciding that as we speak, so you'd better tell me everything, or I'll drop you into the canyon of ghosts myself."

The relief in his eyes as if that was an acceptable way out of his predicament told her a lot about his state of mind.

"I don't know what to do..."

Pandora grabbed his jaw, made him look into her eyes. He looked like an addict at the end of a two-week bender. "She's giving you drugs of some kind?"

He nodded. "I feel euphoric, never better in my life, and then crushing disappointment until I can get more. It's like her voice is in my head even when I'm not in her shop."

"Fuck. It's called menya. They use it to create child soldiers in other places. Or turn people who would never consider going against their own people otherwise," said Pandora.

"Is this what happened to you?"

She punched him in the shoulder. "No, you baka. I told you already to stay away from the Mod. She's someone I knew from before, but we're not friends." The comment brought bubbles of introspection, but she pushed them down. Pandora lifted the satchel, which brought shame to his face. "See? This is why."

"Who is she? Why is she doing this?"

"Those are questions you'd best leave unanswered."

Garret hung his head. "I don't know what to do."

"Shut up, I'm thinking."

This was a problem. A big one. She knew what menya did to people. Turned their thoughts inside out until they could do the most awful things just to get more. She thought about leading Garret to a less traveled place and cutting his throat. It was safer than letting him stay free. Maybe even kinder to the kid. Getting off the drug would be brutal. There were too many things that could go wrong if she didn't. He could go back to the Mod, or even worse, betray her. It was the whole reason she'd told the Mod not to use him. But she'd used her own daughter to further the cause. Why would a fresh-faced boy with a knack for mechanics cause even a moment of regret? Killing him was easier and safer. The old her, even a year ago, probably would have done it without much consideration.

Pandora put a fist around his gold chains and yanked them off, shoving them in her pocket.

"Hey! Those are mine."

"They're going to get you killed if someone ever wonders why you're suddenly flush with cash, buying bottles of Lone Magus at the Onyx, or wasting your money at the pachinko parlors."

"How do you?"

"That's how obvious you are, you idiot. Other people have noticed. It won't take long for someone to start wondering why certain things about the Drops have been leaking to other parties," said Pandora.

Garret turned white. He looked like he might be sick.

"When you start getting urges to return to the Mod for more menya, think of all the things that Duro would do to you with that opal of his. He can slice you up, then put you back together for another round. The pain could go on for weeks, or months."

"But I have to. Elani sends me to the Terreno because I get the best deals."

"Facilitated by your favors?" she asked.

He nodded.

"Tell her that someone threatened you, or that you're afraid of going through the Undercity by yourself. Something, anything, just make sure someone else goes in your place."

"But how? She won't believe me."

"Piss yourself with fear when you tell her."

"Piss myself?"

Pandora put a finger in his chest. "Better than the alternative. If I don't hear that you filled your pants with piss, I'm coming after you."

Garret swallowed as he nodded.

"Now get the fuck out of here and if I hear that you've been back in the Terreno, or any other bullshit, you won't even know that I'm coming. I'll cut your throat in the middle of the night, or catch you on the road to the Terreno."

Before he could speak, she shoved him down the path. He stumbled and glanced back, so she pointed to her black cotton trousers. He hurried away with his head down.

"Fuck," she said, squeezing her hands to fists.

She shouldn't have been surprised, but the last year and a half in the Drops had lulled her to complacency, made her believe that she was in charge of how things would unfold in the Undercity. How foolish she was to believe that after everything that had happened before.

It wasn't that she wasn't still working for the Mod, but she'd thought she could do things her way. There was a way to consolidate the clans under new leadership without mass casualties, but it required a more delicate touch, something the Mod was not known for. Thinking about the overall goal of her mission had her thinking back to Kuma and his offer. Had it not been for the bad luck at Shade's End, they might have been able to push the two clans towards each other. With the peace at its last tattered end, she wasn't sure how to make it happen now, but the Mod's potential sabotage told Pandora that she needed to start thinking about it.

Remembering the satchel of explosives on her shoulder, Pandora hurried towards the Academy. Along the route, she spied a small cave high upon the wall near the ceiling. Using her sapphire, she shimmied up to it and shoved the satchel deep into the hole, hoping that its remoteness would ensure that it wouldn't be found.

With the explosives hidden, she slowed her passage to the Academy, using the time to consider her options. The Mod was clearly running out of patience, which meant that once she learned that the explosives hadn't been detonated, they would try something else. She couldn't tell anyone in the Drops about the attempted sabotage, or risk her own position, but she could get a message to Kuma. Maybe between the two of them they could figure out how to encourage an alliance, or at the very least, how to avoid being played against each other. It was a narrow path that Pandora was treading but she hated the idea of putting her new family at risk when there were better ways forward. The idea that she could be reunited with Kuma made the option even more appealing.

Sixteen

The word that Botan had been found reached the Academy during a break between training sessions. Kuma had been sitting with his friends sucking down water when Carlos arrived in a dead run, strangely out of breath. He'd been on guard duty at the main entrance to the Machi. The devastation in his gaze and the way he glanced at Yara first clued Kuma to the reason for his arrival even before he opened his mouth.

Yara had been leaning on the stone wall next to Deacon, who'd been in the middle of telling them a story about how he'd robbed a corner bodega when he'd only been nine years old using a banana hidden in a brown paper bag. She let out a scream that would have put fear into one of the maetrie, and ran towards the front of the settlement. The rest of the students followed, even though Instructor Helena was due back any moment to resume their training on how to counter an emerald waku.

The body was about a hundred meters away from the guard post. Botan had been laid over a large rock, exposing his naked body and the bloody "D" carved into his chest. His eyes were open, the blank stare containing multitudes, even as nothing remained behind those empty windows. Pink scars littered his limbs, signs that he'd been tortured and then healed repeatedly with an opal. It was the worst of fates.

Yara picked up a rock the size of her head and launched it at the wall as if it were a piece of crumpled paper. It exploded into chips that flew in all directions. Then she curled upon Deacon's shoulder, sobbing between intermittent screams.

Niran and Uncle arrived moments later. Any emotions that might have been revealed were hidden behind the mask of leadership. His father had never looked older, the wrinkles around his mouth deepening. He looked like he was chewing his words to keep them from coming out.

Kuma approached his father. "We're being goaded."

"Shut up, boy."

The rebuke made Kuma step back. His father's face had turned beet red.

"Everyone out," said Brazio.

Kuma turned to leave with the others, but Brazio grabbed his arm. "You were the last to see him. We might have questions. You too, Deacon."

There was more by the look in his uncle's eyes, but it couldn't be said around his classmates. Deacon joined Kuma with his head down, his arrogance tempered.

No one spoke while Niran paced, not even Brazio, who examined the body with a clinical detachment. Kuma shared glances with Deacon, who was clearly in unfamiliar territory, then moved over to the boulder. He'd grown up with Botan, and even though he'd been one of Yara's closest companions—which meant they'd been rivals—he'd never felt animosity towards him. The wise-cracking Botan had been comic relief at worst, a fine soldado otherwise. He hadn't deserved what happened to him. No one did. It wasn't rage that Kuma felt but a twisted pity and an acknowledgement that it could have been him on that rock had things gone differently that day.

"Tell me again what happened," said Niran with his hand cupped beneath his chin.

Kuma repeated the tale. It was probably the fourth time he'd explained it to his father. Deacon added what he knew. Questions were peppered into the conversation.

"Braz?"

His brother had been crouched by the boulder, examining the ground. He shook his head.

"It was an opal who killed him, that's all I can say. It wasn't long ago either. A few hours at most. No signs of anything else. Whoever did this covered their tracks when they dropped the body off. I can't even tell that anyone besides Botan was ever in this space."

"There was the footprint I found," said Kuma, reminding his father.

"The only proof we have that it was a real person and not a demon," said Brazio.

"Some demons wear shoes," said Niran.

The hard stare between the brothers spoke of an experience they weren't going to explain.

"What are we going to do?" asked Kuma.

Niran smoothed the whiskers of his goatee. "You're going to keep your mouth shut until I ask you a question."

Kuma dipped his chin towards his chest while his uncle raised an eyebrow.

"This looks like Duro's handiwork," said Brazio. "Even if I don't understand why now."

The last comment surprised Kuma, triggering a memory from the day he was taken.

"It was a sneaker print," said Kuma, receiving a stern glare from his father for the interruption. "That's what we found in the cavern near the canyon."

"Drops don't wear sneakers," said Brazio.

It wasn't just the Drops that didn't wear sneakers, but most clans in the Undercity wore soft-soled slippers that allowed them to move quickly and silently in the darkness.

"Which means it was one of the new alliance clans like the Blue Daggers, or someone else entirely. They're trying to start a war between us and Drops. You see that, right?" Niran asked his brother.

"I can't deny that it's a strong possibility. However, the clan will not see it that way. Already the news of this killing is spreading through the clan like wildfire."

"By the word of your daughter," said Niran with uncharacteristic venom.

The tension in Brazio's expression bent like metal warping under heat. "She's your niece too."

Niran's nostrils flared before he stepped away, shaking his head. "My apologies. This killing brings me great anger."

"As it does me," said Brazio coolly. "We must strike back at whoever did this."

Niran swiped a fist down. "That's not why I'm angry. I'm angry because once again, this act pushes us into a corner, reducing our options. They're shaping the battlefield and we're blind to our enemies."

"Then we should take the initiative to them," said Brazio.

Niran's mouth worked as if he found his words distasteful. He snapped his fingers at Deacon, who'd been standing quietly observing.

"I need you to take a message to Gregor. We need a meeting as soon as the shadows allow. There must be a response," said Niran.

Deacon bowed deeply as if he'd been born in Razor. The months of training had knocked off the arrogant shine. As Deacon left, Kuma thought to how he'd first seen the Black Crows gang member: as a crude thug. Now, despite his relations with Yara, he thought of Deacon as a friend and an ally.

Brazio waited until after Deacon was gone to speak. "You know we don't have a choice."

"We?" spat back his father. "If I do not act, then the clan will see me as weak and put you in my place, which means we end up at the same result. A war with Drops which would be disaster for both sides. Can't you see that we're being manipulated?"

"You were right when you said we need to take the initiative. This gives us an opportunity, brother. Even if we believe this was someone other than the Drops, the alliance would agree with us that this was their doing. We could use this to press our advantage. Use the treaty against the Drops."

"It surprises me to hear you suggest a diplomatic alternative," said Niran.

"You mistake me, brother. I want to win, whatever way that requires. My desire to hit the Drops has always been to that end. I see the trap that they're laying."

"What if that's what they want?" asked Kuma, receiving twin glares as if they'd forgotten he was still present. "The alliance forged this death to get us to bring it up, giving them a reason to eliminate the Drops. Once they're out of the way, then it gives them a clear shot at us."

Niran grunted softly beneath his breath. Kuma hadn't yet convinced him, but he'd garnered his interest.

"It's like that movie, where the three gunslingers have their weapons trained on each other. Whoever shoots first loses. Someone's trying to get us to shoot first," said Kuma.

Brazio smirked. "Your boy is right. But I think the right path is to eliminate the Drops using the treaty."

"Is this because you want to fight Duro? Prove who the best waku in the shadows is once and for all?" asked Niran.

"It's not my concern."

"I know you, brother. The need to be the best has always driven you, even if you don't recognize it yourself anymore. It's why I've always believed it would be a mistake for you to be the clan leader," said Niran.

The dead stare from Brazio sucked the oxygen from the room. The muscles in his uncle's upper arms twitched. Kuma couldn't sense any trigger of stones, but it felt imminent, like a storm on the horizon. He was waiting for the pressure drop. His father stared back with no hint of fear. Even though the lack of stones made his brother superior in a fight, his position within the clan gave him the upper hand.

Then to Kuma's surprise, Brazio's shoulders relaxed.

"I do what I must to support the clan. I will support whatever path you set us upon. Relay your orders, Solrei."

The formal acknowledgement of his brother's leadership of the clan relaxed the tension that had been ramping up. For now. Kuma allowed himself to breathe again.

"I must speak to Gregor before we decide." Niran glanced to Kuma. "But we must retaliate. The clan will not accept any other course of action."

"Then war?" asked Kuma.

"Not if I can help it," said Niran. "We must satisfy the more bloodthirsty of our clan while keeping the peace. And in turn, send a message to whoever did this that we will not be goaded into reckless acts. When you return to the Academy, keep your finger on the pulse of the students. I cannot have anyone acting of their own accord."

Kuma bowed deeply.

"What about Botan?"

The body had been an afterthought during the discussion. He'd been a living breathing person once, but in death had become a pawn in a dangerous game. One in which his removal from the board had created a precarious unbalance within the Undercity.

"Send for Natsuo. We shall lay his body in the Hall of Warriors as befitting his position within the clan."

Kuma left his father and uncle, not daring to linger because they would know if he were trying to eavesdrop on the rest of their conversation. He wasn't sure who he agreed with, but he knew that whatever direction the clan took, the balance of power was perilously perched upon a fulcrum. A simple tip one way or another and the entire Undercity would erupt in war. Kuma had never been afraid to fight, but he knew that would be the worst possible outcome. And not only for his friends. Deep in his heart lingered the desire to reunite with Pandora.

Seventeen

The rock hung in midair between Pandora and the wall, quivering under the strain of an opposing Push and Pull. The tendons in her neck stood out as she exuded every effort to keep the object aloft. The constant readjustments to ensure the rock didn't spin away under the pressure of counter-forces left a damp sweat on her forehead.

Her entire class watched from the sidelines as she passed the one-minute mark. None of the other sapphires, except Instructor Irina, had reached this mark. But Pandora was a long way from the record of five minutes, which the Iron Bitch held.

"Come on, Pan," cheered Choo-Choo, receiving severe looks from the instructor.

Pandora's whole body was attuned to the hovering rock. Her sapphire radar radiated outward like dense webbing, where she was the spider at the center, reading the vibrations. The effort was making her jaw hurt. She was in the middle of readjusting her Push when tremors came through the outer walls of the cave, an unexpected sensation that distracted her from the task. The rock spun out of control as her Pull overrode the Push, and she had to throw herself to the ground as the rock sailed over her head to tumble down the path, nearly hitting the instructor, who never let a single muscle twitch in anticipation or fear.

"Did you feel that?" Pandora asked from the crouched position.

"This is no time for excuses," said Instructor Irina. Her ponytail was extra tight, which raised her eyebrows into a permanent surprised look. "Until you learn to use your stones without resorting to physical effort, you will continue to fail." She raised her head towards the class. "This is the same for all of you. Razor would wipe up the lot of you, just like that boy did to Pandora last year. None of you are worthy of the title of waku, because you do not lean into the pain. If my hands weren't being tied, I would show you what real training means, but until that time you'll have to overcome the weakness of our Academy on your own."

"My apologies, Instructor, I did not mean to imply an excuse. But there was some shaking, like a tremor or something else."

She had a good idea what the something else was, but didn't want to voice the idea, fearing it would make it true.

"I heard it," said Hector. "I was running my amber, trying to see her sapphire like that Razor did in the duel. It came from the main area. Like an explosion."

The word brought fear to their faces. Pandora felt it as well.

"Enough of this panic. You are waku. You do not fear, but even the earth and rocks should fear you," said Instructor Irina.

The sound of soles slapping brought their heads around as a runner approached. She pointed back to the main settlement, speaking through breaths.

"Someone blew up the processing building. They need an opal bad."

The announcement brought the class off their feet, led by Instructor Irina, who propelled herself ahead using her sapphire. Pandora's first thought as she ran after the others was to check the safety of the explosives she'd taken from Garret. Her second thought was that she was going to drop him off the edge of the canyon of ghosts if she learned this was him. Then her third was the remembrance that Triana was probably working this moment, a fact that Choo-Choo knew as well. She glanced back to see the dread in his eyes as he careened down the path, desperate to catch up with only an amber stone.

Smoke roiled from the collapsed structure upon arrival. Pandora saw old men, women, and kids wandering around with soot-smudged faces in a daze. Small fires continued to burn near the rubble. It looked like the building had been knocked down by the hand of a giant.

"Where's Triana?" she asked a kid who was standing along the path staring into the destruction. When he didn't answer, Pandora shook his arm. He was in shock. She left him in search of other answers. If she could find out the truth before Choo-Choo maybe she could shield him from the worst of the pain.

People were milling everywhere. Someone was screaming near the building. Instructor Irina was crouched over an old man with a glazed look in his eyes. Pandora slowed long enough to see the instructor shake her head at the bystanders, a signal that her healing energies had come too late.

The longer Pandora went without finding Triana, the worse she knew reality was going to be, because if she was alive, she'd be helping the others. That she was nowhere to be found meant the worst.

"I will kill them all," she muttered under her breath, not even understanding who she meant.

Smoke drifted into her eyes, reminding her of past days. A thousand primes drifted into her vision, none of them worthy of being counted. No. She didn't want to avoid the pain. Pandora leaned into it. Rage. That would be her fuel.

"Pan!"

The voice cut through the fog. A woman's voice. Triana. She waved from the other side of a fallen water tank, blood splattered across her jaw. Relief flooded into her system, followed by a strange wetness at her eyes, which she wiped away before it was spotted.

Upon arrival, Pandora saw the problem that Triana wanted her to solve. A timber lay across an older woman with nut-brown skin, soot-covered dark hair, and a grimace that spoke of the pain she was under.

"It's too heavy for me to move. Fila's stuck."

Pandora hesitated. She wanted to throw her arms around Triana and tell her how happy she was that she wasn't dead, but the old woman needed her help. She carefully analyzed the arrangement before attempting to use her sapphire. The stone required linear directions. She stood at the end of the fallen beam and Pulled the top of the obstruction toward her, careful not to yank too hard and let it fall on her. As the beam lifted, Triana and two men carried Fila out of the way. Pandora let the beam down when she was free.

"Come on, there are others trapped," said Triana, leaping towards the collapsed building.

"You're hurt," said Pandora.

Triana waved her away. "It'll stop on its own."

"What happened?"

Triana led them to the pile of timbers and crumpled corrugated steel. She crouched on her heels and peered through a gap.

"I think there are others in here. Someone said they heard voices," said Triana with pinched lips.

Pandora was about to comment that she needed more than herself to move the pile when Choo-Choo, Navos, and a few other waku appeared. Choo-Choo's face cracked with relief upon seeing his mother, but he pushed away the fear that had haunted him the entire run and focused on Pandora.

"There might be more inside," Pandora told them. "We have to lift this pile without causing a collapse. I need the sapphires with me for the major lifting, and the topazes ready to catch falling beams or haul people out if we reach them."

The flat expression from Choo-Choo had her adding, "I'll need you to watch and listen with your amber. You'll have to guide us as we work to reach them."

He stared back as if he hadn't heard.

"Choo-Choo?"

"Yeah, got it," he said, swallowing, then when she glared, added, "Got it."

Pandora set herself before the destruction. It looked like a haystack with timbers and other support beams sticking out everywhere. As she analyzed it to find the order that they needed to remove them, a part of her recognized a scene from her past, which made her adrenaline race into the stratosphere until she dug her fingernails into her palms. The smell of smoke, the creak of steel, and the crunch of glass threatened her hold on the moment until she rallied and pushed it back.

"Okay, sapphires, we're going to lift these beams off the pile. You need to crouch down here to get leverage. Navos, I want you on the opposite side making adjustments as they fall, making sure nothing disturbs the main pile."

The exhaustion from the long trials in class was trivial compared to the need. Pandora found reserves to spare, the collective effort adding fuel. The first beam came away easily. The second, fifth, and tenth weren't difficult either, but as they had to disentangle the twisted pieces without threatening the integrity of the entire structure, it required multiple Pushes and Pulls at different angles to work through the pile.

"Stop!" yelled Choo-Choo, holding his arms out. Even though he was only using his amber, sweat gleamed on his bald head. "I hear voices." He crouched nearby for a moment and then the twitch of hope appeared on his lips before he clamped it back. "They're still alive. I hear them. But some are injured. They need out soon."

"Then let's get them out. Everyone ready for one big Push on this sheet metal? I think we can use it to lift the rest like a lid. Topazes, be ready to support and everyone else to haul them out when we can see." Pandora positioned herself at the center. "Okay, on my count. One, two, THREE!"

A long day of training and then the removal of the beam had left Pandora with little remaining energy to give. The sheet metal quivered upward, groaning and clicking as the remaining pile shifted. The sheet wasn't thick enough to hold the weight and started bending, so Pandora shifted herself beneath and used her sapphire Push to hold the weak spots. As the lid lifted, a hole formed in the back where lights flashed out. No self-respecting clan member was ever without their emergency kit.

Choo-Choo threw himself down by her, reaching into the hole and yanking out a young boy covered in dust and blood, a wound on his forehead. The boy was handed over to the team of opals ready to heal the wounded.

As the pile lifted further, the hole became large enough for the other survivors, but the weight was making it hard to maintain.

"No higher!" someone yelled. "If you shift it any more the water tank might slip into the crawl space."

Pandora had hoped to flip the sheet metal over, but when that possibility was taken from them, she said through gritted teeth, "Get them out quickly."

Choo-Choo hadn't stopped working during the adjustment, helping an older woman with a halo of gray hair around her head. The others came one at a time, but not fast enough for Pandora, who felt her jaw and stomach threatening to spasm from the effort. The instructor's earlier words came to mind about using her physical body to aid what should have been her sapphire force only. She tried to relax her muscles, but the metal sheet bent, and trash fell into the hole, slapping across Choo-

Choo's back.

"Sorry," she grunted and reapplied her effort.

As the minutes went on, she didn't think she could hold it any longer. A migraine was brewing at the base of her skull. Spots formed, pinpricks of light surrounded by shadow, forcing her to clamp her eyes shut. She feared she was having a stroke, but then the strain reduced and she peeked out, finding the sturdy frame of Duro along with three other older waku standing with her, holding up the pile.

When the last survivor was pulled from the hole, the waku slipped out from under and let it crash with a resounding clang. Dust flung up in all directions, making people cough and sputter until it dissipated.

Pandora collapsed to the ground, her side seizing with a cramp from the effort of holding up the pile.

"Do you need assistance?" asked Duro, but she waved him off.

"Heal the others."

As she shuddered in the aftereffects of using her sapphire for ten minutes straight, Triana appeared with a cup of water, which she drank greedily. Pandora couldn't even make the effort to speak when Triana kissed her on the forehead.

"You did good."

"What happened?" she rasped out.

"It would have been worse had it happened a minute before. Most of us were on break outside the building when it blew."

Pandora pictured dropping Garret from a ledge and hearing his screams as he flew down the cliff to crash into the rocks below. She hoped it wasn't him, but how could it be anyone else?

"How many...?"

"Only three. Two caught in the collapse and the other died from injuries. All three were much older. None of the children."

Three. It could have been so much worse. Pandora nodded.

"I'm going to check on the others," said Triana, leaving Pandora alone, leaning her elbows on her knees.

As she stared at the wreckage, it wasn't Garret that haunted her thoughts, but the Mod. Her mother. She'd been behind the attack. The purpose was obvious. They wanted to start a war between Razor and the Drops. She couldn't imagine how it wouldn't happen now.

Pandora stared at the grime on her palms. There was no blood on her hands, but she didn't feel that way. This attack was as much her fault as her mother's. When she'd been sent to infiltrate the clans and help soften them up for a takeover, she'd been willing to do whatever it took to make that happen. But now as she stared at the destruction around her, doubts crept in.

Who am I? When she'd arrived in the Undercity, she thought she knew the answer. But now she wondered if that person was just who she'd been trained to be from an early age. The ties she felt to her mother were frighteningly thin. Click. Click.

The sound of footsteps was followed by the heavy frame of Choo-Choo taking a seat next to her. His mouth twisted with anger.

"I want to kill every last one of them. I know it was Razor."

The answer the Mod wanted her to give was poised on her lips but she saw the hurt in his eyes, pain reflected in her own soul. A fight between warriors was one thing, but killing old men and women, and children?

"We don't know that," said Pandora.

"I thought you were on our fucking side, Pan."

The tendons in his neck were at attention. Sweat dripped from his nose.

"You remember the first time we fought?"

He leaned back. "When I kicked your ass?" She raised an eyebrow, which made him add, "With Navos' help. Like all my scraps, I remember it well. No self-respecting waku forgets a single punch."

"Then you remember when I set you up with those leg kicks, two of them, and then on the third, flipped you on your back and almost ended the fight there, until Navos intervened."

His shoulders sagged.

"I should have seen it coming."

"Now you have your chance. Someone is setting us up," she said. "Don't fall for this trap."

Choo-Choo leaned down and ripped away a piece of dusty plant material that had gotten trapped under a beam. He folded it in his hands as he contemplated her words.

"You can't know that," he said.

"Know? Without proof, I can't say for certain, but it seems more likely than Razor. Do I have to remind you that I've won every game of Undercity we've played?"

"Or you're trying to deflect away from them," he said harshly.

A knot formed in her chest. Before she could speak, he said, "I'm sorry. I'm just so fucking pissed. If that Kuma was here, I'd punch a hole straight through his skull."

Pandora put her hand on his massive bicep. "If you must fight, then fight, but don't let someone push you into unnecessary battle, especially when other enemies are on the horizon."

Choo-Choo chuckled, raising an eyebrow. "You sound like some sort of bullshit guru, or maybe you've not always been honest with me about your past. Sure, you know krav maga, but with everything you've done, it's gotta be more than that."

"You're right. There were other teachers. I had a chance encounter with a very, I don't know, wise isn't the right word, maybe cunning teacher. He set me on the path to finding myself even as I failed in his teachings."

A shadow passed over them, which revealed itself to be Duro. His hands were covered in blood. Choo-Choo quickly vacated the area and Pandora started to rise, until Duro held up a hand. She returned to sitting.

"You did good."

"I did what was necessary for the clan," she said, inclining her head.

"I see a lot of myself in you."

"I'm not a tenth of the warrior you are."

Duro chuckled. "This is true, but even our terraces weren't built in a day. You're like a strike right to the target, powerful and true, without consideration for yourself. This is the way of the waku."

She said nothing, because nothing should be said. Eventually he touched her on the shoulder.

"Come see me in a few days. I have something for you."

"Yes, Shadowmaster."

In other circumstances, her thoughts would have chased the possibilities of what he meant down a thousand dead ends, but she was exhausted and there was something she needed to verify first.

She found the old cave near the ceiling. The emergency at the processing building had pulled all resources for the recovery, leaving her free to investigate. Pandora shimmied up the wall without resorting to her sapphire, fearing a return of the migraine. She pulled herself up into the mouth, clicking on her headlamp to reveal an empty hole. Drag marks in the dust showed where someone had grabbed the satchel and yanked it out.

Back on the cavern floor, Pandora cupped her hands around her mouth. She didn't think Garret had taken the explosives. There was no way he could climb the wall without stones of his own—his arms were toothpicks. That meant there was another spy in the Drops, one that had followed her and Garret during the exchange, and then to the cave. There was no way anyone would have randomly found the satchel. They'd probably been following Garret to make sure he finished the job and that's how she'd been spotted.

Pandora remembered very clearly checking the area with her sapphire for observers, which meant that whoever had taken them must have other ways of observing, or was a powerful waku. She craned her neck in all directions, looking for cameras or other methods of spying, but the space was clear.

Next, she visited the maintenance building. Oriana, one of the older ladies who'd been working for Elani for a long time, was gathering supplies in a duffle bag with a tool belt hung over her shoulder.

"If you're looking for Elani, she's already at the site," said Oriana.

"Have you seen Garret?"

Oriana wrinkled her forehead as she slung the sagging duffle bag over her other shoulder and headed past Pandora.

"Dunno. Check the map in Elani's office and you should be able to find where he's at."

The entire building was empty. Everyone who'd been available had been sent to the scene of destruction. Elani's office was neat and organized, with labeled notebooks on her desk and a map of the settlement with marks and lines indicating the power, water, and sewage lines that crisscrossed the area. A pin with a red head and a tag with the name "Garret" on it was in the back region near a secondary generator.

Pandora was about to head out until she noticed a crumpled satchel in an empty wooden box. She pulled it out, noting that it was the same style and brand of bag that the explosives had been contained in. There were no obvious markings that suggested it was the same one, but even if it wasn't, it'd come from the Mod's store: The Rush. It didn't necessarily mean anything, since the shop had mining and maintenance supplies, which Elani needed for her projects, but the coincidence was suspicious.

She set the satchel back in the box and continued to the back of the Pajot, where she heard music playing long before she saw Garret. His back was to her as he worked inside the generator, humming to himself, his head bobbing with the music. Her blade was against his neck before he knew what was happening.

"Hey—"

"Shut up, and you might live past the next few minutes. I'm going to ask some questions. Answer quickly and truthfully." She let the blade part his flesh, releasing a trickle of blood. Garret inhaled.

"Have you been back to the Mod?"

"No. I did like you said. I pissed myself when she asked me to go back."

"And the drugs?"

"The first week was awful, but I'm over them now. Elani thought I had the stomach flu when they found me near the pit toilets covered in my own vomit. I wanted to die. Like really die."

It was possible to go cold turkey, but she wasn't sure she believed him. Menya was a powerful drug that created hard-core addictions. If he'd been able to break the link, he'd be in rare company. She spun him around and looked into his eyes.

"You look entirely too fucking healthy. How do I know you're not using now?"

She pointed the blade at a spot near the generator. "Sit."

When he did as she said, Pandora grabbed his tool belt, rifling through it until she found a plastic baggy full of little blue pills. His hands went up and he started sobbing.

"I wanted to stop taking them, but I had a stash. It's enough for another two weeks, and then I'll be clean. I swear. I tried for a few days, but I couldn't. It hurt too much."

"What about the explosives?"

He screwed up his face in a believable manner. "You took them from me."

"You didn't find them and take them back and set them at the processing facility?"

"What? No."

She studied him, looking for clues to the truth, but he was unreadable.

"Why?" he asked eventually. "Did something happen?"

"Someone did what you failed to do."

She held up her arm, which was covered in dirt and soot. His face broke with emotion, the lines of his face dripping with sadness.

"I didn't. I swear. I don't even know what you did with them," said

Garret, on the verge of tears.

"Fuck. I don't know how I can believe you, not when you lied about the drugs. I should cut your throat right now, just to be sure."

His eyes darted towards his path of escape.

"Try it. We'll see how far you get."

Garret broke into a sob, followed by a stream of tears. Her nose caught the whiff of piss.

"It's not gonna work on me," she told him, but he continued to cry openly, not even trying to hold back. He started mumbling about wanting to be a better person and give up the drugs, and how big of a mistake he'd made. A puddle of piss formed near his ankle.

Pandora paced away. He was a liability, that much was for sure. The safe thing to do was to cut his throat and dump him in the canyons for the critters to feast on his body, but on the other hand, she'd been seen in Elani's office asking about his location. She could claim she never found him. Given what she'd done to save lives at the processing building, she'd probably be given the benefit of the doubt. Plus, she was a powerful sapphire waku and Garret was a maintenance tech of middling importance.

If she was her mother, she'd have already cut his throat. It was the only thing staying her blade. Pandora was already doubting the path she'd been set upon. It didn't help that the Mod had said she'd have to clean up her mess. A part of her feared that her mother had manipulated events to force her to kill Garret. If only to remind her of who was in control.

Click. Click.

"Shut up."

"I didn't say anything," said Garret as he wiped the tears from his cheeks with the back of his hand.

Pandora took the baggie of pills, dumped them onto the hard ground, and ground them into dust beneath her heel. Then she poured Garret's thermos of soup onto the dust and kicked sand and dirt on top. The empty devastation in his gaze was a portent of things to come. She left him in his puddle of piss, knowing that she needed to have a word with the Mod on a very near timeline.

Eighteen

Kuma was returning to the Academy after a patrol in the northern fields near the well of earth. The region was ripe with fungi, mostly ghosteye, long-stemmed mushrooms that gave off a faint light from their translucent bodies. They shifted as if a strange wind had somehow reached the caverns nearly a thousand feet beneath the earth, but it was well known the fungi created that illusion to lure insects and critters into their midst, where smaller red threads paralyzed them to be consumed through the soil.

The ghosteyes weren't dangerous to humans, but they provided an ominous backdrop to the patrol. He'd been with Adrenalynne and Carlos. They'd found a campsite near a deep stream, the remnants of a sorcerous fire suggesting that it wasn't one of the clans, but the crimaza from above. Carlos thought it could have been one of the clans, since the presence of mages within their ranks wasn't forbidden, but rare. They never determined who had been on their territory, but it was on Kuma's mind as he returned.

On the rock wall outside the Academy cavern, a neon green *D* had been painted with a red *X* through it. The chatter about an upcoming attack on the Drops had been circulating through the clan for a week since Botan's burial.

He was coming through the archway, cycling his emerald while running his amber, working on his endurance, when he caught a pair of voices from a distant location. Kuma dropped the emerald and focused on the amber, which always left him a little overwhelmed until he could sculpt the region he was listening to.

"...it's gonna be glorious. They won't know what hit 'em until it's over. Now come here."

The sound of kissing was followed by a grunt. It'd been Deacon's voice, and then he heard Yara's.

"You're as dumb as one of them Hall mages if you think a group of Crows are gonna hit the Lazona, a heavily guarded enclave, without getting wiped out. I know we gave you some stones, but besides you, I wouldn't trust any of the others to knock over a street vendor, let alone take on our enemies in a place they've controlled for decades."

"That's the beauty of it. It ain't gonna be Crows, not all. Most of 'em will be Razor in our gear. I'm pretty sure your father is going to be leading the raid. Disguised, of course. But you didn't hear it from me, and let's not waste our break with all this talk. Can we go to that one place?"

Kuma tuned out while he assumed they were kissing, but kept his amber trained in their direction in case the conversation resumed. He wanted to hear when this raid might happen.

The idea that his father would risk a hit on a major commerce hub for the Drops spoke to the pressure he was under to respond to Botan's torture and murder. Even though both of them knew it wasn't the Drops, they'd still taken the bait. On the other hand, using the Black Crows was at least acknowledgement of the riskiness of the venture. He knew there'd been other activities in the city using the Crows against the Drops, hitting their businesses, both legal and illicit. It surprised Kuma that the Drops hadn't hit back yet, or maybe it was in the works.

The scuff of soles brought him back to the moment. He turned to find Camina and Tick headed down the path.

"You holding back a fart?" asked Tick, mirth in his grin.

"No. I was—"

Camina gave him a funny look. She made the sign for "need a quiet place to talk?" which consisted of rubbing the top of the ear with a quick head nod.

Kuma rocked his fist and the three of them headed towards the Maze. The runed archway that led into the place of training always reminded Kuma of an eye. He started to speak, but Camina shook her head and pulled a little black box from a hidden pocket. She pressed a button and set it on the ground between them.

"Where'd you get that?"

"Last time I was on patrol in Big Dave's Town I picked one up. Sick of everyone hearing everything I do or say. It's the one part of the Academy that's made me very tired."

"Not the arc runs or every other weird training technique ol' Frog Lips tries on us?" asked Tick.

"What's up, Little Bear? You look like someone put a centipede down your pants," said Camina.

He gave them the rundown from what he'd overheard about the raid on Lazona.

"Shit," said Tick, looking down at his shoes as the muscles in his face spasmed. "I was hoping the war wasn't going to start until I graduated. I'm gonna get murdered in a scrap."

Camina elbowed him. "You know we got your back."

"Sure, but what if they have black diamonds?" asked Tick, swallowing.

"This raid is a mistake," said Kuma.

"Mistake? That duel last year really messed with your head. Those fuckers killed Botan. They deserve what they're going to get," said Camina, her lip curled in a snarl.

"It wasn't the Drops."

"The fuck it wasn't. They put a big fucking D in his chest and all those healed scars. You know that was Duro's work," said Camina.

"I'm telling you it wasn't the Drops. Even my father and Brazio know this, but they needed to make the clan happy. Hit back in a way that satisfies the bloodlust. That's why they're using the Crows, so it doesn't look like us."

"Then who is it?" asked Tick.

"Probably the alliance clans. If we battle with Drops, whoever is left will be easy to clean up, especially with their stones and allies."

Camina picked up a rock and tossed it against the wall. "I don't think so. All the alliance clans together add up to a bag of warm turds. They scrap like shit and have no discipline. Even a black diamond doesn't make them that formidable, just as your uncle proved."

"He almost lost that fight," said Kuma.

"What are you suggesting, Little Bear? You look like you have something you want to say," said Camina.

He paced away, rubbing the back of his head. "I don't know. Lot of strange things happening. Patrols are finding evidence of visitors all over our territory. The day Botan died I nearly got trapped alive in that mine. The black diamond. We're missing something."

"Missing what?" asked Tick.

"I don't know. That's why we need to go to the Terreno. Ask around, stop looking to the other clans for every answer, and open our eyes."

"If you want to see Leesa again, you don't have to make up a convoluted reason to go to the Onyx," said Camina.

"We need to talk to Leesa, but not that kind of talk," he said.

Kuma hadn't intended to use the signaling system he'd set up with Pandora, but with everything coming to a head, he thought it best if he could set up a meeting with her. His friends didn't have to know about this secondary goal.

"You know I'm always down for a visit to the Onyx," said Tick. "I got bills burning a hole in my pocket. The siren call of the pachinko machine is whispering my name."

"We're not going there for pleasure," said Kuma.

Tick frowned. "If there's gonna be a war and I'm gonna die soon, at least let me have a bottle of Lone Magus with Leesa."

"You know that's not how it works. It's not just about money," said Camina.

"I never should have kept the amber during attunement week," said Tick. "I could have just acted like it hadn't worked on me. Everyone would have believed it."

Kuma put a hand on his friend's shoulder. "When the time comes to scrap, we got your back. But in the meantime, help me figure out how to stop the war."

Camina stared at him with pinched lips. "What happens if your father finds out you're going against his wishes? I know you're his son, but he won't have a choice but to punish you severely. It'll be much worse for Tick and me. Not sure I'm excited about this idea."

"I'm not doing anything against his wishes. Yet. For now, we're just gathering information. Look, I was there when they discussed the implications of Botan's death. They want a better way out of this problem, too. If we learn something that will help steer the clan in a better direction, I'll take it to them."

"You'll take it to them," said Tick. "Your uncle scares me. I always feel like he can see inside my soul, tell exactly what I'm thinking."

"It's pachinko and masturbation all the way down," said Camina dryly.

"Will you come with me?" asked Kuma with his hands pressed together before him.

"I don't know, Little Bear. This sounds like the path to doing something really stupid. I'd rather get off before the ride crashes," said Camina.

"I promise I won't do anything without both of your agreement. Please. I need you two."

"You need us to share the blame," said Camina.

"I swear on my mother's grave that I'll listen to your counsel once we learn what's really going on."

Camina crossed her arms with her mouth shifted to the side. "I'm not sold."

Feeling desperate, he turned to Tick. "I'll pay for your pachinko if you come with me."

"Bribery, really? You really think that's going to work?" asked Camina.

"Throw in a regular bottle with Darina and I'm your man," said Tick, grinning.

"Tick? Have some self-respect," said Camina.

"Really, Camina? You've known me how long?"

She rolled her eyes. "Ugh. On your mother's grave?"

Kuma put his hand over his heart. "She'd support this plan. She always believed in acquiring more information before making big decisions. She advised my father to do that many times."

"Fine. Only because I know how much you loved your mother will I entertain this foolishness."

"It's not foolishness."

"We'll see," said Camina.

"Great. We have a few days off soon."

"But we're not allowed at the Terreno right now," said Tick.

Kuma nodded. "I know. We need a good excuse why we're not in the Machi."

Camina raised an eyebrow. "How about that we're camping near the Great Arch? It's relatively safe and we used to do it all the time when we were younger."

"Perfect," said Kuma, grinning. "See? This is why I needed you."

"What did you need me for?" asked Tick.

"We'll figure that out eventually. But I know when it happens, it'll be amazing."

"Yeah, right," said Tick, rolling his eyes. "But I'll forgive you because of pachinko and Darina."

The three of them returned to the Academy. The idea that they were going to do something about the potential war had his thoughts careening around his head. Maybe they'd find nothing, but at least he would feel better that they'd exhausted all options. And maybe—he knew this was highly unlikely—he'd get a chance to see Pandora again. Her black eyes haunted his dreams each night and left him burning with desire.

Nineteen

The meeting with Duro was set for the wild lands north of the Pajot and east of the Lazona. On the way out of the settlement, she passed the skeletal processing building, which was being rebuilt larger and sturdier. Unlike the ramshackle version that had served for many years, it would be composed of steel and reinforced concrete.

Elani and her crew were working diligently day and night to get the center back up and running. The loss of profits was hurting the Drops, who were already under strain due to the attacks on their legitimate businesses in the city. Pandora saw the older woman, who was going over blueprints on a table near the construction site. The idea that she'd been the bomber seemed ludicrous in retrospect given how hard Elani worked at keeping the settlement running in the harsh environment of the Undercity. Pandora decided that the presence of the satchel had been purely coincidental.

Before she reached the cavern where she was to meet Duro, she wondered if it was a trap. That her false pretense for joining the Drops had been found out and the Shadowmaster was going to kill her. But that had always been a lingering concern. Pandora entered the prescribed meeting place and found Duro waiting.

He stood on a rock with his arms by his side and his eyes closed. He looked like he could have been sleeping, but she knew the truth even without an amber. Rumors were that Duro slept but a few hours each night. Many a younger clan member had seen the warleader in the earliest hours of the day scrambling up cliffs or carrying small boulders through the caverns on his shoulder, maintaining his relentless training schedule.

She crept in as silently as possible, using her sapphire to keep her feet light.

"Did you bring the pistol?" he asked without opening his eyes.

Pandora halted, pulled the weapon from her waistband, and held it out on the palm of her hand. When he opened his eyes, she gave the pistol a Push, sending it in an arc until he snatched it out of the air.

"You're getting better."

"Not good enough."

He inclined his head. "Good. Never be satisfied. It's the only way you'll survive." Duro quickly inspected the weapon and then shoved it in the back of his pants. "It's the reason why Irina will never be the war-leader. She thinks she's reached her peak. The problem with excellence is it blinds you to the possibilities that you have yet to uncover. I've had to invent challenges to keep myself progressing."

Duro reached into a pocket and casually tossed an ornate box to her. She caught it easily, giving him a questioning eyebrow.

"Open it."

Inside, an opaque stone sat in a velvet catch next to a small vial of electric blue liquid.

"An opal?"

"You've only one stone, not enough for a waku of your ability."

She hung her head. "I failed to attune to the amber and topaz. Maybe I'm destined only to be a single stone waku."

"That's what the vial is for," he said with a smirk.

"This is Eclipse?"

Duro nodded. "A quarter of the normal draught, but I think it's all that will be required to attune."

Pandora wasn't sure she agreed. She looked around at the cavern they were standing in. It was wide, with multiple levels, a section with stacked stone pillars, and a grotto that looked like teeth. There was plenty of illuminating fungi to see by, which made her wonder why he'd asked her all the way out here to give her the gift of a new stone and the Eclipse.

"Drink it."

She popped the top and threw back the liquid, which burned like peppermint schnapps on the way down. She was tasting the cool coating across her tongue when she looked up to see Duro aiming the pistol at her. A heavy punch in her shoulder knocked her on her rear. The bullet had ripped right through her muscles. Pandora couldn't catch her breath as he approached without the weapon in his hand.

"Now heal yourself."

"What?" she asked, holding a hand over the wound as she gasped for breath. "I'm not attuned."

"Better hurry before you bleed out."

The agony in her right shoulder made it hard to pull the opal out of its velvet catch. She fumbled with the sticky bandage as she placed it against her wrist while Duro observed passively.

"Why did you shoot me?" she asked as a wave of disorientation hit as if she'd just been spun around a dozen times and had fallen on her rear.

"Focus on the task. Answers will reveal themselves."

The warleader was unassuming. A man with dark hair and a medium build. Had it been anyone else, she might have wondered if this was a sick game, but his reputation gave her the impetus to trust, even if her mind was screaming alarms.

A gurgle in her stomach had her closing her eyes, rocking against the pain and nausea. The smell of damp stone filled her nose.

"Why aren't you healing yourself?"

Pandora could barely sit up straight. The world spun around her, but she put her hand to the wound. *How do I make the opal work?* Deciding that any questions would be met unanswered, she imagined her flesh knitting together at the same time she focused on the stone against her wrist.

Nothing happened.

She checked her shirt to find it soaked through down to her pants. She'd lost a lot of blood and was growing dizzier by the moment. Duro could heal her wound, but he was making no move to help.

Rather than interact with the wound, Pandora pressed her thumb against the opal, pushing it into her skin. A flash of a vision startled her. It was as if she'd seen her entire body revealed by an X-ray in her mind. She saw the veins pumping blood, the spark between neurons in her mind, the way her muscles stretched and bunched providing locomotion.

In the afterimage of the vision, Pandora was beset by another wave of vertigo. She fought to maintain her seated position while trying to claw back to the picture of her body, sensing it was an opportunity. A window to the opal.

Pressing her hand against the wound a third time, Pandora could feel the way her heart pushed the blood out of the severed veins, the torn muscles trying to shift as she breathed but because they were missing mass they sent alarm signals down her nervous system letting her know that something was terribly wrong. Had she not had the hole in her shoulder, leaking life fluid, she might have stayed seated exploring the wonders of her body with the opal for hours, but she renewed her focus on the wound.

Convincing the flesh to knit back together felt like molding with clay, except that her fingers knew the ways of shaping. Maybe it was because it was her body and she carried great subconscious knowledge about it, but once she'd attended to the hole, she was able to convince it to grow back together.

"Done," she said.

The effort left her weak. Duro handed her a water bottle filled with thick green liquid that looked like juiced vegetables.

"Drink. All of it."

The liquid tasted like spinach and chalk. It took effort to swallow the mixture given how dense it was, but she managed to get the entire bottle down, releasing a belch for good measure.

"Satisfied?"

She hadn't meant the question to be disrespectful, but she knew how it had sounded the moment it came out.

Duro took a seated position across from her, resting his wrists on the bend of his knees.

"Quite. The green drink should help you recuperate from the energy it took to attune and heal. It's a mix of natural foods with some elixirs that I've found help with recovery. As for shooting you, I needed to put your body in a state of shock and emergency. I feared even telling you might lessen the impact. Do you understand why?"

"It's how I attuned to the sapphire. It was in the middle of a fight," said Pandora, nodding slowly.

"I gave you a quarter draught of Eclipse to ensure that it happened, but yes, your rapid attunement was facilitated by the body's shock response. Otherwise, as you know, it can take much longer."

"How long have you known this?"

He chuckled. "This is only the second test. Next time I need to confirm with other subjects in case this technique only works on you." Duro leapt to his feet from the cross-legged position, a movement that appeared almost instantaneous. "Now, training can begin."

Joining him on her feet with her uniform soaked in blood, Pandora offered a steep bow.

"Most waku think of the opal stone purely for its healing components. The faez crystal allows for great feats of bodily repair, but there is a hidden skill which few besides myself have unlocked. The ability to modify the body extends to manipulating the muscle tissues, adrenal glands, and other important functions that aid a warrior in a scrap."

Duro leapt away, landing thirty feet behind where he'd been previously standing, then ran across the cavern, bounding over stones until he ran sideways along the wall for a dozen feet before returning to the ground.

"Use your opal to enhance your muscles. It's almost like warming them before a fire. Once you get the feel of it, you won't be able to forget it."

Using the opal was unfamiliar, so it took her a moment to refocus her mind towards the newly acquired stone. She did as he suggested and then leapt away, attempting to follow the same path as Duro. She barely jumped further than she could without the stone, and then in bounding over the obstacles, overcompensated and slipped off a pillar, crashing to the ground.

The urge to stay prone was strong, but she regained her feet and continued on the path. She managed to prod her body to be faster, but it made her unsteady as her feet didn't land where she expected to be.

"The adjustments will come in time, but you're understanding the technique. I want you to follow that route until you can achieve wall running."

The next three hours Pandora spent attempting to repeat what Duro had so easily shown her. She managed to enhance her speed on every run, but fell frequently, smashing into boulders and rocks, scraping her skin and nearly knocking herself unconscious at least twice.

Duro never said a word during the entire process. He watched with the passivity of an old man bobber fishing in his boat on a warm summer day. Each time she fell, she healed herself and returned to the start.

"Now I know how a foal feels after birth," she muttered to herself at one point, catching the twitch of a smirk from the warleader.

He gave her a brief break. Enough to squat in the corner of the cave, down another bottle of the thick green liquid, and patch up the little wounds she'd missed earlier. Then she was back at the course, finding her limbs even less steady than during the first three hours.

After a time that started blending together—during which she'd suffered countless more injuries—Pandora grew frustrated by her lack of progress. She could reach the wall with speed but as soon as she put her foot on the vertical surface she could barely take two steps before gravity took hold.

"You fight like you're mad at the world," said Duro.

Pandora couldn't recall the last time words other than her cursing had been uttered in the space.

Duro tilted his head. "Don't force the stones. You have much power, but you wield it like a sledgehammer. It makes you tired. It's why you lost against the Razor boy. Had you not worn yourself out, you could have Pushed the rocks and him off of you, but you were tired."

The denial died in her throat. She saw the truth as soon as he said it. It was the same thing Instructor Irina had been admonishing her for during the last few months.

"Whatever it is that you're holding onto inside, you need to let that go before you can attain your true power. Come. Today's training is complete."

"But I didn't run the wall."

"You're not capable of it. Not yet. Not until you address these internal issues. I want you to spend time meditating on these ideas. Think deeply about who you are and what you want to become. Nothing else matters on this path."

Pandora glanced back to the rock wall, which brought a shifting of his mouth.

"I want you to come here every morning before class and practice with your opal until you've mastered the wall. Keep it hidden otherwise. I want no one to know that you've a second stone. Not even your friends Choo-Choo and Navos."

"Understood."

"Dismissed. You may return to the Pajot and clean up. You can charge your new uniform to me since I ruined this one."

Pandora chewed on the inside of her cheek. "Why isn't the Academy teaching how to use an opal this way? I've never seen Instructor Irina move like this, and she has an opal."

"You have not earned the right to ask this question. Nor do I think it necessary that you hear me speak the words." He pulled the pistol from his waistband and handed it over. "See me tomorrow after your training. I have an errand for you to run."

"The Terreno?"

The corners of his eyes creased. "The Lazona."

She tried not to show her disappointment, but with his amber, she knew it was unlikely that he hadn't sensed it. Duro left the chamber, moving at a speed she couldn't follow and in a direction not heading back to the Pajot.

Pandora made her way back slowly. The training had left her muscles spent, even with the elixirs. She was disappointed that the errand wouldn't take her back to the Terreno as she wanted to confront the Mod about the attack and figure out who she'd convinced to do the deed after Garret.

Before she reached the outer guard stations, Pandora removed the sticky patch on her wrist and reapplied it to her inner thigh until she could get a proper setting for the opal. Two stones. She smiled to herself. There were a lot of questions about why Duro was keeping this gift hidden from the Academy and Instructor Irina, but for now she didn't care because it'd given her more ways to protect herself should events slip to war.

Twenty

A woman screamed the moment Kuma and his friends stepped into the Onyx. His whole body went on high alert until he realized it'd been Darina squealing as her customer had grabbed her rear. The rest of the club was almost empty, except for two older alliance waku at the bar and a group of Blue Daggers in the back singing karaoke in a private room with a younger waku outside the paper door.

"You sure this is a good idea?" asked Camina. "What if word gets back that we came here, or someone from the clan spots us?"

"Then we'll be in trouble." He approached the bar. "Seen Leesa?"

The bartender was refilling the brand-name bottles of alchohol with cheaper generics. He appeared annoyed by their presence. He set down the bottle and jabbed his thumb into a little black box.

"Leesa. You got customers."

A minute later, the redhead appeared looking bleary-eyed and a little gaunt. A silver dress hung loosely on her frame, exposing bony shoulders. The delay in recognition was followed by a forced smile.

"Kuma? What are you three doing here?"

"Buying you a bottle," he said.

Leesa blinked. "Celebrating?"

"Sure," he said, gesturing towards the booth furthest from the private party on the opposite side.

She gave them hugs, ordered the bottle from the bartender, and led them to the booth. The hostess had always been impeccably prepared, speaking to him as if she'd known what he was thinking already. But her appearance made him think she'd just woken up, or had been under the influence of drugs, which were plentiful in the Terreno.

"What's wrong?" he asked her.

"Nothing." Pinched lips were followed by an angry glare. "I'm fine. Business has been slow. I was sleeping when you arrived."

Leesa popped the bottle of champagne when it arrived, pouring a glass for the four of them. She held hers aloft, which they matched. Her smile was obviously forced.

"To unexpected friends."

With the glass set down, Kuma nodded to Camina. The little black box set off a faint humming. Leesa tapped a crimson fingernail on the box, frowning.

"I don't like this."

"You'll just have to get over it," said Kuma, under his breath.

"So you didn't come to visit me?" she asked, crossing her arms.

"Think of the bottle as a down payment," he said.

Leesa considered them with half-lidded eyes. "I don't spill secrets."

"We're not asking you to. What we want to know is less specific."

"And?"

"The war between the clans is coming soon," said Kuma.

"No shit," she said, throwing back the fluted glass of yellowish-gold liquid and pouring herself a second. "The Terreno has been as dead as my sex life, but what do I have to do with that?"

"We want to avoid it, if possible," said Kuma.

Leesa checked over her shoulder. "You're kidding, right? I thought you wanted to scrap with the Drops. The way I see it, the war between you two has been inevitable."

"That's the problem. If we were the only two clans in the Undercity, the peace would have never been brokered, but the alliance waits to clean up the survivor. It puts the winning clan in a perilous position."

"I still don't see why you came to me," she said.

"Something happened in our clan that was made to look like it was the Drops that caused it. It's not the first, nor will it be the last. I suspect the same thing has been happening on their side."

"You want to know who's behind it," said Leesa.

"You've always said that you know everything going on in the Terreno. Not just because you hear us all run our mouths when we're in our cups, but because you keep your eyes and ears open. I'm not asking for secrets. That's your prerogative. But I am asking about what you've been seeing around here."

"Or lack of seeing. This place is dead. Profits have dried up and our illustrious owner is being stingy with our benefits."

"Then you've a vested interest in the Undercity returning to a calm stalemate."

Leesa stared back with an unusual animosity. "Or maybe I'd like to see you fight it out and let the winners return to the Onyx for a victory celebration which involves buying me more bottles of bubbly than I can count. I didn't come here for my health, Kuma. I came here to make money."

"I told you this was a waste of time," said Camina, starting to rise.

Kuma put a hand on her forearm. "Please."

Camina grumbled and returned to her seat.

"Have you noticed people in the Terreno you haven't seen before? Someone who looks out of place?"

Leesa snorted behind her hand. "Really? This is your line of questioning? Stick to your stones, Kuma, you're embarrassing yourself."

Shame burned in his cheeks. "I'm serious. The alliance clans have always been a bunch of collective fuck-ups. Then you have what happened to us. I want to know who's behind it. Who are we really fighting against? It sure as hell doesn't seem like this is only an Undercity battle."

The dead silence was a sign of recognition. He saw right through her with his amber. She'd seen things, but he smelled her fear. Kuma put his hand over hers and gave it a squeeze.

"You've seen something, or someone," he said.

"A few weeks ago. Whoever it was had a Look-Away enchantment. I couldn't see anything about them except that they existed, but their entourage was nothing I'd ever seen before in the Terreno."

Her nostrils flared as she reviewed the memory. Camina and Tick leaned forward in anticipation.

"And?"

Leesa shrugged, took another drink. "I told you. I couldn't see the person."

"What about the guards?" asked Camina.

She checked around the bar before lowering her head. "Real badasses. Fully enchanted Kevlar gear, automatics that looked custom, though I don't know shit about guns. Earpieces and their glasses shimmered." Leesa inhaled slowly. "I spend a lot of time when I'm not down here watching out my window from the apartments above the Onyx. My windows are tinted, and I was half hidden by a curtain. There's no way anyone should have seen me but one of those guys, neck as thick as a tree trunk, looked right up at me. I was afraid he'd come into the Onyx and strangle me."

Remembering the day of Shade's End, Kuma asked, "Blackstone Security?"

"No," she said right away, shaking her head. "Like them, sure. But not them. I've seen enough of Blackstone over the years to recognize their insignia. This group wasn't wearing any."

"Where'd they go?" asked Tick.

"I couldn't tell you. They turned right, headed towards the other end of the Terreno."

"Anything else?" he asked.

Leesa nodded slowly as if the memory had been burned into her mind. "One of the guards wasn't like the others. He made my skin crawl. Gray, chalky skin and a smile that would have given a serial killer the creeps."

"City fae?" asked Tick, breathlessly.

"Yeah. Seen 'em from time to time down here, usually on their own, but this one was part of the security detail. Probably in charge of it."

"Shadows below. Whoever this is must be a big player, being able to afford a maetrie as their head of security," said Kuma.

"We don't know that's who's behind all this," said Camina.

"No, but it's weird for someone to visit the Terreno with all those precautions. It's not like this is a grand destination that pulls in tourists from the light."

Leesa elbowed him. "Hey, I think we put on a pretty good time down here."

"Sorry, Leesa. You know what I mean." He tapped on his glass, then threw it back. The bubbles made his nose itch. "I'd put all the money Tick's lost at pachinko on that our visitors have something to do with the alliance clans. They might not be behind them, but they certainly could be business partners."

"Buying up the stones?" suggested Camina. "Maybe that's how they're recruiting so many new waku and soldados."

"Fuck," said Kuma. "You're probably right. They're treating them like a business, expanding rapidly, bringing in new partners. Soon they'll be big enough to eat us both for lunch."

Leesa refilled their glasses, taking care to wipe the rims with a white silk napkin.

"No offense, but what's the point of all this? It's not like you're going to suddenly change the power balance in the Undercity. Not the three of you."

Tick grinned and jabbed his thumb at Kuma. "He singlehandedly screwed things up last year at Shade's End when he let that Drops girl live."

"Shut up, Tick."

He opened his palms. "Am I right?"

"You're not wrong."

Leesa stared at him with the truth of what really had happened clearly on her mind. Camina hunched her forehead as she checked between them.

"What? There's something else that happened."

"No," said Kuma, holding up his glass to Camina to distract her.

Camina looked back and forth. "You sure? Seemed like something passed between you there."

"Anything else?" he asked Leesa.

"Nothing out of the ordinary. You know we get mages down here sometimes. Either curious, or probably to do a deal. More traffic since the stones trade started, but nothing that unusual considering."

"Anyone in particular?"

"I'm a hostess at an Undercity club. All those mages look the same to me. They usually disguise themselves anyway. It could be Celesse D'Agastine herself at my booth and I probably wouldn't know it."

"Let's look around," said Kuma, finishing his glass.

"For what?" asked Camina.

Kuma lifted his shoulders. "Dunno. But the shadows don't reveal their secrets from the light. Figure we can head the same way that group did, maybe see where they might have gone."

"There are hundreds of businesses and apartments in the Terreno," said Camina.

"You don't have to go."

Camina pursed her lips. "You know I do."

Leesa joined them on their feet, giving hugs and kisses on the cheek. Kuma lingered afterwards as his friends moved towards the exit. He slipped a note that he'd written for Pandora into her palm, giving a curt nod.

"In case."

He started to move away, but she pulled him back. Leesa checked with the rest of the bar before leaning towards his ear.

"I heard something happened at Drops recently. Around the same timing as what happened in Razor. Rumor, but, you know."

"Thanks."

Outside the Onyx, the sad chimes of pachinko rang through the nearly empty streets. An old woman who looked like she'd been chain-smoking for the entire day was working her pachinko machine inside the Bogo. Two trays of silvery balls sat by her seat along with an ashtray stabbed with a half dozen old cigarettes.

"Where to?" asked Camina.

When he didn't answer, Tick gestured towards the Bogo. "You know, since we're here..."

The last bit of information swam around his mind. "I don't know."

The idea that he might learn something by coming to the Terreno seemed foolish standing outside the Onyx.

"What was that with you and Leesa? Before, when you were talking about Shade's End," Camina said.

Kuma checked over his shoulder. "I told you, nothing."

"Didn't seem like nothing."

"When we left, she told me that the Drops had been hit recently. Around the same time as Botan. What if those heavily armored visitors had something to do with it? They showed up and then both clans get hit in a way that suggests it was the other?"

"Sounds good, but what are you going to do with that information? Even if it was true, which I doubt, your father wouldn't believe you," said Camina.

Tick was staring longingly at the pachinko machines. Kuma pushed him forward.

"Let's walk. I need to think."

Twenty-One

The Lazona wasn't what Pandora expected. The other settlements in the Undercity were spread out in caverns, linked by tunnels, and form-fit to the space given. This place was like the inverse of a skyscraper. The cavern was circular and the ceiling so high it was out of sight. Bulb lights were strung across the space at various levels, providing illumination for the silo-like settlement. A collection of businesses and an open-air market populated the ground section, but stairs carved into the walls or ladders reached caves and other spaces further up.

Pandora was reminded of a time her father took her into a mega-hotel in downtown Chicago. The interior had a garden with a big fountain at the bottom and balconies from the interior rooms overlooked the lush greenery.

The Lazona wasn't unlike that place as every ledge and balcony sported plants and colorful flowers. The businesses didn't look as profitable or organized as the ones in Big Dave's Town or the Terreno, but there was something organic and alive about the Lazona. She spotted Drops guards lurking in the shadows, but not as many as she would have expected given the importance of the region. Either there were others better hidden, or the tension with Razor had pulled resources to other locations.

The business name Duro had given her wasn't visible from the bottom of the Lazona. She found a street vendor sitting on a blanket with trinkets that looked like common wire twisted into pleasing shapes and attached to bits of quartz or other unusual rocks. His face was smudged with dirt as if he hadn't showered in weeks.

"Lucky ducky trinkets here, get 'em hot, oozin' with the good stuff, fresh from the earth. Protect you from the creepies and the crawlies lurkin' out there. 'Allo, pretty. Care to buy one, or six? Keep a hard-workin' man in the green?"

Pandora dug into her pocket for a small bill. "Where's the Lime Duck?"

His smile faltered. "Third level. Up them steps over there."

She craned her neck, spotting the neon sign gleaming into the space. It showed a lime green duck smoking a cigar. Pandora tossed the bill onto the blanket and headed to the stairs.

She passed a hewn tunnel leading to a heavy construction site, which she assumed was the elevator that was being built to make the Lazona a better hub of commerce for the Drops. Welding torches sparked in the dim light amid the shouts of the construction workers. Burnt metallics reached her nose, making it wrinkle.

The stairs to the upper levels including the Lime Duck were narrow and without a guardrail, forcing her to turn sideways as she passed a drunk coming down. She imagined more than a few patrons took the fast way down by mistake.

The Lime Duck looked like it could be any tavern in a major city. The bar's mascot, a cigar smoking duck, was plastered all over, including a wooden version sitting at the end of the bar with a half-full tip jar in front. The resemblance to a city establishment ended the moment she laid eyes upon the bartender. The chalky gray skin opened a pit in Pandora's stomach a mile deep. She had a pretty good idea that the maetrie behind the bar was the Najani she'd been sent to deliver the message to.

Pandora found a spot at the bar furthest away from the other customers, which set her near the wooden duck. Seven bills and sixteen coins in the jar. If she'd had a single coin she would have thrown it in with the others to make it seventeen. As the maetrie bartender approached, Pandora was surprised by unexpected features including blonde streaks in her hair, a nose piercing, and, most striking of all, a pleasant smile. Nothing like the maetrie she'd known in her lifetime.

"You look like you've seen a ghost," said the bartender with the lilt of an Undercity accent and amusement lurking in her black eyes.

"Najani?"

"Present and accounted for," said the woman with her hands splayed on the countertop. "You gonna stare at me like that all day? I do have an establishment to run."

"I, uhm..."

"Care to tell me about that ghost you think you've seen?"

Najani was clearly messing with her, but Pandora couldn't get her mind around what she was seeing.

"City fae."

"Only partial. More looks than attitude, and given this clearly isn't your first time, I'd say this rightly shocks you. Most maetrie are rather cold, impersonal. Cut you from gut to gullet given the opportunity."

"You're not."

"No," said Najani, shaking her head. "Like I said, more looks than attitude. My father was half-maetrie at best, probably less. I'm probably no more than a quarter." She smirked. "You probably didn't even know they could conceive with humans, but it happens from time to time. Not often. But it happens. What can I get for you?"

Pandora pushed away the maelstrom of thoughts that had her twisted up inside. She was here for a job. Nothing more.

"A bottle of Hornhammer whiskey."

The order brought an arch of Najani's eyebrows. "I see." She checked back to the other patrons, who were too busy in their cups to notice. Najani jerked her head.

"Come on around back to my private tasting room. I'll buzz you through the door."

The back room smelled like rich leather. A trio of black couches sat around a mahogany table. Najani entered from the opposite door with a bottle of dark liquid in her fist and two tumblers held with her fingers.

"Get comfortable," she said, setting the glasses on the table, rattling the ice. She pulled a knife out and cut away the wax around the seal.

Pandora remained standing and reached into an inner pocket, producing a thin box barely bigger than a match container. A simple latch held it closed, but Pandora hadn't risked opening it in case Duro had left an enchantment. She had a good idea that it was a faez crystal in the box even without looking, but she didn't understand the why.

"This is for you."

Najani stared at the box as if it were a bar of pure gold. Her eyes lit up. She set it on the table and continued removing the wax, then poured two glasses of whiskey and offered one to Pandora.

"What's this for?"

"Celebrating."

They clinked glasses. Pandora took a drink while Najani threw hers back, grimacing momentarily before shooting her a wink. The whiskey burned on the way down in a pleasant way.

With the drink consumed, Najani turned her attention to the box. She opened it towards her, the slow smile spreading to a face-splitting grin.

"Beautiful yet so small."

"Satisfied?" *A faez crystal for sure, but which one?*

"Very." Najani closed the box and left the room. She returned a moment later with a wrapped box suggesting a second bottle of whiskey. "Here's a gift for Duro."

Pandora accepted the box with both hands, inclining her head. "I must attend another errand after this. Must this reach him right away?"

"No," said Najani with a half smile. "I can send this by courier later."

"Anything else?"

"Tell him he'll have the Lazona's full support."

"I will pass the message on."

Najani raised an eyebrow. "If you didn't have to head back right away, you and I could finish this bottle."

"I have other errands and I shouldn't be away from the Academy too long."

"I understand. Good luck. I'm sure we'll see each other again."

Najani buzzed her out the door. She might have stayed to learn more about the Lazona, Najani herself, and the reason for the cryptic message, but she wanted to get to the Terreno. If she hurried, and used her stones for speed, she could make it to the Mod's shop and back to the Pajot without anyone suspecting that she'd been gone longer than expected.

Twenty-Two

The Chinese store owner sat across from Gregor with her hands in her lap, head bowed and eyes averted. Wisps of graying hair floated around her face, blown from the ceiling fan, but she made no move to adjust them.

"Three times, Mr. Anderson," said the woman in a thick accent. "Three times those punks have stolen from my shop. This is just the last three days. I cannot continue this way."

Gregor drummed his fingers on the table and let out a calculated sigh. "Thirty percent."

"Thirty percent?" she asked incredulously, lifting her head and daring to make eye contact. "I cannot stay in business with thirty percent."

"That's the going rate. It costs a lot to maintain my network of guards. The seventh is a big ward with lots of streets. If you want the thieves to stop hitting your place, it'll have to be thirty percent."

The old woman jabbed a bony finger in his direction. "You probably sent them after my business. I not pay thirty percent. I prepare to pay ten at most. No more."

She swiped her hand through the air defiantly. Gregor admired the old woman. Most came into his office, shaking in their boots afraid he was going to drop them into a deep hole or splatter their brains across the wall. He done it once, in the early years, just to let them know he could, but it wasn't profitable to keep killing the people he needed for cash. Besides, he rather liked the old woman. It'd be a shame to make her an example.

"Thirty, Ms. Chen."

"Mr. Anderson, I am so very sorry. I cannot do that. I told you, ten percent is my max."

Gregor reached into a drawer and pulled out a remote which he pointed at the wall television. An image sprung to life revealing the back office of a crowded tea store. Ms. Chen was the single person in view, sorting her bills and marking notes in a ledger. The Ms. Chen before him gasped when she realized what she was seeing. She started to speak, but he held up his hand and motioned for them to both watch. The woman on the screen took a third of her bills and stuffed them in a jar then poured ground tea over them and set the jar on a shelf.

Ms. Chen bent at her waist, her head nearly touching the desk. When the number twenty-five came out of her mouth, he had to laugh. Almost no one continued negotiating after he'd thrown salt in their plans.

"Fine, Ms. Chen, twenty-five percent, but it'd better be a true twenty-five or I'll come back and take forty if I find you skimming, or hiding profits."

"Thank you, Mr. Anderson."

As she rose from her chair, she put on a show of frailty, even after they'd just both watched her moving around her shop spryly. After one of his men led her from the room, a message came through his phone about the visitor he'd been waiting for. He switched off the television and pulled out a small dark bottle, using the eyedropper to release three cold drops of the elixir in each eye. A strange calm overtook him. He didn't like the way it muted his thoughts, but it was a necessary precaution against the aura of his visitor.

"Send him in," he told his assistant through the intercom.

The gray-skinned city fae sauntered through the door as if he owned the place, smoking a cigarette as if he were thinking about putting it out in someone's eye. He was more broad-shouldered than Gregor knew most maetrie were built, and wearing body armor. If he'd been human, Gregor imagined he'd have been a corrupt cop who dealt the drugs he confiscated on the side and killed the occasional dealer for fun.

"Titus," said Gregor, gesturing towards the chair opposite. "It's nice to finally make your acquaintance."

The maetrie made no move to sit. He finished his cigarette and pinched off the smoldering embers before throwing it into the wastebasket.

A wave of euphoria passed through Gregor as Titus focused his attention on him, but then the elixir kicked in and the deep need to be agreeable washed away. The maetrie henchman put his boot on the chair and leaned on his knee, which revealed the enormous handgun on his hip. Gregor would have to have a talk with his personal guards about letting people into his office with their weaponry.

"This doesn't bother you, does it?" asked Titus.

Gregor leaned back.

"No, not at all," he lied. "How is—"

Titus snapped his fingers. "We don't talk about him. Soon, everyone will know his name, but for now, we don't want any loose lips to spoil the surprise."

Had it been anyone else, Gregor would have beaten his brains in with his television remote, but given the promised benefits of their relationship, he was willing to let it slide. Titus raised an eyebrow and smirked as if he knew his inner thoughts.

"Is your team ready?" asked Titus.

"Teams. I put my best with the first. We need to take out Brazio right away. If he's alive he could cause problems. The rest can hit the Machi with guns and the few waku we have, plus the ones on the inside, which will help them get in undetected."

"My boss wants a minor tweak." Titus held up his forefinger and thumb and made a tiny twist while clucking his tongue. "My team will ambush Brazio to make sure he's dead. He'll be so focused on the Lazona hit that he'll never see me coming. No offense, but you'd be sending your men to their deaths and we need to make sure the rest of Razor clan is destroyed. They'll never bend the knee."

Gregor tried to see if there was an advantage he was missing, but without one, he nodded.

"Understood." He cleared his throat. "What about the rest of the Eclipse?"

"It's en route to the alliance clans, and once they've been paid, they'll mobilize. With Razor out of the way, between the alliance clans, your Crows, and my team we'll wipe Drops from the Undercity."

"Are you sure it'll be that easy?"

Titus licked his lips. "Our person on the inside tells us that it shouldn't be a problem. They'll have a large group of their forces headed towards Big Dave's Town for a revenge hit. That should split them up sufficiently to make cleanup simple. When it's all done, they want to lead the waku that remain."

"And the Undercity will be yours, neatly wrapped up with a bow."

Gregor smoothed his fingers across the table. "The drug operations?"

Titus inclined his head. "Under your purview as agreed. There will be unrest."

"Expected, but I'm not unused to subduing unwilling participants. Once they're eliminated, I'll have their operations at full strength in a week."

"Good. Once the Undercity is under our control, we want to fully exploit the mining opportunities. If there are any...*unwilling* participants, you can always send them our way for the deep mining operations."

"Excellent," said Gregor, feeling a weight lift off his chest. "I like the way you run things. How much does someone like you cost? Not you, of course, I know you're spoken for, but if I were to hire a maetrie mercenary, what would that set me back?"

The way Titus stared back made Gregor think he'd made a mistake in asking. The half-lidded glare had him imagining Titus leaning over him with a curved knife, gently teasing his intestines out of his chest cavity.

"You can't afford me."

Titus sauntered out of the office, leaving Gregor to close his eyes and lean back in his chair. He pulled out a silk handkerchief and blotted the sweat from his forehead. Once he'd composed himself, he called his assistant to have his lieutenants meet him in the basement.

They were waiting at the bottom of the stairs when he arrived. A half dozen sets of eyes waited for his command, but he said nothing, heading towards the steel wall on the far side of the space. Bullet scars in the concrete remained from when the Drops raided them many months ago. He'd left them as a reminder of the danger.

Vibrations grew stronger the nearer they got to the wall. The handle tickled his palm as he opened the door, revealing a second group of men and women in construction hard hats and talking into walkie-talkies. A steel cage and spools of thick wire sat to the side of a thirty-foot-wide hole in the ground.

The foreman, a man whose name he'd forgotten, approached with a clipboard.

"Sir. A pleasant surprise. How can I help you?"

Gregor squeezed his lips flat. "How close?"

"A few days. The rock is weaker at the bottom, but it carries the vibration. I don't want to give our position away."

"Forget your caution. I need that hole open by tomorrow morning."

"But that's only twelve hours away. I can't do that."

Gregor grabbed the foreman by his shirt. The clipboard clattered to the concrete as he pushed the man back to the hole, holding him at an angle over the edge.

"That hole better be fucking open in twelve hours or I'll throw you down the shaft myself. Use explosives for the last bit if you must."

"Yes, sir," said the man with fear in his eyes. "I'm sorry, sir."

"Don't be sorry, get it fucking done!"

Gregor pulled him back from the edge. He gathered his lieutenants outside the drilling room so they could hear him speak.

"Ready the troops. We're hitting Razor in twelve."

"What about the cage?" asked one of his men. "It'll only fit ten. The original plan was to make a rendezvous spot at the bottom and ferry everyone down before the assault. It'll take a half hour between trips."

"Pick your best ten for the elevator and the rest will go through the tunnels. Send a message for Deacon to open the doors when we're ready."

His lieutenants dispersed, leaving Gregor to his thoughts. If everything went as planned, he'd have significantly upgraded his empire. The Undercity clans had always vexed him, hitting his operations with impunity and then disappearing below before he could retaliate. Their arrogance would be their downfall.

Twenty-Three

Pandora hesitated at the door before barging in with the fires still burning in her chest. She'd made it from the Lazona to the Terreno in half the time it would have normally taken.

Her mother was seated at the desk, scribbling in a ledger with her good hand, the one made of steel and bone and gold holding down the book.

"You're not supposed to be here. Go back to the Pajot," said her mother without looking up.

"I came here to talk, and that's what we're going to do," said Pandora.

The glancing glare was like a shock to her system. Pandora hated the way her mother had that control over her.

"You'll be lucky if he lets you live, considering you did everything you could to sabotage our plan in the Drops."

"It was old men and women and children in that building. Three died. Lucky it wasn't more."

"That's good. Maybe you should have thought about how to minimize casualties yourself. It seems whoever did it for you knew how to do their job," said her mother with a smirk.

"This isn't how it's supposed to go down," said Pandora, regretting the words as soon as they left her lips.

Her mother looked right through her. "That's not for you to decide. Now leave, before I grow cross."

She reached inside the top drawer. When the brass clicker appeared, Pandora Pulled it to her hand. The object's sudden departure left her mother snarling.

"I don't think you realize how big of a mistake that was."

Using the opal, Pandora enhanced her muscles, squeezing the clicker until it bent to an unusable state. She shoved it into an inside pocket so it couldn't be repaired later.

"Mother. Selena. Let's forget this place. If you want, we can leave right now. Look what he's done to you. Before long, you won't be human anymore. There'll be nothing left but spite."

"Cutting out the weakest part would be a boon. It's what's driving you to mistakes, letting that human need for connection blind you from your path. You could be great. That ability is in you, but you must carve away the weakness."

"No."

Her mother set down the pen and gave Pandora her full attention. Her expression was a mix of pity and contempt.

"It's Emilio's family that has you confused."

"It's more than that," she said, but didn't want to air her thoughts knowing that they'd be used against her.

"If you want to save them from the coming storm, I can give you an elixir with which to knock them out, keep them safe until it's over. Once they see how their world has changed, they will acquiesce." She blinked. "Or they won't."

"It's happening soon?"

Selena tensed. It was barely perceptible and quickly smoothed over with a contemptuous smile, but Pandora knew she'd seen it.

"As you can see, you were not trusted with this knowledge because of your past failures. Had you killed the Razor boy, or set the explosives, things might have been different. As I said, you'll be lucky to come away with your skin intact after all is over. I had to *beg* for your life, and you know how much that cost me."

The war was coming. Not soon, but now. A hundred thoughts raced through her head, none of them supporting her mother's plan. *Is this who I am?*

"Leave me," said her mother, slamming the book shut with authority. "I have errands to run. You'd best get back to your precious Drops if you want to save your friends." The half of her face that had been replaced with steel and bone after the accident twitched. "A word of this to anyone will ensure your fate. Do not tempt him to remove your disobedience once and for all. A second round of training would eliminate what's left of your weakness."

Adrenaline flooded her body. Pandora wanted only to flee the room and the Undercity. Anything other than being sent back to *training*. What a benign word, hiding the truth in its torturous claws.

"I don't need retraining."

Her mother hesitated before her office door. "Good. But prove it. Be the daughter I've always wanted you to be. Dismissed."

Pandora found herself outside the building before her mind had caught up with her actions. The earlier defiance seemed foolish. Childish even. What had she been thinking? If the plan was at its final stages, then there wasn't anything she could do. Her best course of action was to stay away from the Pajot and wait for it all to be over and then hope that the punishment for her failures wouldn't be too severe.

She headed the opposite direction to clear her thoughts. As she rounded the bend near Hotel Endless, Pandora glanced back, catching sight of her mother in a hooded cloak, hurrying the opposite way with a stainless steel cylindrical cannister in her bone–and-steel fist. There was an insignia on the top, but she couldn't tell what it was other than the color black.

Curiosity battled with her mother's authority, the former winning out as Pandora hoped to have more information for a decision. Using the sapphire radar to keep tabs on her mother without being in eyeshot, Pandora followed at a meandering pace.

When she disappeared down an alleyway, Pandora feared she'd lost her until she realized that it was an exit into the caverns outside the Terreno. She kept up her surveillance, finding the tunnel leading in a direction she was unfamiliar with. Voices stilled her feet. Pandora leaned against the wall, determining that there were eight figures in the cavern with her mother. She risked a peek to see a group of Blue Daggers circled around her mother, licking their lips in anticipation. When she lifted the top of the cylinder, revealing a carousel of blue vials, Pandora realized what was happening. The Blue Daggers were being paid in Eclipse for their support.

Pandora retreated back to the Terreno before one of the Blue Daggers scanned the area with their amber, revealing her hiding place. She wandered through the wide streets, ignoring the few vendors hawking their wares as she wondered what she could do to stop the war. She was deep in planning before she realized she was opposed to her grandfather's plans. Pandora had come to the Undercity prepared to carry out his wishes in subjugating the clans. She'd been willing to do anything. At least until she'd lived with the Drops and met Kuma. If her grandfather's plans came to fruition, all the people she cared about in the Undercity would be dead. She couldn't let that happen, but she was only one person. Stopping the shipment of Eclipse might slow or halt the plan, but there was no way she could take on eight Blue Daggers by herself.

Vertigo overtook her with the realization that she was no longer following her grandfather's plan. Defiance would come with a price, one that she'd have to pay eventually, but she couldn't carry out his brutal mission. All the *training* in the world couldn't convince her to kill the people she'd grown to love. Triana and Vasy's faces rose into her vision, followed by Emilio's and finally Kuma's. The last came with more than fondness.

When she'd been sent to the Undercity, she'd thought the clans were like the gangs of her youth, undisciplined and brutal, their purpose almost entirely criminal. While the Undercity clans certainly carried out the same ruthless illegal acts she was well familiar with, they seemed to be trying to create something larger than themselves as well. Had created. She looked around the Terreno to see a place that had been built with that purpose in mind. Even if they didn't know it, they wanted to come together into a larger society. The Terreno was proof of that.

Her grandfather's rule would strip away the society that had been built. She knew all too well how he operated. There would be obedience. Period. Nothing less would be tolerated.

Lost in thought as she wandered the Terreno, she didn't realize there were three people staring at her from the shadows of an alleyway until her mind caught up with her eyes. A warmth filled her midsection as she found Kuma staring at her with equal interest. Had his friends, Camina and Tick, not been standing at his side, she would have thrown her arms around him with the same exuberance as a drowning person to a lifeline.

But this was the Terreno. Snooping eyes were everywhere. She acknowledged their presence with a barely perceptible nod, then turned the opposite direction, heading to an exit while watching them with her sapphire. They didn't follow right away.

Outside the flashing lights of the Terreno, Pandora waited for them in a side cavern with her exit to her back in case she'd misread their intention. Not long after she set up, the three Razor members entered.

The girl with the slicked-back hair and darkened eyes turned towards Kuma with a snarl on her lips.

"We're here to kill her, right?"

Twenty-Four

She was standing about thirty feet from his location. Pandora. He could smell her as if she were pressed against him, fingers clawing at the back of his neck. The memory of her lips against his had him aching inside.

"We're here to kill her, right?"

"What? No," said Kuma, turning on his friend. "Why would you say that?"

"I knew it," said Camina, gesturing across the cavern. "There's something between you two. That's why you didn't kill her in the duel. Don't fucking lie to me, Little Bear. I've known you your whole life. I know what it looks like when you have a thing for a girl. You might be a strong waku, but you have a shit poker face."

The way his friends were staring at him had his stomach in his knees. He felt like he'd betrayed them even if he'd had the clan's interests in mind.

"She was spying for me."

Pandora made no motion to speak. She watched from her perch passively.

"Bullshit."

"I'm serious. I was following her last year and saw her kill one of her own. I made her a deal. I wouldn't expose her if she'd spy for Razor."

"Seriously?" asked Tick, glancing between them.

"I hate to be the bearer of bad news," said Pandora, "but our two clans have a big problem right now. Much bigger than a little spying."

"What's that?" asked Camina, stepping forward with her hand on her hilt. "Is it that you're a traitor to your own clan?"

The comment brought a twitch to Pandora's jaw as if she'd been smacked.

"There's a war coming."

Camina stepped forward, her blade whispering out of its sheath until only the tip remained.

"And when it does, Razor's going to be the last clan standing."

"Neither clan is going to be alive unless we wake up to what's really happening in the Undercity," said Pandora.

The parallels with what he'd learned with Leesa had him surging forward with his hand on Camina's arm.

"What do you know?"

A cloud of conflicting thoughts passed through Pandora's black eyes, too quickly for Kuma to understand, even with his amber. The only thing he knew was that she was a boiling cauldron of emotion. The urge to collect her in his arms was strong.

"Only pieces. I just watched a batch of Eclipse being handed over to the Blue Daggers. A prepayment on what I can only assume is some action on the alliance's part."

"Eclipse?" he asked.

"Right. You don't know. It's an elixir that helps with attunement. Not a guarantee, but you can almost ensure you have the right stones with the right waku."

The implications staggered him. Even his friends saw the possibilities.

"Imagine if Duro had a black diamond," said Tick with a shiver. "He'd be unstoppable."

"Duro's the least of your problems," said Pandora. "I don't know what's going on in your clan, but someone hit ours in a way that only spilling Razor blood can satisfy. We're being manipulated."

Camina turned to him. "Why would she tell us this? She's the one manipulating us. She's trying to get us to reveal something we shouldn't. She's the enemy. We should kill her and be done with it."

"Didn't we just determine that someone's trying to get our two sides to scrap? If she's right about the Blue Daggers, then we should go back to Razor and tell my father."

Tick scratched the back of his head. "He'll never believe you. You said it earlier. He *has* to go to war. Without proof, he won't lift a finger."

"Fuck," said Kuma, realizing his friend was right.

"There's an alternative," said Pandora.

"If it's you dying, I'm all in," said Camina.

Pandora kept her eyes on him. "We could go after the Blue Daggers. Kill them and take the Eclipse for ourselves. If we each take half back to our clans, then maybe they'll understand the real danger."

"Half?" asked Camina incredulously. "There's three of us and one of her. She should get a quarter at best."

"You want to go after Blue Daggers?" he asked.

Camina screwed up her face. "I wasn't suggesting that. You know, if we did, we should get more."

"What do you think, Tick?"

He furrowed his brow. "She could be leading us into an ambush."

Kuma couldn't explain that he knew she wasn't doing that, but the question was valid. He looked to Pandora.

"If my presence worries you, then I'll stay in the lead. If there's an ambush, then I'll be the one to trigger it, but if we're going to track them down, we'd better hurry. They have at least a ten-minute head start on us."

He turned to his friends. "We already know we're being goaded into action. If this is true, then the alliance might be taking this opportunity to hit us while we're distracted with Drops." He glanced back to Pandora. "If we get the Eclipse, we can halt whatever the alliance planned to do *and* bring back a valuable elixir for our clan."

"She'll have some too," said Camina, her upper lip curled in a snarl.

"Sounds like they already have some," said Kuma, catching a twitch of recognition. "But more importantly, this will help prove that we're being manipulated."

"I'm not sure it does that," said Camina.

"Let's get it and find out."

Camina checked back to Pandora, then shook her head. "This feels like a really bad idea. The clan might go to war soon and here we are, working with the enemy."

"The enemy of my enemy..."

"I hate that fucking saying," said Camina, scowling.

"There are three of us," said Tick with a shrug. "And Kuma already beat her once. It's not like we have anything to fear."

"Sounds like Tick's in. What about you, Camina?"

She looked from him, to Pandora, and back to Tick. "Fuck."

"I think that's a yes," he said to Pandora. "Where are these Blue Daggers?"

She described where she'd seen them make the handoff. Tick spoke up right away.

"I know a shortcut that gets us there faster, but once we're on their tracks, you should lead, Kuma. Your amber is the best."

"I thought she was supposed to lead?" asked Camina.

"I'll see any ambush with my amber. You two can keep an eye on her."

"Fine," said Camina with a sign. "Let's get moving before I change my mind."

As Tick headed in a perpendicular direction that would skirt around the Terreno, and Camina fell in behind him, Kuma gave Pandora a slow nod. She held up her arm, and he felt a ghostly tug Pull on his hand from her Sapphire. She smiled and they turned their attention forward.

The chase was on.

Twenty-Five

Camina ran at the back of the group, keeping the traitorous Drops member in front of her. Pandora kept glancing back at Camina as if she expected a blade in her back at any moment. *You should be worried.*

The idea that her friend—no, best friend—was working with the Drops brought unending heat to her face. She wanted to smack him. Hold him down under a cold stream until he came to his senses. What was he thinking? He was the clan leader's son. Why would he risk his father's position for this girl?

Unless she'd ensorcelled him? The idea had merit. There was something about Pandora that tickled the back of Camina's neck. Something familiar that suggested the girl wasn't being level with them.

"Fucking wayhos."

That brought another head turn. Camina gave her a grin that would have curdled milk at a hundred paces, but it washed over Pandora without acknowledgement.

They passed through caverns at speed, but Camina barely noticed. Not even when they cut through a nest of cave crickets. Gossamer wings rose up around them, then flew away. Camina crushed one against her shoulder, keeping her eyes on the traitor's back the whole time.

Nothing about Pandora's appearance in the Undercity made sense. She showed up as a waitress, and on the very first day saved the life of two major clan figures and gained an invite to the Drops. No one was that lucky. Which probably meant she'd made her luck.

And now she showed up at the most opportune time when they suspected there was a larger scheme afoot? How convenient. It was planned. Maybe even Leesa was involved. They'd laid a trap for Kuma. The question was, who was behind it? If she was willing to spy against her own clan then Camina doubted she was truly loyal to Drops.

Camina would put a large pile of cash on the fact that Kuma had slept with her. She could see it in his eyes, the way he pined after her. What if it was an enchantment? Or an elixir? There were ample ways to break a person's mind, make them subservient to another.

She brooded on these ideas as they ran through the caverns, relying on Kuma's amber to keep them safe. She knew she should be keeping her senses on high alert, but Camina kept them focused on Pandora. Even though she couldn't see the vibrations of the stones like Kuma could, Camina could sense that there was something strange going on inside Pandora's body. She moved in fits and starts, sometimes making long leaps that to the visible eye were unaided by her sapphire.

What are you up to?

They ran for fifteen minutes straight, pausing occasionally to pick up their quarry. Kuma was an excellent tracker, made better by his amber, and the Blue Daggers appeared not to care if they were leaving a trail. Candy wrappers occasionally marked their passage. Camina could smell the sweetness in the air, the remnants of sugar on the interiors of the packaging.

Kuma had them slow when they caught up to the Blue Daggers. His sensing range was huge, which meant they could follow without being seen. He made the silent gestures of Undercity speak, proposing a plan to overtake them from behind, but Pandora suggested circling around and ambushing them.

Camina made angry gestures of disagreement, pointing to Kuma to confirm his plan, but they agreed with Pandora. Frustrated, Camina wanted to shake him. She'd tricked Tick as well. He seemed enamored by the Drops member.

As they cut up a side passage, intending to set an ambush, Camina sensed the change in Pandora. Her muscles were tensing at odd moments and she kept looking to Kuma. Camina was sure she was going to do something soon. They were being led into a reverse ambush. Whoever she was working for was waiting for them, and then as they were defending themselves, the Blue Daggers would come up from behind. It'd be a bloodbath.

They were about to make a right turn into a cavern so they could set up the ambush. Camina unsheathed her blade, which brought a head twitch from Pandora. As Kuma positioned them behind a wide stone pillar, Camina saw Pandora reach into an inner pocket. It was a signal, or compact weapon. Camina peeked over her shoulder. It looked like a brass button. It'd been through hard times, half-crushed, but the way Pandora caressed the slight dome had alarm bells ringing in Camina's head. She reared back her blade, determined to stop Pandora before she could press it.

Twenty-Six

Yara snorted lightly in Deacon's arms, eyes fluttering faintly, but quickly fell back asleep. He reached up and grabbed the loose flesh of her cheek, pinching and tugging. Yara continued to snore, oblivious to his increasingly aggressive attentions.

He slid out from under her, letting her settle back onto the wide cot. The hut still smelled like sex. After he'd gotten the message from Gregor, he'd plied Yara with drinks, spiking the last one with a knockout drug that would keep her under until after the raid was complete.

"I'm sorry," he whispered. "I hope you'll understand."

Deacon knew there was a good chance that she'd hate him for what he'd done, but on the other hand, she was more bloodthirsty than the average Razor member. She might see it as an opportunity to scrap, even if it was for a new clan. And if not, well then he could always find a new girlfriend.

After slipping into his city clothes—he didn't want to be confused for a Razor clan member in his Academy uniform—he stepped outside and stretched. Yara had pinched a nerve in his shoulder when she'd passed out on his arm.

"Going somewhere?" asked Juliana from her perch on a rock wall. She stared at him suspiciously then gestured with her beer bottle towards him. "Where's your uni?"

No answer came at first. He looked back to the hut. "Got it dirty."

Juliana smirked as she hovered the bottle before her lips. "I heard." She jutted her chin. "What you mean when you told Yara that you're sorry?"

A chill went through him. "You creepin' on us?"

She cocked her head, looking to the ceiling. "Not on purpose, but you know, you're both kinda loud. I was enjoying the fresh air when I noticed dust falling from the ceiling. When I really concentrate, I can feel a vibration."

The drill. He smiled at Juliana to hide his concern.

"What do you think it is?"

Juliana pumped her shoulders. "Dunno. Some weird wayhos project, or maybe it's a generator going out."

"Seems plausible."

He cracked his neck. "I'm gonna stretch my legs."

"What did you mean?" she asked when he hadn't even gotten ten feet. "*I'm sorry, I hope you'll understand.* What kinda bullshit is that?"

The urge to draw his blades and attack her was strong. He knew he could kill her even though she'd recently gained an emerald. She was too new to the stone. Barely made it past the rings on the training course. He could overpower her with his topaz, break her neck. He'd have to hide the body. Probably shove it into his room with the unconscious Yara.

Deacon put his hand on his side, bringing it close to his hilt as Juliana stared at him, the bottle slowly returning to the top of the wall. Their fight felt inevitable. He sent out a quick burst of amber to confirm no one else was near.

"You're not fucking some other girl, are you? I will tell Yara and then she'll cut your balls off."

Laughter broke from his lips. Juliana appeared offended by his outburst.

"What the fuck's wrong with you?"

"That's what you thought? I'm sneaking off to fuck some other girl?"

"You look like the type," she said, cocking a grin. "Besides, if you weren't with Yara, I'd let you sleep in my hut."

He gave her a two-finger salute. "Noted." He took two steps and turned back. "I was sorry about her father. I know there's been a bit of conflict between Niran and Brazio, and my boss asked me who we should support if it came to a clan vote. I know, I know, we're Crows, we don't get a say in how Razor does things, but these little things can sway people. Yara's father's a badass, but if Razor and the Crows are going to take over the Undercity, I think Niran's the man for the job."

He left Juliana musing on his words. It wasn't a lie. He truly believed Niran was the better clan leader. Yara's father saw things only in black and white. My enemy or my friend. The reality was somewhere in between. That's what he'd learned working for Gregor all these years. He'd turned a two-bit gang into a major force in the city, and now he was expanding his empire beneath the ground, and as an up-and-coming member of the Crows who had facilitated the takeover of Razor, the rewards would be plentiful.

There were three main entrances into the Machi. One of them went directly into the main building and was heavily guarded, including warding enchantments and other surprises. It was the one that led to the tunnels, making it the most heavily trafficked. The second entrance was the one that went between the settlement and Big Dave's Town. At any one time, there were at least five clan members—usually two waku and three soldados—at the station. The last entrance was the one that they took to the Terreno. It was guarded similarly to the second, except for one major difference. It was at the far edges of the Machi, where even gunfire wouldn't be heard by an amber. The third entrance was also where his fellow Crow, Syn, was working. After five months, Razor saw the Crows as almost clan members. A mistake on their part.

On the way, Deacon picked up a small black bag hidden beneath a carpet of edible fungi. He slung it over his shoulder, pulled out a compact handgun and checked it for bullets, then switched off the safety.

Each entrance to the Machi had two halves. The front half, well hidden with clever placement of stone walls, was manned by two guards. The inside part had the other three, as well as the controls for an enchanted door that couldn't be blasted through even with heavy explosives. The Machi could be locked down with a simple press of the button and then alarms sent through the settlement on wires.

Before he reached the third entrance, he slipped into a climbing harness and shimmied up the wall, finding the insulated black wire running along the stone. He drove a piton into the rock and hooked on a carabiner from his harness so he could work hands-free.

Clipping the wire would only sound the alarm, so he had to bypass it. He pulled out a simple box from the bag, something he'd rigged up with materials he'd pilfered over the months. Making simple tech was something of a specialty for him. Deacon snapped the ends of clamps over the black wire. The serrated ends bit through the rubber shielding and a green light appeared on the box, signaling that the alarm had been disarmed.

Back on the ground, he headed to the entrance, letting his hand rest inside the black bag on the handgun. If everything went to plan, Syn would be working at the inner door. But when he arrived he found two soldado and one waku, each one he barely knew, seated at a table playing cards.

"You aren't on duty tonight," said a soldado as he shuffled the cards.

The waku, an amber named Mika, reached for her blades. Deacon pulled the handgun from the bag, firing twice into her chest. The second soldado kicked out the fourth chair, which hit him in the knees, knocking him onto his side. As an automatic weapon was brought around, Deacon fired into the soldado, catching him in the shoulder. The spray of bullets sent chips of stone into Deacon's cheek. Before the third soldado could reach his weapon, Deacon fired three more times, killing them both.

"Fuck," he said, climbing to his feet while holding the side of his face. Blood was running down his shirt, but he ignored it and moved to the warded door. He pressed the release button, then pointed his weapon at the entrance. It slid open, revealing a lone Syn. He sighed in relief and let the weapon drop by his side.

"Broke his neck as soon as I heard the shooting." She wrinkled her nose. "Get hit?"

"Exploding stone."

"Clean yourself up. I'll make sure they're all dead."

Deacon found a first aid kit in the little kitchen that served the guard station, bandaging his neck and cheek. He'd have an opal heal it later once they were finished mopping up the Razors.

With the station firmly in their control, the only thing they had to worry about was replacement guards, or unexpected visitors from the Terreno.

Syn had the black automatic weapon clutched to her chest. "I'll keep an eye on the inner path."

He nodded.

"You have any idea how long until they get here?"

He shrugged. "Soon is all I know. The drill is almost through the ceiling near the Academy."

Syn grinned. "They'll never know what hit them."

"Nope. And then we'll have control of the Undercity." He slapped a new clip into his weapon. "Keep sharp. Don't want anything to stop us now."

Twenty-Seven

Pandora stared at the crushed brass clicker in her hand. Whatever she did next would end the pretense that she'd been operating under. When word of the Blue Daggers demise reached her mother, there'd be no doubt that she'd been involved. Coincidences were one thing, but she'd just been seen in the Terreno. Once the loss of the Eclipse had been confirmed, Pandora would no longer be welcome.

The internal debate was interrupted as Pandora heard the whisper of steel leaving a sheath. Animosity radiated from Camina.

"What's that?"

"A leash," said Pandora, tossing it to the Razor member.

Camina caught the brass clicker, gave it a once-over. "Doesn't look like a leash."

"Neither does family, but that's what it is sometimes."

"Hey, chatterboxes, shut up before you give us away," whispered Kuma.

When Camina looked to her clanmate, Pandora stepped up close and grabbed the woman's knife arm.

"If you're going to do it, do it now before the Blue Daggers get here. That way your friends can escape. But if you're not gonna do it, then let's focus on our mutual fucking enemies."

The crinkles at the corner of Camina's eyes smoothed away. She checked back to Kuma only to receive a shrug.

"Fine," said Camina, pulling her arm away. "Let's do this. But I swear—"

"Just don't," said Pandora and joined Kuma at his side, placing her back to Camina. "What's the plan?"

"Still good with your sapphire?" he asked, a grin teasing his lips.

"Almost got you."

"We don't know what stones they got, but I figure with surprise and your sapphire, we should be able to create a fair amount of confusion. Once they know we're there, we'll need you to keep them off our backs while we take them down one at a time."

"And if they have a sapphire of their own?"

"Kill them first."

"Any stones beyond amber?" she asked the other two.

Twin headshakes left Pandora disappointed. Camina produced a pair of throwing blades from an inner pocket and twirled them on her palms.

"Stones only get you so far."

They fell to silence when Kuma gave the sign. The wait before the fight was the worst part. It was the time when her mind tried to remind her that she might not walk away from the scrap. The odds were against them, and it was well known that the alliance clans had been discovering new and unusual stones like the black diamond. A wrinkle in the fight could be disastrous.

The sound of laughter preceded the glow of headlamps weaving across the rocks. Pandora smiled at their overconfidence. Between their numbers and location deep into alliance territory, they thought themselves untouchable.

Pandora peeked around the corner, looking for the best target for her sapphire. None of them seemed particularly unusual, except for the tall waku in front who was busy telling them a story about his latest sexual conquest. Three of the Blue Daggers held automatic weapons, which suggested—but did not guarantee—that they were soldados.

Kuma held up three fingers and pulled them down, signaling the countdown to the scrap. When his hand was a fist, he surged into the lead.

With a healthy Push, Pandora launched herself thirty feet through the air, using small Pulls to aid her leap. The first few seconds of the fight would be the riskiest part. She was arcing downward when she heard a cry of alarm. Pandora wasted no time, hitting them with a heavy Push that due to her still airborne self, resulted in a hard tumble into the rocks.

Gunfire echoed. Lights flashed with muzzle fire. Pandora flipped back onto her feet, aided by opal. A Blue Dagger brought the barrel of his weapon towards her, only to fall to his knees, a thrown blade in his throat.

She Pushed a soldado, knocking him backwards before he could bring his automatic around. Keeping her blades at the ready in case someone rushed her, she flung Pushes and Pulls to keep them off-balance as her companions engaged.

The glare of a headlamp blinded her as a Blue Dagger rushed her position. She managed to block his blades, then kicked out, hitting him in the midsection. The follow-up was lost amid the sounds of chittering wings. Before she knew it, thousands of tiny insects surrounded her. Cave crickets. A frantic Push did nothing to clear the clinging insects from her face and arms. Normally they quickly fled discovery, but the nest had attached themselves to her as if they though she was a carcass to be devoured. Tiny, sharp legs brought back the horrors of training. She couldn't breathe without feeling wings and jagged feet entering her mouth. Somewhere in the depths of her mind, she realized she was screaming as thousands of cave crickets turned her into a living cocoon.

Pandora Pushed.

Fear fueled the act. She heard the crunch of bones and cries of pain. Pandora scraped the clinging insects from her flesh, smashing and crushing them in her desire to remove their feet from her skin. Deep in her mind, she knew she probably shouldn't be alive. The insects had blocked her eyesight, making her vulnerable to enemy blades.

The remaining insects, as if they'd collectively decided to stop tormenting her, flew away. Tiny wings sounded like a thousand sharp whispers receding, until she could see the remaining carnage.

Pandora witnessed Camina leaning down and cutting the throat of a Blue Dagger who'd been grievously injured. A mercy given the heaving of his breath and the fear in his eyes.

She didn't see Kuma. Only bodies strewn about the rocks. Pandora spun around, looking for him, emotion rising up in her chest like floodwater until she was choking on it. Then she spotted him climbing over a pile of rocks, wiping his bloody blades on a piece of cloth. He gave her a little wave.

"I think my arm's broken," said Tick, who was sitting next to two dead Blue Daggers, his arm hanging limply at his side.

Camina approached him. "Not broken. Dislocated. Let me fix that."

She yanked his arm back into the socket. Tick screamed momentarily then clamped his lips shut.

"What the fuck happened with those insects?" she asked them.

"Beats me," said Kuma.

"It was one of their waku," said Tick as he searched the bodies of the fallen. "I saw him lift his arms and then the insects rose from the rocks like a locust swarm. I didn't think anything about it until they covered you like a blanket."

Pandora shivered.

"But how?"

He grinned as he lifted the uniform of the dead Blue Dagger lying sprawled across the rocks with gashes in his chest. Tick ripped the stone from his left nipple, removed the dangling flesh, and held it up.

"I think this is it." He peered at it closely. "Whoa. I haven't seen this one before. I think it's new. It's what controlled the insects."

"I bet that's what happened when they took Botan," said Kuma. "First a tunnel rat, and then a group of tumblers attacked us. Didn't make any sense until now."

Tick held up the stone. "If we can show your father this stone, maybe he'll believe you that it wasn't Drops behind it."

Camina glared at Tick.

"It won't work unless we can show him, and it could take weeks to find someone to attune to it. The war will already be started by then," said Kuma.

"Not if you use Eclipse. Won't take a lot. Half a draught," said Pandora. "You could be attuned in minutes."

Tick's eyes lit up like a firework display. "Kuma? Can I?"

"Yeah, but let's collect the other stones and weapons, move to a different tunnel in case someone comes this way."

It took a few minutes to gather the stones—mostly ambers, one opal, and the new yet unnamed stone. They retreated a few hundred meters to a safer location. Pandora brought the cannister of Eclipse, which brought a lot of scrutiny from Camina, but the Razor member didn't say a word.

The electric blue liquid had a faint glow in the dim light of the nearby fungi. She removed the stopper and handed it over to Tick. He threw it back, drinking half the vial, giving a little whoop of joy when he was finished.

"There's one other thing I can do to help make sure you attune," said Pandora. "Are you okay with that?"

"Sure, anything to make this happen."

"Then I'm very sorry about this."

Pandora grabbed his recently injured arm and punched him right in the shoulder, dislocating it again. His scream was followed by a cold blade against her throat.

Camina whispered in her ear. "Dare so much as a gentle Push and

I'll cut your throat."

"Camina, stop!"

Kuma held his hands out. No one moved except Tick, who lay on the ground moaning.

"Tell me why I shouldn't kill her. Look what she did to Tick. We can take all the Eclipse for ourselves."

"We need her."

"Why?" asked Camina.

"So she can convince the Drops that it wasn't us. She didn't have to tell us about the Eclipse."

"Why are you defending her, Little Bear?"

He glanced her direction. If there had been any doubt in Pandora's mind that he had feelings for her, it was silenced by the ache in his brown eyes.

The tension grew until Tick started laughing. The laughter was intermixed with cries of pain as he climbed to his feet, wiping his eyes with his good hand, shoulder hanging limply at his side.

"What the fuck is wrong with you?" asked Camina.

He rocked on his heels with his dislocated shoulder held close. "Oh, it hurts, but it feels so good."

"Kuma, will you check on him? I think that new stone is driving him mad."

"No, I'm fine," said Tick, grimacing. "Except for the shoulder.

Could you put it back for me?"

Kuma yanked it back into the socket, producing a yelp.

"Much better," said Tick, rotating his shoulder tentatively.

"Are you going to explain the crazy?" demanded Camina.

He cocked a grin in their direction as he held his arms out as if he were the ringmaster in a big tent circus. Pandora didn't understand until she heard the skittering of feet and a half dozen eyes reflected out of the darkness.

"You're attuned."

"See, Camina? She was only helping."

Camina growled under her breath. "Fine. But can you make those creepy fuckers go away? I hate rats."

The tunnel rats, a few of them as big as a small dog, faded into the darkness.

"Thanks, Pan," said Kuma.

She caught the way Camina wrinkled her nose at the shortened version of her name.

"Only trying to help." She glanced over her shoulder. "But now that we've taken care of the Blue Daggers, I should head to the Pajot. The sooner we can stop this nonsense between our clans, the better."

"Agreed.

Pandora reached into the open cannister, taking out a handful of the vials and tucking them into her inner pocket. The hardened glass would protect them as long as she didn't fall on a rock.

"I only took a third. Don't really have room for any more. You can have the rest."

Camina stared at her suspiciously. Pandora gave a little wave and moved towards a tunnel.

"I should get moving. It was good working with you."

"Wait!" said Kuma, hurrying after. "I need to talk to you."

He checked over his shoulder. Camina gave him a shrug. Pandora followed him into the next cavern.

"I'm sorry," he said.

"For what?"

"For almost killing you."

She chuckled. "I almost did the same to you and I wouldn't have offered yield."

He nodded. "I know. You didn't have that choice. Which was why it was good that I won."

"A dirty trick, leaping through that wall." She put her hand on his chest. "What is it that you wanted to say?"

She cocked a smile, tilting her head.

"Just that. I'm sorry. After this is over, after we show our clans that we're being manipulated into a war, I thought...maybe we could see each other again?"

Pandora nodded towards the cavern. "You know they're listening."

"I think they've figured it out already." He bit his lower lip. "I think about that night in the Onyx all the time."

"Me too."

"Pan..."

"I have to go. We both do. Otherwise there won't be any reason to make promises to each other."

He started to speak again, but she Pulled him to her, smashing her lips against his. The kiss went right through her, filling her with warmth and desire. When they finally pulled apart, she winked.

"See ya around."

Twenty-Eight

The cavern where Brazio stood was a back way to the Lazona, barely used due to the narrow and obstacle-strewn tunnel that connected the two. Terrible for commerce, but perfect for a raid. His spies had determined that the Lazona was barely defended. With the Undercity in high tension, and Drops thinking offense, they'd pulled a quarter of their guards in the last week.

Jando made a series of hand signals, asking when the Crows were due to arrive. Brazio checked his watch. They were a few minutes late, which didn't surprise him. The Crows were undisciplined gangsters with a minor talent for violence. Allying with them wasn't his first choice, but he didn't think his brother's idea had been a bad one. The only difference was that he would have used their numbers to take down the Drops right away before their alliance was well-known. Strike fast, strike hard. The tenet had served him well in the Undercity. As soon as doubt was allowed to creep in, then death was around the corner. He loved his brother, but his indecision as of late had cost them valuable momentum. The war for the Undercity would not be won with half measures.

Brazio motioned back to Jando. *Stay ready.* There were eight of them. Four waku. Four soldados. The Crows would double their numbers, but not the reach of their raid. He planned on using them to protect their flanks, not trusting their trigger discipline in a tight firefight. The Crows were used to wide city streets where wanton bullet spray could be forgiven.

At the edge of his amber, Brazio sensed movement towards their location through the tunnels they'd agreed upon using. He gave the signal for "soon." His warriors made last-second checks on their gear.

Brazio did the same. He adjusted the placement of the sword on his back. It'd been specially made by an alumni of Metallum Nocturne. He hated the name Reaver, but couldn't deny its effectiveness. The blade could cut through wood or thin metal sheeting as if it were paper. It'd been his preferred weapon before the stones. A quick confirmation that his twin pistols were off safety was followed by confirming the looseness of his curved blades. Finally, he checked the pouch on his hip for the little surprises that he'd brought to help create chaos.

The scuff of a shoe against the rocks announced the arrival of the Crows. Brazio had expected them to come in with headlamps as they had few ambers. He'd supplied his four soldados with elixirs that would provide the same quality of vision as an amber. He assumed that the Crows had done the same, which gave him hope that they'd sent their best to support the raid.

The leader of the Crows stepped into the cavern, a good fifty feet from their location. He was well-built with wide shoulders and wore thick armor. The rest of his team wore an equal level of protective gear, while his side wore only loose clothing. His brother had suggested body armor for the raid, but Brazio didn't like the way it slowed him down. He gave them a welcoming gesture. Brazio might not agree with the over-all plan, but he'd do his best to carry out his brother's wishes, and that included making the Crows feel like equal partners.

The Crow leader returned the wave, an awkward gesture that struck Brazio as peculiar. The Crows wore coverings that hid their faces. Brazio had a few trinkets to drop during the raid to throw blame towards the alliance clans.

Their partners crossed the cavern not in single file, but in an arc. It wasn't the kind of formation one used during peaceful times, which made Brazio give a covert signal to his companions that something might be wrong. Brazio drilled his amber into their leader, sensing an alien aura reflected back.

Jando responded to his gesture, but Brazio never saw it as the tips of the Crows' automatic weapons rose in unison. He switched to Lightness, and using his topaz, he threw himself forty feet through the air towards a rocky ledge.

Gunfire erupted. Muzzle flashes hurt his eyes, but Brazio squinted through the glare, taking down two Crows with his twin pistols before he landed.

He barely threw himself behind the rocks before the Crows lit up his part of the cavern with overlapping fire. Rocks exploded all around him. Brazio kept his face down to protect his eyes as they wasted their bullets.

A brief pause gave him the opportunity to check back to where his fellow Razor members were standing. He saw only bodies. It didn't look like anyone had gotten away. Brazio ducked behind the rocks as they fired once again. Not a great position. Brazio cursed himself for not running for the exit, but he'd thought he would take a flanking position.

"Fucking Crows," he muttered.

Their leader called out. "You're trapped and outnumbered, Brazio Santos. The rest of your crew is dead. Surrender and promise loyalty to my boss and you'll have a chance to live."

As the silky voice hit his ear, he knew exactly why their leader's aura felt different.

"Maetrie are nothing but liars and thieves," said Brazio.

"That's no way to negotiate, insulting the person who can grant you life under terrible circumstances."

Brazio had no intention of surrendering, nor did he believe the city fae. The promise of submission would only get him a hail of bullets to the chest. There was no way that Gregor Anderson would agree to let the brother of the clan leader they wiped out go free.

He risked a peek over the rocks to see five remaining Crows. He'd killed two with head shots during his flight through the air. One of his mates must have gotten the other. Five against one. He'd feel better about his position if their side didn't include a city fae. They were powerful in ways that were not well understood.

"I know you're thinking that I won't honor the surrender, that I'll shoot you in the back the first chance I get, but that's not how I operate."

"That's how Gregor does," said Brazio.

"And if I was working directly for Gregor, that might be true, but the truth is I'm on loan."

"From who?"

"Gregor's business partner."

"And who is that?" he asked, hearing the echoes of his brother's arguments in his own head.

"He's not ready to reveal himself just yet."

"You're not exactly giving me fucking good feelings when you won't tell me his name."

"You'll just have to trust me. After all, I hold all the cards. But I will tell you mine. Titus Cabone."

Brazio sensed that two Crows were moving into flanking positions. Once they had him cornered on both sides, they could mow him down with ease. He rolled to his left, firing at the Crow on that side, sending him scurrying back.

"You're only delaying the inevitable," said Titus.

Brazio reached into his pouch, pulling out two small silvery cannisters with pull rings. Smoke bombs. He'd intended to use them when they hit the Lazona. Two were enough to cover the entire space, and with their superior senses, they would have been able to take out any opposition more easily.

With the rings pulled, he lobbed the cannisters at forty-five-degree angles, hoping to cover the entire cavern in smoke. They bounced amid the rocks, immediately spilling out white mist that quickly filled in the space.

"This won't work, Brazio. The right move is to surrender."

As the smoke reached his ledge, Brazio calmed his muscles, the beating of his heart, and even the adrenaline rushing through his veins. The stones worked best when the body didn't interfere, and escaping was going to require absolute perfection.

He leapt with Lightness. A trigger-happy shot barely missed his left thigh as he rotated through the air. More shots flew underneath, where they expected him to land, but he'd pushed off heavily with his right foot, spinning through the air until he "landed" on the ceiling. Holding his Lightness between his teeth like a bit, Brazio ran across the ceiling, sensing the locations of the Crows in the fog. He fired twice, killing one and wounding another, leaving the odds three to one.

The furthest he'd run inverted was thirty feet. He estimated that it'd take him sixty to reach the exit. He could land, but that would slow his escape and place him where they thought he eventually had to be. Gunfire sprayed beneath him, bouncing off rocks and stalactites, but never coming close to his location.

He sensed the hardening of focus before the shot. *He sees me.* Brazio lurched to the left and the bullet hit him in the back of the ribs, dislodging him from the ceiling. He crashed into the rocks, nearly knocking himself unconscious, but he'd been running his opal at the same time and his body recovered from the impact quickly.

Brazio wanted to leap away, but he had to cycle Heavy. The run across the ceiling had taken too much. A cracked pebble shattered under his foot. He leaned down and scooped up two handfuls of rocks, throwing them in a wide arc as bullets flew hot.

The obstacles deflected the wild firing of the Crows, but Brazio felt Titus focus again and knew he wouldn't miss. Brazio fired faster, forcing the maetrie to lean to the left, then, ready to cycle Light, he leapt towards the tunnel. He was sliding around the side when a shot took him in the neck.

The world went sideways. Brazio crashed to the ground. He held his hand to his neck, trying to staunch the bleeding. Lifeblood ran through his fingers as he struggled to heal himself with the opal. The efforts of escape had drained him. He managed to regain his feet and ran almost unaided by stones as he poured all his energy into closing the dangerous wound.

Brazio ran for ten minutes, sure that the Crows were on his tail, but not able to use his amber. He found himself in unfamiliar territory. The cavern had a small waterfall in back and he sensed small critters amid the rocks. He found a deep corner and fell into it as unconsciousness delayed finally caught him.

Twenty-Nine

"I think I'm going to be sick," said Camina, stumbling to the side of the tunnel and bending at the waist.

"You shouldn't have tried to attune to the opal," said Kuma. "Not now."

She looked up, her normally deep brown skin faintly green. "It worked for Tick."

A moment later, liquid exited her mouth, splashing amid the rocks.

"You heard what she said—adrenaline and pain helps the process."

Tick was holding his hand out. A cave cricket balanced on his palm, singing a tune. "I could have punched you in the face, Camina."

She wiped her mouth with the back of her hand and gave Tick the finger.

"I still can't believe you slept with her. She's the fucking enemy, Kuma."

"I don't think she is," said Kuma. "She was right about the Eclipse and the Blue Daggers."

"She's playing you."

"What do you think, Tick?"

Tick was petting the cricket on his palm. "What? Huh? I dunno. Seems risky. If anyone finds out about you and her. Not gonna go well."

"I assume you two can keep your mouths shut," said Kuma.

Camina held two fingers to her head. "Only because we're friends. But I still think it's a bad idea. We might be at war with the Drops by the time we get back."

"Not if we can help it. Come on, Camina. We need to hurry. The faster we can get back, the better. My father's going to be really happy about the Eclipse and to finally have proof that it's not Drops that killed Botan."

Camina struggled upright. "It'll be worth it when I'm better. You'll be glad too when I save your asses with it."

"You couldn't heal a hangnail right now," said Tick.

"Climb on my back," said Kuma. "I'll carry you awhile."

"Nope. I'd rather move on my own. If I had to ride on your back I'd probably puke on your shoulder," said Camina.

When they'd left the Terreno to go after the Blue Daggers, they'd headed in a northwestern direction, but to return to the Machi they would have to head east. The tunnels and passages were less well-known to Kuma, which made their progress slower. Outside of the protected areas, the Undercity was a dangerous place. After an hour of meandering progress they stopped in a wide cavern that held a brackish pond at the center.

"Don't like the look of that water," said Tick.

Kuma nodded. "Intuition? Or something from your new stone?"

Tick tilted his head as he stared at the motionless surface. "The stone. Something large and tentacly in that water."

"Could you control it?"

"Unlikely. When I reach out to the little insects or tunnel rats, it's like molding putty. But connecting with whatever's in that water was like it saw me at the same time I saw it. I don't think the stone works on intelligent creatures."

"That's frightening," said Camina, who held her arms around her chest tightly. "Don't like the idea of a thing with tentacles and thoughts lurking in that water."

"Haven't seen a safe passage sign in a while. We're off the beaten path. Should we find another passage or you think it's safe to skirt the water?" asked Kuma.

Tick was chewing on his lower lip as he stared at the brackish pond.

"Tick?"

"What? Me? You want me to decide?" he asked incredulously.

"Yeah. You're now the resident expert in creepy-crawlies. Can we get past safely? Going around will probably add another hour to our journey."

"And we need to get back soon?"

Kuma nodded.

"Shit." Tick extended his arm. "If we cross over there, maybe we can avoid the creature."

"Can you keep it back if it attacks?"

"I can try."

"Camina?"

She looked hazy-eyed. "Whatever. Just get us back home so I can lie on a cot for the next week."

They picked across the rocks. There was no natural path. Clearly the other clans avoided the area. Kuma wondered if they were making a mistake, but they'd been so slow already because of Camina's sickness.

"Don't be shy with your updates," said Kuma. "Otherwise I'm going to jump out of my skin if a bug lands on my arm."

"Sorry," said Tick, frowning as he looked to the water. "The creature kinda disappeared from my radar. I sensed it a moment ago, but then it, I don't know, fled into the depths?"

"Is that a guess? Or do you know? This is kinda important."

They stood near the narrowest point. The dark waters were about fifteen feet from their location with a wall on the other side.

"I don't know, Kuma. I really don't. I've had this stone for all of an hour now? Maybe two?"

Shaking his head, Kuma said, "Let's move then. Get this over with."

"It needs a name," said Camina.

"The creature in the water? What, like Ralph or Bob?" asked Tick.

"No, the stone," said Camina, shaking her head. "Like topaz or emerald."

"Quiet, you two. Move quickly and let's get this over with."

They scrambled over the rocks. As they passed the narrow section, Kuma couldn't help but constantly glance at the pond. He sent his amber in that direction, but the water made it difficult to see beyond the surface. The wall curved around, making them travel near the pond for longer than he'd originally intended.

"We good, Tick?" he asked as he climbed over a boulder.

No answer came. Kuma turned to see his friend staring towards the water with his jaw slack.

"I think it's—"

Black, bug-infested water exploded from the pond as glistening deep purple tentacles extended. One of them grabbed Tick around the midsection and started dragging him towards the water. Kuma leapt over a tentacle coming for him, landing near Tick and grabbing his hand, making himself Heavy to keep him from being dragged in. A second tentacle coiled around Tick, squeezing him until his face was purple.

Behind them, Camina battled with three smaller tentacles that weaved around her as she sliced at them with her blades. She lobbed the tip off one, which made them retreat.

"Help me free him!"

Camina slashed the thick purple tentacles that had Tick with her blades, only to have the metal bounce harmlessly off the skin.

"Oh shit."

"I can't hold this Heavy much longer."

One of Tick's arms was trapped in the coil. "It's crushing me."

Remembering how his uncle beat the black diamond, he told Camina, "Cook it! Use your opal."

"How?"

"I don't know, but you have about three seconds to figure it out before I have to cycle away from Heavy."

Camina put her hands on the tentacle. "I can't!"

Tick grunted out. "Please."

Straining to hold Heaviness for a little longer, Kuma finally had to switch. As soon as he did, Tick was dragged towards the water. Kuma tried to go after him, but the three smaller tentacles appeared again, preventing the rescue. As Tick screamed, Camina followed him into the water with her hands on the slick surface of the tentacle.

Kuma tried to reach them but the smaller tentacles forced him to defend himself with his blades. Then suddenly, they retreated into the water. When he checked back to his friends, he found the edge of the pond empty. Bubbles floated up. The tentacles had dragged them beneath the surface, leaving him alone.

Thirty

The kiss lingered on Pandora's lips long after she left Kuma, a salve to the self-flagellating thoughts about betraying her mother and grandfather. Whenever the ache grew to be too much, she pictured the dead bodies of Triana and Vasy and the other Drops she'd come to love. It reminded her of the price of fealty. The unwavering loyalty to a family that didn't offer her the same.

It wasn't fair.

They'd asked her to throw away everything she'd gained in the last two years, and for what? A new set of chains and responsibilities that would only be more of the same. It'd been a mistake to send her, she realized. Or maybe the clans weren't the brutal regimes they'd thought they were. Sometimes people did terrible things for survival. The clans were proof of that. They were trying to carve civilization out of an inhospitable place. Would have succeeded, except for the introduction of the faez crystals.

She moved through the caverns in a southerly direction, taking care to confirm the safety of each space before passing through. As a lone traveler, the Undercity was perilous. Especially so with a war between the clans on the horizon.

But the war was the least of her problems.

Am I deluding myself? Am I so enamored with Kuma that I'm convincing myself peace would be possible?

She wasn't sure how truthful she could be about how she'd acquired the Eclipse. She wasn't even supposed to be in the Terreno. It'd be even more suspicious if she told them who she'd been with. She'd have to tell them that she ambushed a smaller number of Blue Daggers and snatched the Eclipse before escaping. But once she did that, word was sure to get back to her mother. Then they would know for sure that she'd betrayed them.

The pathways took her back towards the Lazona. She could circle around the canyons east of the Fire Well, but it would look better if she came back through the tunnels that led from the Lazona. Safer too.

The rattle of distant gunfire had her throwing herself to the ground. Was the war starting already? She stayed low, expanding her sapphire radar to its furthest radius. Pop. Pop. More firing gave her a good idea of the location. She was probably a couple hundred meters from the battle. The question now was which way to go. The nearness to the Lazona suggested a raid.

She heard voices approaching. The scuff of soles against the rocks. A few of them were injured. Then she heard *his* voice and her chest went cold. Titus Cabone. A notorious mercenary from the Eternal City who'd made his name exporting the cutthroat ways of the maetrie to downtrodden realms. It didn't surprise her that her grandfather was using him.

Pandora hurried across the rocks, attempting to make no noise, but having to move with speed. The echoes made it difficult to tell which direction they were coming from. She paused at a tunnel, unsure if she was running away from or towards Titus. She thought about revealing herself to him, but there were too many risks. Putting a bullet in her head just to take out a rival down the road was a regular part of his playbook.

Running out of time, she leapt to a higher ledge using a combination of Push and Pull, then threw herself on her stomach and prayed that Titus hadn't heard her.

"He can't be far," said Titus from around the corner. "My shot took him in the neck. Not even an opal can heal that."

Who'd they try to kill?

She sensed Titus stopping beneath her ledge. Pandora willed her heart to stillness, fearing he could hear even that. There was no sound or suggestion that he'd moved, but she worried that he'd detected her presence.

With her heartbeat thundering in her ears, Pandora remained as motionless as the rocks. It wasn't until she heard his voice further away that she allowed herself to relax. *Too close. Too fucking close.*

Given the location near Lazona, Pandora wondered if it were Duro that had been ambushed. But why would he have gone there after sending her on an errand? No, the more likely reason was that this was a raid by Razor, and they'd expected support from the Crows, only to be betrayed.

Whoever had been shot was important and skilled enough to evade Titus. There were few waku who could accomplish that, and if it wasn't Duro, then it was likely to be Kuma's uncle. Saving him would help their cause against the alliance. If the Crows were attacking the Machi, then they'd need everyone they could to take it back.

When she was certain that no one was near, Pandora crept down the wall. She moved in the opposite direction that Titus had gone. Using her sapphire was great for sensing physical objects, but wouldn't do shit for finding a trail of blood. If she were going to find him, it'd have to be with logic and a little luck. It was well-known that Brazio had four stones: amber, topaz, emerald, and opal. Like Duro, he'd found ways to make himself superhuman. She'd seen him in the duel against the black diamond last year and knew that even on her best day she could never beat him.

He had to have moved away fast, using a combination of his emerald and topaz. Lightness combined with strength was a potent combination. Based on where the gunfire had come from, she had a good idea where the ambush had been. It was in a back tunnel to the Lazona.

While she wasn't as familiar with the caverns in the region as members of the Drops that had been born in the clan were, she'd learned enough not to feel lost. Pandora pictured the layout of the area in her head, deciding where Brazio would have fled to if he'd been injured.

If she'd been standing at the map in Duro's office, she would have jabbed her finger in the place she suspected. Since the drawing was entirely in her head, she let the twitch of a smile rise to her lips before she padded in that direction.

When she reached the place, she feared she'd guessed incorrectly when she saw no sign of him. Her sapphire detected no other souls. She thought she'd made a mistake until she heard a moan near the trickling waterfall in the back. Tucked between the rocks was a waku she knew only by reputation. Brazio Santos. He was unconscious and soaked with blood. Insects climbed over him, feasting on the fresh food. After clearing them away, she knelt by his side, finding that he'd healed the worst of the wound in his neck, but enough blood was trickling out that he'd be dead in less than an hour.

Pandora placed her hands against the gash in his neck and flooded it with healing energies. She felt the flesh knit together beneath her palms, and the vein that had been ripped in half reconnected and allowed the blood flow to resume to his brain. When she was finished, she sat in the cubby and prayed to the shadows above and below that Titus Cabone wouldn't find her.

Thirty-One

Kuma sat alone in the darkness with the cannister of Eclipse. The surface of the pond had stilled. He'd been so high from their fight against the Blue Daggers thinking he'd have solved the problem that had vexed his father for so long and now his heart was twisted with pain.

But he had a task to finish, even if it was without his friends. When his father had told him about the scraps of their youth, when friends had fallen to enemy blades, it'd sounded heroic and a little bit romantic. Now, with the ashes of his failure resting heavily on his heart, it felt like devastation.

As he lifted the silvery cannister, a huge bubble of air hit the surface. His hopes were dashed when nothing followed. He waded into the water, reaching out with his amber, but the dark liquid blocked his senses beyond a few feet below the surface. He listed around as a great weight formed on his chest. Kuma dove in, swimming into the water a dozen feet, but not able to see through the murky depths or sense his friends, he returned to the shore.

Kuma left while he still could, making haste with barely any consideration for his own safety. He knew his headlong rush through the Undercity was a mix of grief and reckless desire to be punished for his hubris, but he didn't care. He'd known Camina and Tick longer than anyone except for his cousin Yara, and she didn't count. They'd given each other their first bloody noses, climbed the starwall together, and given blood oaths to protect each other in a scrap.

Despite knowing the dangers that lurked in the shadows—the demons, forgotten creations of Hall mages, and other dangerous outcasts—he'd never thought it'd be one of them to take his friends down. He'd always expected it to be the Drops, or another clan. To die by the blade, not by a watery doom.

He wasn't far from the Machi when he sensed a group at a crossroads ahead. Kuma threw himself into a cubby and prayed to the shadows that they weren't paying attention, or that they were friendlies. He focused his amber in their direction, but they were right at the edge of his range. He smelled a cigarette burning. There were a few of his clan that smoked. Should he reveal himself or move closer to find their identity? Once he did, he'd be exposed to their ambers and if they were the enemy he'd have a hard time escaping. He was near the western entrance to the Machi. No one else but Razor should be in the area. He was being foolish. He should hurry and take the cannister to his father to put a stop to a potential war between them and the Drops.

He was so focused on the group ahead that he didn't hear those behind him until they were in the same cavern. If they had ranged weapons, they had the drop on him. Kuma spun around to find two familiar faces staring back at him, still wet from their incursion into the pond.

The joy that wanted to leap from his lips was tempered by the nearness of unknown others, but he hurried across and threw his arms around them, tears flowing freely down his cheeks.

"I thought I'd lost you both," he whispered.

Camina put a hand on Tick's shoulder. "He managed to keep the tentacle beast from crushing us outright until I figured out how to do the opal trick like your uncle and cook the creature from the inside. Once I gave it a good hot-fist, it released us and we swam back to the surface. It's a good thing we can hold our breath for a long time. I'll have to thank ol' Frog Lips when I see him next."

"What were you doing?" asked Tick. "You looked like you were meditating over there."

"There's a group ahead in the tunnels. Something about them seemed off. Didn't feel like Razor."

"Let's check 'em out," said Camina.

Together they crept ahead until they were near enough to identify the other group. Kuma felt much safer surrounded by his friends. Once he heard them speak, he knew their identity. Crows. He signaled to his friends, but they'd already confirmed what he had. What were they doing so near the Machi? If it were a mixed group he might understand, but a patrol made entirely of Crows was unusual enough to concern him.

Plan?

Kuma thought about it before answering. They couldn't reach the western entrance without passing the group of Crows. He made the gesture for "approach with caution." Camina held up the handguns she'd taken from the Blue Daggers as her answer.

There were six Crows at the juncture, sitting in a small cavern that had been widened years ago. An electric lantern hung above them.

Kuma was able to reach the edge of the warm light before they noticed him. They stiffened to alert, grabbing weapons, but not pointing them at him.

"Hey," said Kuma casually with his hands empty.

He stood in the dim shadows, forcing them to squint. If this had been a guard post of Razor and they'd been this distracted, the entire group would have earned a week of punishment with Uncle Brazio. Their surprise was met with questioning stares between them. He kept his amber alert.

"It's Kuma, right?" asked one of the Crows, trying his best to act informal.

Kuma stayed to the center of the tunnel. He made a gesture to his friends at the same time he felt the will of the Crows hardening.

"What's going on?"

More glances were followed by an awkwardly obvious gesture from the leader.

"We're, uhm—"

Before they could bring their weapons around, Kuma dropped to the ground. Camina started firing before a single Crow could squeeze a trigger. She killed five and the sixth ran, but she took him in the back down the side tunnel.

"Nice shootin'," he told her.

"Dumb fucking wayhos."

"Well, we either averted a problem or started a war with our allies," said Kuma, staring at the bodies.

"This doesn't feel good," said Tick, staring at the open-eyed Crows.

"No, it doesn't."

"Let's keep moving."

After grabbing the cannister of Eclipse, they hurried towards the western entrance, but stopped when they heard gunfire. Kuma crept forward alone and used his amber to sense the way forward. What he "saw" made him want to scream.

"The war is already started," said Kuma upon return.

Camina screwed up her face. "With the Crows? Fuck."

"I'm afraid so."

"Let's hit 'em in the back."

Kuma shook his head. "I sensed a lot of Crows ahead. At least a hundred, probably double that, and they're all heavily armed."

"What the fuck?" asked Camina.

"Let's go to Big Dave's Town," said Tick. "If the Machi is being hit, then we need to find others to take it back. Isn't that what your father would counsel?"

Camina shook her head vehemently. "We should hit 'em with whatever we got. Let the shadows take them. It's what your uncle would do." Her lips squeezed white. "But it's your call."

They were both right about his father's and uncle's takes on the situation. Niran never rushed into danger. He always planned and strategized while trying to minimize casualties. His uncle had made a career on rashness. Even before the stones the stories of his reckless adventures—dragging his brother into countless dangers—were legendary. But wasn't it his father's caution that had gotten them into this mess? If he'd taken his brother's advice the Undercity would be a much different place. On the other hand, rushing into a heavily armed and massively outnumbering group of Crows seemed suicidal.

Niran or Brazio? What kind of clan leader would he be? Either?

Both?

"Kuma. We need to do something and fast," said Camina.

He closed his eyes. He'd come so close to losing his friends just an hour ago. Kuma wasn't afraid to die, but living without them seemed like pain eternal. Sending them into the fray would only end in tragedy.

"To Big Dave's Town. It's the strategic choice."

Thirty-Two

Brazio woke a few minutes after Pandora had stitched up his neck with her opal. She hadn't bothered cleaning him up, there was far too much blood, but she kept the critters from feasting on the sticky substance covering his skin. Pandora hadn't realized he was awake, as her focus had been on the surrounding area, keeping watch with her sapphire. He held up a blade, pointing the tip at her.

"You're as weak as a babe. I can take that from you whenever I want. But I don't know why you'd want to kill the person who saved your ass."

"Drops?" His question came out weakly. He'd probably lost three liters of blood. There wasn't much more to lose.

She was surprised that he hadn't recognized her but remembered that they were sitting in darkness with scant illumination to see with his amber.

"Pandora. I fought your nephew last year."

He wheezed out an acknowledgement.

"I just came from him actually. Him and his friends, Camina and Tick. We took down some Blue Daggers who'd been given a big batch of Eclipse for payment."

She held out a vial and his eyes widened with recognition. She wasn't surprised that he'd heard of it.

"They're headed back to the Machi with their half of the haul. The Eclipse was a payment to the Alliance to wipe out both clans and claim the Undercity for themselves."

It was a simplified version of what was happening, but she assumed he knew the stakes already. She left out the part about her mother and grandfather. That was too complicated to explain. Brazio struggled to sit up, but he could only make it a quarter of the way before he collapsed. Pandora pulled out her water bottle and let him sip some.

"You need to restore your blood volume. I have a candy bar around here somewhere."

He managed to get a few bites down along with more water.

"Crows," he said.

"What about them?"

"Betrayal."

He pointed to his neck.

She started to say "Titus Cabone" but quickly rectified her near mistake and said instead, "The people who did that to you are working for the Crows?"

"Yes," he wheezed again.

Pandora looked in the direction of the Machi. It was all the way across the Undercity.

"Those were your allies."

Her grandfather's plan was becoming clearer by the moment. He'd either sent the Crows to Niran Santos or bought them out later. Imbedded in Razor, they'd learn their secrets and have a prime spot for betrayal. It was the same reason they'd sent her to join the clans, but he'd done it on a much larger scale. She'd been thinking too small.

"The Alliance is supposed to join the fight, probably to wipe out the Drops once Razor is taken care of, but hopefully we put a stop to that. For now."

"Machi..."

"You can barely move, old man. Am I to carry you the whole way?"

Brazio burst into a coughing fit. He sounded like death. Then he surprised her by sitting up and motioning for the water bottle. He took a long drink and finished the candy bar, shoving the wrapper into a pocket.

"Why helping?"

I fucked your nephew? She chuckled. "Because there are a lot of people I love in my clan, and if Razor goes down, then Drops will be next. If we don't work together we're both screwed."

He stared at her for a long moment before nodding, then motioned for her to help him up. As she pulled him upright, she said, "You're going to have to walk without too much of my help. I can offer a shoulder, but if that asshole who tried to kill you shows up, you're on your own. I know my weight class and he's way above mine."

Brazio smirked. "Smart girl."

The next ten minutes of helping him down the slope and getting him to walk were excruciatingly slow. Brazio had to lean on her shoulder and rest every fifty feet. After finishing another bottle of water after she'd strained it through a filter, he seemed to gain a little energy. Enough they were able to move at a steady, but crawling pace. It'd take them all day to make it to the Machi. If someone didn't find them first.

She took them by the northern route around the wild zone that held the well of fire. To reach the Machi they'd pass near or through the Terreno. The Drops and Razor areas were on opposite sides of the Undercity.

When she stopped to give Brazio a rest, he leaned against the wall and sipped the water.

"You know who's behind it?" he asked.

Pandora had a good idea he was using his amber. "I have my suspicions."

"My brother was worried that there were shadows behind shadows pulling strings. I'm beginning to suspect he was right." He handed her the water. "Come on. We need to go faster."

He was one of the most feared warriors in the Undercity, second to Duro, but she saw the concern in his gaze. Almost everyone he loved might be dead for all he knew.

Brazio sensed the intruder before she did. A figure stood on the far side of the cavern. A bright spark of phosphorus glare was followed by a flare being tossed into the center. A second and third followed the first, providing a red-orange dome of light.

Irina Stevya.

The Drops Academy instructor wore a black tracksuit. Her hair was pulled into a ponytail that should have given her a headache, and the hilt of a sword stuck above her shoulder.

"What a surprise. I was expecting to find a half-dead Brazio Santos but not one of my own students helping him. Has betrayal become a habit for you?"

The meaning of Irina's appearance and her words connected dots in Pandora's mind. How did she know Brazio was out here unless she was working for her mother? It was well known she coveted Duro's position as warleader. Had she been promised the position after the dust settled?

"You were the one to plant the explosives."

Irina smirked. "You saved Garret's life when you stopped him. I was planning on killing him after the deed was done because I knew he wouldn't be able to keep his mouth shut out of guilt, but then to my surprise, I saw you steal the satchel, disarm the explosives, and hide them in that cave. I'd always suspected you were the other spy but that only confirmed it."

She caught Brazio's furrowed brow. These truths would complicate things later, assuming she survived.

"I'm not a spy," she said, annoyed at her own lack of conviction.

"Spy or not, what does it matter? What matters is your choice now. Are you going to give up Brazio Santos? Or do I have to kill you too? Your choice. Killing him would go a long way towards appeasing the new lords of the Undercity."

"Do you even know who you're working for?" Pandora spat back.

The tension in Irina's body as she flinched said everything it needed to. "I know enough. Do you?"

"I'm working for the Drops. I'm not willing to sacrifice my family to get ahead."

"It was going to happen anyway, especially with Razor clan out of the way. I just got word from the Crows that the assault on the Machi is underway, which means his brother should be dead or soon to be dead. Maybe his daughter too. The Drops will be next. There's nothing left to stop it from happening."

Brazio grunted and tried to take a step forward but his knee gave out and he had to grab the wall to stay upright. His ashen expression was warped with grief.

"Better to get ahead of it and profit from the exchange of power." Irina pulled the sword from the sheath on her back. "Time to make your decision."

Pandora checked back to Brazio, who leaned against the wall, barely able to stand. He stared into the distance, the news of his family's death a shroud around him.

"Are you sure about this? There might be nothing left to defend soon."

Pandora pulled out her curved blades. "I have faith that Razor is stronger than the Crows, even after betrayal. If we're going to have any chance for survival, we need you. But you have to promise me that you'll make amends with Drops and band together to oppose the Crows and whoever else is behind it."

Brazio shot a surreptitious look at Irina, who was advancing across the cavern. She'd reached the dome of sputtering light.

"Here, you're going to need this," he said, pulling his sword from its sheath. "You know how to use one, right?"

She nodded. "Better than my blades."

He handed her the sword, which she accepted with both hands. The steel whispered from the sheath, revealing an exquisitely crafted weapon with arcane runes etched along the side.

"Its name is Reaver."

"I will treat it well."

"I don't care if you break it in half as long as you kill that bitch."

He gave her a gallows grin. The loss of blood had turned his normally brown skin ashen. He appeared ghoulish. She left the sheath behind and marched towards the center of the cavern, knowing that the chances of her beating Irina were slim.

The flares cast a reddish glare across their faces. Irina waited in a wide stance. Her blade was a version of the longsword, but thinner to support quick, two-handed strikes. Pandora had seen the instructor working out alone during quiet times between training sessions. She was a master at her weapon.

The blade in Pandora's grip was slightly curved, but not quite a katana. A non-straight blade was best against a non- or lightly armored opponent, while Irina's sword style had been made for piercing heavy armor. Pandora had no doubt that Irina was the better practitioner, but it wasn't just a fight with weapons. They each had their stones, with the sapphires being the main component.

"May the shadows keep you safe," said Irina, extending a shallow bow.

"And the light blind you," responded Pandora while staying upright.

"Your insult will mean nothing when you're bleeding out on the rocks."

Pandora snapped her body into a ready stance, feet parallel and facing forward. "And your arrogance will be your undoing."

"Time to die."

Thirty-Three

Niran was meditating before his dead wife's shrine when an explosion ripped through the Machi. He'd been thinking about her advice during the years of their happy marriage. Never let the storms of the day prevent you from planting the seeds of tomorrow. Her words had been sage. A tenet that had served him—and Razor clan—quite well.

When the shaking knocked over her picture, he knew that sometimes one had to survive the storm to worry about future crops. He peeked out to see a hole the size of a bus in the ceiling of the cavern. Small rocks and dust streamed from the cavity, along with probing spotlights. Before he could figure out what was going on, gunfire erupted from the opposite direction.

Niran moved to his bedroom. He took his sword from its perch on the mantle and strapped it to his side, followed by a hefty handgun. He allowed himself a moment's thought for Kuma's safety, but quickly recognized that he had to take stock of the situation first. His son's training as a waku would be his best shield. It was his only hope.

Outside the house, he witnessed a yellow elevator cage descending from the hole like a spider on a silken thread. The interior of the cage was packed with men and women bristling with automatic weapons. They fired at the members of his clan approaching. Was this the Drops? He worried that he hadn't heeded his brother's advice, thinking him too bloodthirsty. It was too late now.

A figure appeared on the nearby wooden bridge: shaved neon green hair and a host of tattoos and piercings.

"Who's attacking us?" he asked Adrenalynne.

The waku had her hand on a sword at her side. "Black Crows. They've hit the western entrance with force while blocking the tunnels, trapping us here. They mean to wipe us out."

Her point was proven as more gunfire erupted from the west, followed by a minor explosion. He gave her a curt nod.

"You know what to do."

She leaped towards the west, while he considered his options. His brother had taken a team to hit the Lazona. They'd probably tried to ambush him, but unless they'd disguised their intent cunningly or brought overwhelming force, Niran assumed that his brother was alive. But he was too far away to help the defense.

He can enact my revenge.

It wasn't a self-defeating thought, but the cold analysis of what was transpiring around him. Whoever had planned this attack, and he doubted it was only Gregor, they'd planned it well.

The competing fire on the western side of the Machi had him deciding to move against the elevator. The Academy was on the far side of it and a small force with automatic weapons could keep the clan's fledgling waku from joining the fight. If he could rally his clanmates to quickly squash the inventive attack, then they could move against the exit, escape to Big Dave's Town, and regroup. The secondary reason for opening the route from the Academy was it would give him a chance to see Kuma.

He ran across the bridges wishing he'd attuned to at least one stone. It'd never bothered him personally except that it made his hold on clan leadership more tenuous. But today, he would have liked the additional speed or versatility from a topaz or emerald.

The cage had reached the ground. He couldn't see it anymore, as there were houses in the way, but he could hear the gunfire and screams. He checked for others, but only saw a few clanmates hunched behind walls. None with guns.

He approached a boy a few years older than his son. He huddled behind a wall with his blades in his fist. Carlos. A three-stone waku.

"Take this," said Niran, handing him the handgun.

Carlos stared at the weapon not understanding.

"Keep them on the bridge. It's our best chance to stop them."

Carlos nodded, even as his face betrayed confusion. Niran stayed low, running to the curved wooden bridge and leaping into the meandering water that ran beneath. Before he could be spotted, he leapt up and grabbed the structural beams, pulling himself beneath. With only four of them against the entire team that had come through the hole, he only had one chance.

As he hung beneath the bridge, his sixty-four-year-old arms holding tight, he wished the younger clan members could see him. To them, the stones had become everything, but discipline and training still mattered. He still woke every morning before the rest of the Machi, performing the exercises he'd been doing for nearly fifty years.

Pounding footsteps on the entrance to the bridge were followed by the blast of a handgun. The Crows returned fire, overwhelming Carlos and the other Razor members with automatic weapon spray.

Holding on with one hand, Niran slid his blade from the sheath and grasped it with his teeth. Then he swung his body a few times for momentum like a gymnast on the uneven bars and flipped himself over the shallow railing, landing in the middle of the Crows. Their surprise was met with a quick blade. The nearest Crow was left with a crimson smile across his throat. The others converged around him, but they couldn't risk opening fire without hitting each other, leaving him ample room to dance through them, cutting and slicing.

A tornado in the storm of chaos, Niran struck lightning quick at the Crows. He took two hands, opened up the side of a third, and knocked a woman with gold teeth off the side of the bridge with a roundhouse.

"Bloody fucking move!"

His luck ended when the big man who seemed to be leading the contingent brought his automatic weapon to bear with no Crows in view. Niran raised his sword and prepared to charge as his last stand.

A big blast had him flinching. When he realized his chest was still intact, he saw the big man fall to his knees without the top of his skull. Blood sprayed in a wide arc. Before the others could make sense of what had happened, Carlos and the other Razors rushed the bridge. They finished off the rest of the Crows.

"Solrei," said Carlos, grinning with pride as he gave a deep bow.

"Take the others to the west, but don't be foolish. Fall back as they push. We can't hold the Machi. Our best bet is to escape to Big Dave's. I'll gather the Academy and meet you at the exit."

Carlos nodded and burst away, eyes alight with the excitement of a scrap. Niran remembered that exhilarating feeling, but after burying too many friends over the decades, he'd lost the thrill. He hurried towards the Academy, running into a group headed his way, led by Instructor Kazuki.

"We're being attacked by the Crows."

Kazuki held up a fist. "We'll destroy them."

"It's too late. The raid was well planned and too many of our best warriors were elsewhere. We're falling back to Big Dave's."

More gunfire echoed in the big cavern.

"Have you seen Kuma?"

Kazuki shook his head, but one of the students, a girl with red hair, spoke up. Juliana.

"He was camping with Tick and Camina."

Niran steeled himself from reacting. Every member of his clan was important, but he couldn't help but feel a profound sense of relief at knowing his son would probably survive.

"Where's Yara?"

Juliana looked back through the tunnel. "Shit. She was with Deacon before he headed out. I'll go back and check on her."

"I'll go with you. Kaz, take them to the exit. Do what you can to get everyone out."

"Yes, Solrei."

Niran ran with Juliana back to the Academy. They found Yara unconscious in bed. No amount of shaking would wake her.

"He must have drugged her."

Niran understood that to mean Deacon. They'd been together since he'd joined the Academy. Niran scooped up his unconscious niece. They ran back towards the exit, not as quickly as he would have liked. He felt hale and fit, but his endurance wasn't what it used to be.

"Do you want me to?" asked Juliana when she noticed he was struggling.

"Please."

He handed her over and wiped the sweat from his white hair. When they reached the main cavern, they met Carlos and the others falling back to their position. There were only a dozen left and half of them had visible injuries.

"Go!" said Carlos, standing defiantly on the bridge with an automatic weapon in his hands. "I'll cover your escape."

Together they ran across the paths. Behind them gunfire erupted, followed by a war cry and then silence. They reached the outer door only to find ashen expressions amid the survivors. There were about sixty people, only half of them warriors, the rest old or young and very scared. The raid had pulled the curtain down on their protected lives.

Kazuki shook his head. "They have us trapped. There are a half dozen men with automatic weapons beyond the door. One step out and they'll mow us down."

Despair threatened to suck him into a hole, the same one that had come for him on the day of Himari's death. But all eyes were upon him. He was the Solrei, the clan leader of Razor.

"Do we have any sapphires?"

When no one answered, he saw their chances diminish. If they'd had a single sapphire, they could have possibly Pushed their way out.

"Niran Santos!"

He knew the voice. Gregor Anderson. He hadn't entirely trusted the head of the Crows, but he'd thought the problems would be smaller issues like skimming profits or stealing stones. Not a full-scale betrayal. Niran didn't peg Gregor as cunning enough for a move of this kind.

"Niran Santos! I know you're back there with what's left of your clan. Surrender to me now and I'll show mercy to your old folk and children. Delay or attempt to fight back and we'll treat you like vermin and stomp out every last one."

"My brother will cut your heart out and make you eat it," said Niran.

"Your brother is dead."

Niran closed his eyes and squeezed his hands to fists. Everything they'd ever worked for was being destroyed. He checked back to the men and women and children around him. The green-haired Adrenalynne was nearly unconscious, sitting against the wall with bloody bandages around her chest. Others had similar wounds. Few had escaped unscathed.

He choked back a sob, cursing the day the stones had been found in the Undercity. He'd always known they'd bring a storm, but he'd thought he could keep them ahead of it.

"Not just the old folk and children. You must give each of my warriors a chance to pledge to you. Let them serve the Crows."

"Why would I trust them?"

Niran checked back to his warriors. Few could meet his gaze and those that did wore a mask of shame.

"Because it is the way of the warrior. My clan is filled with those that we defeated. Never once have I questioned their loyalty once they made that pledge. There will be some that will refuse, but offer them a quick death by the blade. A warrior's death. Promise me that and I will surrender."

The silence was punctuated by the crying of a child.

"I accept your offer."

Niran turned to what was left of his clan and bent at the waist until his head nearly touched the ground. Before he could leave, they returned the gesture—even the grievously injured. They collectively climbed to their feet and bowed as deeply as he had.

Before he left, Niran approached Adrenalynne and held out the sword.

"Give this to Kuma. It was a gift from his mother on our wedding day."

Adrenalynne accepted the weapon with both hands, even as she struggled to stay standing. Her wounds had left her reduced. She returned to the others.

Niran closed his eyes, inhaling the sweet air of the Machi. No one ever believed their time was at an end until it arrived, suddenly, the warnings obvious in retrospect. He thought to his son, Kuma, and then his dead wife, Himari, knowing that he would see her soon.

He strode forward. Heavily armed men grabbed his arms when he appeared. They brought him to Gregor Anderson, who had a lit cigarette dangling from his lips. He flicked it away into the stream beneath the wooden bridge they were standing upon.

"Were you always planning on betraying me?"

Gregor smirked. "You should have known there's too much at stake. This isn't about the Undercity anymore. The value of the faez crystal trade is too great."

"And what makes you think the ones that put you in this place won't turn on you when they feel you've outlived your usefulness?"

The dead stare from Gregor revealed his intentions. "Who's to say I won't turn on him first? But for now, I see no need. Profits are going to be generous. There'll be enough for everyone to go around."

Niran scowled. "Whatever you plan to do to me—make it quick. I earned as much."

When Gregor reacted with a surprised grin, Niran knew the deal wasn't going to be honored.

"I'm afraid that's not going to happen. I'll be delivering you to my new boss. He'd like to extract information from you first. As for your kin, I'm very sorry. There was no way that we were ever going to trust a single one of them."

Gregor nodded to a knot of men with automatic weapons.

"Make it quick. We have to deal with the Drops next."

Niran tried to break away and grab Gregor, but someone slammed the butt of their rifle in his gut, sending him to his knees. He watched in horror as the men marched away to slaughter his clan.

Thirty-Four

Irina came at Pandora like a windstorm of blades. Each block took every inch of her skill to survive, and on the final blow, one that should have taken her head off, Pandora twisted away using a combination Push and Pull.

"You're no match for me," said Irina with the sword at her side. "If there were no stones, you'd be dead already. Your sapphire will only delay the result you know is coming."

Pandora stayed in a crouched ready position, expecting a renewal of attacks at any moment.

"I don't know how you expect to win. I've seen you fight countless times, I know your tendencies, your flaws—"

Irina leapt forward, another flurry of strikes which had Pandora using her sapphire in concert with her blocks to survive. She'd so far declined to use her opal, fearing her inexperience would only lead to a fatal mistake. But on the other hand, if she didn't find a way to surprise Irina, it wouldn't matter. The conclusion of the fight seemed inevitable, even to Pandora.

Before Irina could move again, she hit her with a heavy Push. The instructor returned with a Push of her own, the forces nearly equal, but as they strained against each other, Irina forced Pandora backward, sending her sliding through the rocks until they collectively released their Pushes.

"You can't beat me with your sword or your stones. Your best move is to run. Flee the Undercity, never show your face here again. Better to survive than die for a cause I know you don't believe in."

Pandora risked a glance backwards at Brazio, who was leaning against the wall, barely managing to stay standing. If it were just his life, she'd probably have let Irina have him already, but the Razor warleader provided the best opportunity for the two clans to make an alliance and if her family in the Drops was going to survive they needed more than what they already had.

The next attack came as a mix of high and low strikes. Pandora sensed she was being set up and used a Pull to yank herself away when Irina came for the killing blow.

"You can't run from me forever. Eventually you'll make a mistake. You fight like you're mad at the world. Have since the first day in my Academy. It might help you against those without much skill, but those of us with real quality, like Brazio or myself, you must learn to fight with stillness. Without fear."

The lessons were meant to mock her. To remind Pandora that for all her instruction, she'd still not mastered the higher arts that made the difference between student and instructor. Feeling like she had nothing else to lose, Pandora allowed herself to relax at the same time she encouraged her opal. The addition of the stone made her muscles hum with background vibration.

The next attack from Irina came after a heavy Pull, then a Push on her legs to trip her up. Pandora was knocked to her knees, but managed to snap the blade into a high block as Irina smashed down with a two-fisted overhand strike.

Pandora kicked out, surprising Irina and forcing her to Pull a retreat. She spat on the ground.

"A lucky block."

But they both knew the truth. Pandora had moved with speed. Without the opal, the sword would have sliced her in half. Irina's expression betrayed her concern as she tried to figure out how that had happened, because her former instructor had no idea that she was the owner of an opal.

Pandora shifted to her feet, then relaxed into a ready stance, breathing with purpose, meditating on the hum of the opal.

Irina advanced again under a cloud of Pushes and Pulls to keep Pandora off-balance, but that was one area that she was better in than her instructor. She countered the attempted interference and was ready with her blade when Irina made her attacks.

This time, the blows were not only one way. Pandora managed to make a single attack for every four of Irina's, an irritating surprise for the instructor, who was still trying to understand what had changed.

When they broke off, a melodic laughter from the back of the cavern had Irina scowling.

"Shut up, old man. I'm coming for you next."

Irina attacked next with a ferocity that had Pandora defending with everything she had. She barely remembered the exchange as thought was too slow and only reflexes, training, and the speed of the opal saved her.

At the end of the exchange when their swords no longer clashed, Irina stalked away, swiping through the air and glancing back at her with supreme annoyance.

"When did you get an opal?"

Sensing an opportunity to get under her skin, Pandora replied with a grin. "Duro gave it to me."

The sliver of fear in her eyes was all Pandora needed. Irina knew that Duro had somehow unlocked the opal to perform superhuman feats, a practice she'd not yet learned to accomplish despite sharing the same stone. While Pandora was moving at a fraction of the speed that Duro could, it was enough to overcome the imbalance of skill in the scrap.

"It won't matter, whatever you think," said Irina.

When Irina attacked again, she came like a hurricane. Sword and sapphire. The combination had Pandora nearly tripping over rocks as she was forced backwards.

But once she recovered from the initial assault, finding the rhythm in the swings, she saw an opportunity. There was a hole in Irina's technique, a place where rage and skill didn't quite meet. She'd overextended herself to end the fight. Pandora saw it coming long before it happened.

High block. Sidestep, kick. Parry, parry. High block. The pattern went on for another ten moves, but Pandora knew what was coming. She knew because it was a strategy she'd used against her classmates and now Irina was using it against her. There was a chance it was a setup, but she suspected that Irina had forgotten where she'd learned it.

When Irina attempted to use a Push/Pull twist, Pandora Pulled herself backwards with a jump and then when Irina attempted to chase, she immediately burst forward using the opal with her sword low. The arc of Irina's leap left her midsection exposed.

Pandora brought her sword tip up.

The curved blade would open her up from thigh to breast. Irina was too slow. There was no way she could block it. The corners of Pandora's lips creased with victory as the blade hit flesh—

And bounced off as if it'd hit steel.

The implications had barely ricocheted off her mind before she threw herself forward. Irina's blade sliced across Pandora's arm, sending a spray of blood in a wide arc. She rolled forward, coming up on her feet with her sword out as Irina casually turned around, skin shimmering with hardness.

"I believe I have you to thank for my gift," said Irina with a smirk.

Thirty-Five

Kuma knew the way to Big Dave's Town by heart but every step he took felt like betrayal. Was he running away or making a strategic choice? It was one thing for his father, who'd survived sixty-four years in the Undercity, first as a soldado, then a lieutenant, and later as a clan leader. He'd proved himself in countless scraps, many of which had left him surrounded by his dead friends.

There was no such storied history for Kuma. He wasn't even a graduate of the Academy, nor had he been in more than a few scraps. Kuma sensed the disappointment from Camina, but she'd said nothing. Like his uncle, she was a good soldier.

When they reached a crossroads that would lead them to Big Dave's

Town if they turned right, and return to the Machi if they went left, Kuma turned to his friends.

"Am I making a mistake?"

Camina wrinkled her nose. "There might not be a correct choice."

"It's like the maze exercise during our first year," said Tick, who was bouncing on his heels. "The darkness made it impossible to know what everyone else was doing. We just had to try our best to find the pebble."

"But the consequences of getting this wrong isn't a hundred arc runs," said Kuma.

"Little Bear, if you're going to change your mind, now's the time. We can always head back and hit them where they least expect it."

Kuma glanced down the tunnel that would lead to the third entrance.

"I've been thinking about the Crows. If they're going to hit the Machi, they don't want anyone to get away. They want to kill every last one of us so there's no chance of reprisal. Which means they'll need to block the exits."

"You don't have to tell me twice," said Camina, foot changing directions.

Kuma found a hole near a pile of fungi and hid the cannister of Eclipse inside before they took off running towards the Machi. The further they traveled the more Kuma was concerned he was right and they were too late. The curves of the passages passed at a blur. Betrayal. Deacon and the rest of the Crows had stabbed them in the back. Kuma couldn't wait to put his blade deep into Deacon's chest.

A burst of automatic fire brought their headlong rush to a halt. Tick ran into his back when he stopped. Kuma held his hand up and sent his amber forward. There were at least a dozen Crows set up outside the exit with a tripod-mounted machine gun pointed towards the hidden door. Another burst was followed by screams. Echoes of gunfire on the inside clarified the situation: his clanmates were getting ground up between the two firing stations.

"Let's rush them," said Camina, looking frantic. "Before it's too late."

"They've got Crows pointed this direction. We'll be running to our deaths." He held up the stolen pistol from the Blue Daggers. "I wish they'd had some grenades or smoke bombs. Anything to help us get past them."

"I'll do it," said Tick, strangely still as he focused towards the tunnel.

Camina turned on him. "And why wouldn't you get gunned down like either of us?"

Kuma put his hand on Camina's arm as he recognized the faraway stare from their friend.

"He's not the one running in."

The sounds of chittering had Kuma checking behind them to see a half dozen tunnel rats running past them along with a cloud of flying insects. Without looking at them, Tick said, "Be ready."

A moment later, gunfire erupted in their direction. Kuma heard screams as the Crows descended into chaos, trying to kill the rats, or keep the insects off them.

"Now."

On Tick's mark, Kuma leapt away with Camina right behind him. When he reached the exit cavern, he switched to Lightness, throwing himself towards the ceiling and firing twin pistols on the downward arc. As the Crows tried to orient themselves towards the new threat, Camina came in three steps behind, picking off the ones that Kuma hadn't killed. In the span of a half dozen seconds, they killed all the Crows blocking the exit.

The steel door that blocked the exit flew open, revealing a shaved neon green head.

"Little Bear!" She turned inward. "The way is open! Go! Go! Go!"

Gunfire chased others out as Kuma pushed his way in to support their escape.

"Where's my father?" he asked Adrenalynne.

Her expression turned to ash. "He surrendered to give us a chance to escape, but they turned on us anyway."

"Never should have trusted the Crows."

Kuma joined the soldados providing cover for their escape. He wanted to see his father.

"Where is he?"

Their expressions betrayed the danger. "On the bridge. There's no way you can save him, Little Bear. They have more coming. We have to go."

Kuma rose and considered leaping into their midst with Lightness. Maybe he could cause enough chaos that the others could rescue his father. He took a step forward and Camina grabbed his arm.

"There are too many. It'd be suicide."

"Where's Tick? His trick could work again," he said, trying to dislodge her grip. She wouldn't let go.

Camina's lips were squeezed white. She looked at him with a mix of pity and concern that only made him want to rage.

"Kuma. We have to go. You have to sense them too. The rest of the Crows are converging here. Whoever is left will be slaughtered, and we don't want to risk them cutting us off before we reach Big Dave's Town."

"He's my father."

Camina cupped his face, placed her forehead against his. "I know, Little Bear. I know."

A memory of their last morning together, when his father made them breakfast and they discussed his training at the Academy, rose up in his mind. He could see the laughing creases around his father's eyes as he told him stories about his and Brazio's shenanigans when they'd been in the Academy. The pair of them had been beaten senseless multiple times by the instructor for their pranks, but it didn't dissuade them from doing more.

That time seemed like a lifetime ago. Kuma could taste the tea, see the way the soft light of the house cast across his father's face. Knowing that for a short time, even with all the stresses of clan leadership, missing his dead wife, and knowing that everything could come crashing down in an instant, he was happy.

"Little Bear. We have to go."

Kuma strained against her pull even as bullets impacted the cavern wall, sending chips of stone overtop.

"I can't leave him."

Before she could stop him, he ripped away from her grip, throwing himself forward in a leap of Lightness. As he arced above the wall, he saw his father on his knees before Gregor with an army of soldiers at his side, including the traitorous Deacon.

Kuma made it ten feet before two bullets ripped into his shoulder and another into his thigh, throwing him to the ground. He felt a hundred barrels point in his direction, ready to wipe him from the earth, but Camina appeared by his side, lifting him up and helping him behind the wall before the hailstorm of bullets sprayed the area he'd just been.

Other hands grabbed him as he collapsed from being shot. He grew dizzy as he was carried from the Machi, fighting against unconsciousness because he knew that if he didn't get to the bridge, it would be the last time he'd see his father alive.

Thirty-Six

Blood ran down Pandora's arm. She risked a glance to Brazio. His earlier excitement had been tempered by the reveal of the black diamond. Pandora cursed the shadows that it'd gone to Irina. What bad luck.

"I commend you for pushing me to have to use it. I wanted the first time in a real scrap to be when I fight Duro. He thinks Daraja took the black diamond. She gave it to me when she failed to attune, even with the addition of Eclipse. I've convinced her that Duro is the traitor in our midst, which kept the truth from his ears. He'll learn the truth when my blade has pierced his heart."

Pandora backed away as Irina approached. No one was invulnerable, but this made an already difficult fight almost impossible. She lacked the emerald that Brazio had used in his duel and Irina's sapphire nullified many of the strategies she might employ.

The next set of attacks came with careless abandon. Irina took unreasonable chances knowing she had her black diamond to rely on. Pandora dared not risk counterattacks, knowing that they might easily be thwarted. They danced across the rocks. Pandora retreated, giving ground when even the barest hint of disadvantage was revealed.

Irina forced her around the cavern, dodging the stalactites and stalagmites, leaping from rocky crenellation to angled wall. The first phase of the fight had been on the flat circle at the center while the second had moved to the edges where the unusual features created additional obstacles. The thrill of the chase was evident on Irina's lips as she pushed their fight to the limits.

Only when Pandora was sure she had a clean shot did she risk a counterattack, hoping to catch her by surprise, but each time her blade bounced harmlessly off Irina's steelskin. As they moved through a maze of pillars, Pandora made a head-hunting swipe only to have Irina duck and the blade sing towards the rocky structure. At best her weapon would bounce off the stone, interrupting her flow, while at the worst, the impact would trap the weapon and leave her defenseless.

But the weapon sliced through the stone as if it were papier-mâché.

Pandora used the follow-through to Pull the crumbling pillar onto

Irina, providing the chance to escape. Backing away as Irina climbed out of the rocks with a sheen of steelskin, Pandora examined the cutting edge to find no chips or dulling. The blade's name of Reaver came back to her.

Irina attacked with unrepentant anger. The length of the fight was frustrating her, and she struck like a berserker with no regard for her own safety. Pandora fled back into the pillars and when Irina tried to corner her, she sliced through a section, releasing more crumbling rocks upon her opponent.

"Stop and face me, you coward!"

Pandora saw no immediate opportunity to kill Irina, so she tried to delay the result as long as possible so she might yet find a way. There were no boulders to somehow trick her beneath, or ponds to drown her in. The way they'd killed the original owner of the black diamond by putting a gun in their mouth and pulling the trigger wouldn't work while Irina was wielding a blade of her own.

As Irina pursued her, Pandora reached out to a piece of the pillar and Pulled it. The rock sailed into Irina's back, catching her by surprise and knocking her down. She'd switched to steelskin a moment too late.

When Irina tried to regain her feet, Pandora sent another rock towards her, but this time her former instructor was ready, dodging out of the way. Before she could get her bearings, Pandora pushed a smaller stone to tumble across the ground, slamming into Irina's legs.

"Why won't you fight me?"

Pandora sliced through a nearby pillar, and as the upper half toppled over, she Pushed it after Irina, forcing her to counter it with her own Push. The rock spun away from the opposing pressures. Keeping Irina off-balance, Pandora kept sending new stones, either Pulling or Pushing them. The one area where she was stronger than the instructor was her sapphire, and unlike her, she'd been practicing relentlessly with the stone.

Irina blocked most of the flying rocks, but every eighth or ninth got through, forcing her to put up her steelskin. Pandora kept the projectiles coming in a steady stream of solid earth. Irina did her best to deflect with her sapphire, but she was wearing her down. Frustrated, her former instructor screamed with the rage of a trapped lion and tried leaping after Pandora. A rock the size of a bowling ball slammed into Irina's shoulder, knocking her down.

As Irina struggled to rise, Pandora poured more rocks over her. She was running out of projectiles, so she swung Reaver through more stalactites, creating new chunks of stone. Every time Irina managed to reach her knees, another rock slammed into her. The effort of keeping her steelskin up to protect from the impacts was making her too weak to defend with her sapphire. Few could run their stones simultaneously and at near full strength like Duro.

Pandora sliced through another pillar. And another. The piles of stones around Irina looked like the beginnings of a burial cairn with the former instructor sticking half out the mound.

Then she was covered.

Pandora kept them coming even as her own exhaustion began to set in from the fight and the unrelenting use of her sapphire. When the pile was as high as her waist, Pandora stopped to listen.

Muffled cursing slipped through the gaps. Irina Stevya was trapped. The rocks rattled as she tried to Push them off, but there were far too many.

Pandora positioned herself over the pile, looking for places to slip the blade through. She jabbed downward, normally a recipe for a damaged sword, but Reaver had been made for such endeavors. It took her a half dozen tries, but she found a narrow space. As the blade hit Irina, steelskin repelled the attack. Pandora lifted and jabbed down the blade again. And again. And again.

Eventually she felt the rigidity of Irina's chest begin to cave in, the steelskin becoming less protective. Not wanting her to have a remote possibility of survival, Pandora kept pumping her arms up and down, sending the blade against Irina. A war cry rose on her lips as she worked, until she was screaming at the top of her lungs.

Until there was no more resistance.

Pandora jabbed downward a half dozen more times, feeling like she was puncturing a watermelon. When she yanked the blade out, the end was covered in blood. There were no more muttered curses rising from beneath the rocks.

She collapsed on the pile, using the blade to keep herself upright. Brazio gave her a respectful nod and to her surprise, moved towards her in a stride that spoke not of exhaustion, but hidden reserves, or worse yet, subterfuge. As he grew closer, she wondered if his visible fatigue had been an act and now he was coming to kill her.

But then he reached the rocks, gently set himself beside her, and handed over a water bottle. She promptly chugged half and dumped the other half over her sweaty, hot face.

"You fight good."

Thirty-Seven

The harrowing march to Big Dave's Town barely registered to Kuma in his grief. Even after Camina healed him, he could barely see anything but his father kneeling on the wooden bridge, the ruins of the stolen Machi behind them.

Kuma had expected a fight. He'd thought there'd be a grand war between sides, not a dagger to the back when they'd least expected it. Where was the honor? Where was the chance to die gloriously in a final scrap? The Crows had robbed that from them. They'd taken everything, including their honor.

The Crows chased them to Big Dave's but Razor knew the paths by heart and the narrow tunnels made great ambush points. They made them pay for every sorry attempt to stop them.

When they reached Big Dave's, the populace was ready for them. Word had gotten out about the betrayal and every resident greeted them with an armory's worth of weaponry, or magical trinkets. In the depths of his grief, it warmed Kuma's heart that they saw Razor not as oppressors, but keepers of their safety. It was a legacy of his father's leadership.

Instructor Kazuki took charge of the defense when the Crows arrived. The clan's mage, Gabrielle Au, was there too. It didn't take much to beat the Crows back. They decided it wasn't worth the effort, not when they had the prize jewel of the Machi in their hands.

When it was clear there wasn't going to be a fight, Kuma collapsed on the ground. The rest of his clan spread out on the streets outside of the Devil's Lipstick. The owner, Delilah, and her crew brought drinks and warm meals, serving them like homeless refugees.

"Little Bear," said Xylos, coming up from behind. "They need you. Want to discuss the future of the clan."

Kuma wanted to tell them that he didn't care. His uncle was likely dead and his father would be shortly, if he wasn't already. Once they'd squeezed any useful information out of him, they'd chop off his head.

The three remaining lieutenants sat at a table inside the Devil's Lipstick, which had no other customers. The cheap basket of fries at the center, next to mugs of golden beer, was much different than the meeting room inside the Machi. Was this to be their future?

"We heard from Camina that you have other news," said Kazuki, lifting the cannister of Eclipse.

He told the tale from their earlier adventure, not leaving anything out, including Pandora's part in it.

"She was the girl you dueled?" asked Gabrielle, lips pinched. Everyone else looked worn from the battle, except for her. She looked like she was about to attend a corporate business meeting.

"She was."

"Why do you think she came to you?"

"Because we were the only ones there."

"Why were you in the Terreno?" asked Kazuki. "I thought you were camping."

"It was a lie. We went to spend some coin at the Onyx and Tick wanted to lose money at pachinko."

The lie was believable enough they all nodded. They'd all done similar things in their youth.

"And what made you think you could trust this Pandora?" asked Natsuo Torres, the clan business manager.

"I didn't. I worried that it was an ambush, but when I was in the Onyx, I learned that something was happening that suggested what she told us was true."

"You learned?" asked Gabrielle.

"The hostess Leesa. She told me that strange parties had been seen in the Terreno, meeting with alliance clans. There've been other things too, which was why I wanted to confirm it. If we could prove that Drops wasn't behind Botan's death, we could avert a war that we were being goaded into."

"And you think the stone that Tick has now is proof that the Blue Daggers were behind it?"

"It's the only explanation. Otherwise, why would the tumblers attack us like that? Pandora told us that an explosion had killed some of their clan and the attack had been blamed on us."

Kazuki rapped his knuckles on the table. "Given everything that's happened with the Crows, I'm inclined to believe his theory."

The others nodded as well.

"Have you seen my uncle?" he asked them.

Tight-lipped shakes of the head were his answer. "He was on a raid at Lazona with a group of Crows," said Kazuki. "I can only assume that he's dead."

"He's not that easy to kill," said Kuma.

"We hope so." Kazuki inclined his head. "That's all, Little Bear. Thank you for your information."

Anger rose up in his chest. "What? That's it? Aren't we going to do something? They have my father, my uncle might be dead, and we have no home. We have to do something quick before the Crows regroup and march back into Big Dave's Town and wipe us out."

Kazuki raised an eyebrow. "And what do you suggest?"

"Send word to the Drops. Pandora was supposed to take the same news back to them. Maybe we can work together, convince them that it's in their best interest to help us get the Machi back before they're wiped out next."

No one spoke. Eventually Kazuki said, "Thank you, Little Bear. We'll take it under advisement."

Kuma returned to his friends, who were sitting in a circle.

"Anything?" asked Camina.

He shook his head.

Yara came up, circles around her eyes. "Do they know where he's at?"

"No word," said Kuma, putting a hand on his cousin's arm. She looked like she wanted to flinch away, but didn't have the energy. "He'll turn up. He's not that easy to kill."

Yara nodded, started to leave before turning back. "I'm gonna kill that fucker."

Everyone in hearing distance knew that she meant Deacon.

"I hope I'm there when it happens."

Thirty-Eight

"We should get moving," said Brazio, handing back the water bottle as they sat upon the rocks where Irina was buried. "I'd hate for you to die by that maetrie's hand after surviving that fight."

"I agree, but I have to get something first," she said, glancing at the pile beneath them.

"Right."

Pandora started pulling the rocks off the body. Brazio helped as he could but he tired quickly. After ten minutes of digging, Pandora reached Irina's body. Using a knife, Pandora cut through the instructor's shirt and rescued the four stones that formed a circle around her belly button: amber, opal, sapphire, and black diamond.

"What are you going to do with that?" he asked.

She dropped them into a little pouch. "Haven't decided."

Brazio's gaze flitted to the vials of Eclipse she'd left near his previous location.

"Not in the mood for attunement right now," she said, prompting a snorting chuckle.

Pandora reached back into the hole, searching for a communication device, but not finding one. So she went back to where she'd first seen Irina. A small backpack had been dropped behind a rock. Inside was a device that looked like a walkie-talkie, but had golden runes around the outside of the casing. When she couldn't get the device to react to her touch, she brought it back to the pile and used Irina's cold hand to unlock it.

After she read the most recent messages, Brazio asked, "What now?"

"Change of plans. I'm taking you to the Pajot."

His eyes widened.

"Your home is no longer yours. The Crows have possession. Some of your clan made it to Big Dave's Town."

"Some?"

Pandora shrugged. "The messages weren't clear. But it's not safe to head across the Undercity, and besides, it's best that you and Daraja have a long talk."

"There's a chance she cuts my throat and makes a deal with the

Crows or whoever else is behind them. She's a cunning businesswoman who likes to make a good deal."

"Then I'll be the one who can claim your capture and the killing of a spy."

He tapped on the rocks. "Assuming they believe you. After all, Irina called you a spy too."

She gave him a long look. He stared back with no hint of concern.

"At least we won't have far to go."

"I'm feeling better already," he said, and nearly fell on his rear as he tried to reach his feet. She helped him to stand, after which he nodded his thanks.

They walked in silence. The Undercity was too dangerous at the moment for casual conversation.

Pandora gave the signal—a combination of tongue clicks and whistles—near the outer guard post. She heard the response, which told her the way was clear. The inner station bristled to attention when Brazio appeared with her. One of them was a soldado she knew from the city raid.

"Are you mad? What the fuck is he doing with you?" asked Dane, eyes wide and making a warding sign towards the darkness.

"It's a long story that I'm too exhausted to explain right now." She jutted her chin at the additional numbers at the guard post. Usually there were only three, but as she saw around the corner a full dozen were camped at the entrance. "What's with the party?"

"The Crows hit Razor, might have wiped them out. Other weird shit's been happening. Reports of a firefight outside the Lazona. No one's seen Duro. Place is going mad. Where you takin' him?"

"To Daraja, assuming she's here."

He nodded. "You can't take him alone."

She wasn't about to argue, when on the surface he was right. "You can send some waku with us."

"What about his hands? Why don't you have him tied up?" asked Dane.

Pandora frowned. "Look at him. He's half dead. A breeze would knock him over."

Dane stared at Brazio, who was doing a good job of looking like he might fall at any moment. The dried blood covering his clothes helped. He looked like a war refugee.

"Let me grab some zip ties at least," said Dane.

After they had Brazio's wrists bound together, Dane and a few waku came with them. The Pajot was different from when she'd left that morning. Everyone was traveling around with weapons and in small groups. The clan was on a war footing. Brazio craned his head in all directions as they traveled down the gravel paths.

"I knew there were gardens, but this is impressive," he said.

"Shut up, fool," said Dane, pushing him forward. Brazio fell to his knees which brought laughter. Pandora quickly helped him up, admonishing the group. "It's not for you to decide how he's treated."

Dane inclined his head. "Sorry, Pandora."

The others averted their gaze. The respect shown surprised her. After years of struggling to find her place in the clan, she'd somehow become elevated in their eyes, probably for being seen with Duro. Brazio gave her a knowing nod as they continued through the caverns.

When they reached the main headquarters, near the in-progress processing building, a crowd gathered around Brazio, who seemed ambivalent about his fate. A chant of "Drop! Drop! Drop!" formed in the younger kids, but when they reached the ladders, one of the older men chased them back to their planting responsibilities.

The entourage stayed at the base of the ladders. Brazio climbed on his own with his wrists still bound with the zip ties, but he had to stop frequently and lean against the bars.

Inside the headquarters, of which Pandora had only seen Duro's room, they were led deeper into the structure. Word had been sent ahead, so there were no more questions. A room that looked like it belonged in the top floor of a skyscraper rather than deep in the Undercity was their final location. Plush leather chairs surrounded a long polished wooden table. Blank screens littered the walls. A towel was thrown over the chairs before they were allowed to sit, and a tray of steaming tea was brought. Then it was only the two of them.

“A cup?” she asked.

“Please,” he said, bowing his head.

She poured them both a cup. Pandora couldn’t sit, so she paced around the back of the room while they waited for Daraja.

The door opened twenty minutes later, revealing the head of the Drops clan. She wore a colorful black, green, and yellow business suit with gold earrings. She entered the room like a whirlwind.

“I hope to the shadows above and below that you have a good story to explain why you’ve waltzed into our home with *this man* at your side, when the entire Undercity is in turmoil, and I cannot find my two most important lieutenants.”

Pandora shared a glance with Brazio at the last part, receiving a withering stare from Daraja.

“I have much news,” said Pandora, bowing her head deeply. “Little of it will be pleasing to hear.”

Until Daraja had arrived, Pandora had not decided what to say. There were many things she could explain, and many things she could leave out. But the more secrets she kept, the larger the danger, especially with what Brazio had heard. Before she could begin speaking, the door opened again, revealing the warleader Duro.

“Where have you been?” asked Daraja, the cracking of her voice betraying the strain.

Duro took stock of the room. His eyes creased as his gaze washed over her, but she had no clue to his thoughts. He approached Brazio.

"You look half dead, old man," said Duro with a smirk, inclining his head.

"Three-quarters," said Brazio, matching the gesture. "But getting better."

"We don't really need these, do we?" Duro asked Daraja as he motioned towards the zip ties.

Daraja shook her head, and before anyone could move, Brazio snapped his wrists, popping the plastic wraps from them. When Daraja furrowed her brow at Pandora, Brazio said, "I didn't want to show any disrespect."

Duro poured himself a cup of tea and plopped himself on the table, receiving a frown from Daraja. He took a sip, then stared into the cup with his nose wrinkling.

"You didn't return right away after the errand. Where did you go?" asked Duro with a casualness that had her alarm bells ringing. "And do you know why Irina is missing in this time of need?"

The way he said it suggested he knew more than he was letting on. Pandora had the sudden realization that the reason he'd asked her to join him on his extra missions was to get a better read on her with his amber. He was known as a skillful interrogator. Pandora saw her carefully constructed personality unraveling at the seams.

She considered continuing the ruse, but realized that her story had far too many holes if she went that direction, and having made her choice about who she supported, better the news came out now rather than later on by her mother's hand. That Brazio had heard Irina's accusation, even if it were from the enemy's mouth, was proof enough that her position was in peril.

"I went to the Terreno."

"Why did you do that?" he asked, setting the cup down.

When she'd brought Brazio to Daraja, she'd expected the Razor warleader to be the one interrogated. Either Duro knew something about her past, or suspected and was trying to get it out of her. Given everything that had happened, she knew she had a choice to make, but if it were the wrong one, she'd likely end up dead. She might even end up that way if she did everything right.

"I met my handler. I've been spying on the Drops."

The cold hiss of in-breath had her averting her gaze, not wanting to feel the heat of their recrimination.

"Explain," said Duro in a flat tone.

Daraja held a hand up before she could speak. "Should we have this conversation without him?"

Duro shifted his mouth to the side. "I believe it will be important for Brazio to hear this as well."

"Very well. Continue," she said.

"I was sent to the Undercity to infiltrate one of the clans and spy on them. The day that we first met in the Pale Sun, I planted the gun on that Blue Dagger and remotely fired it."

The news seemed to surprise Daraja, but not Duro, who stared at her with a flat expression.

"My handler owns the Rush. That's where I would meet her. My job was to find cracks in the cohesiveness of the Drops and exploit them, but I failed miserably. I thought I was joining a gang, but I learned it was nothing like what I'd experienced in the light. When she asked me to bomb the processing building, I refused. I never agreed to killing old men and women and children."

Daraja surged forward and grabbed Pandora round the neck, squeezing hard enough to make her choke. Daraja's eyes bulged with anger and spit flew from her lips. "You? I'll have your skin flayed off before I drop you in the canyon to let the scorpics eat you alive!"

With the gentleness of a snake handler, Duro placed his arm between them, leveraging Daraja's hands away from Pandora's throat.

"Let her speak, Daraja. There's more to her story," said Duro.

When her throat was released, Pandora had to take a drink of water before she could speak again. Pandora explained the whole endeavor with the explosives, including Garret's part, and how she'd taken the satchel and hid it afterwards.

Daraja was spitting mad, pacing and squeezing her hands into fists.

"Tell me why we don't have both of these traitors in chains. And who was the real bomber? Or is this all a lie?"

Duro pulled a gold chain from a pocket and tossed it on the table. The necklace slid across the smooth surface before stopping. Pandora recognized the jewelry as one of Garret's, which meant the kid was no longer alive and that Duro already knew most of this story, which made her inhale with relief that she'd chosen the truth.

"I came from questioning him. He confirmed everything she just said."

"Then why was the processing building bombed?"

Pandora bent at the waist. "I can explain, but it is best if I continue the story in order so I don't miss anything."

"Very well," said Daraja. "I am liking this less and less."

Pandora went on to explain how she'd confronted her mother and followed her to the meeting with the Blue Daggers. When she reached the part of the story when Kuma and his friends appeared, Daraja slammed her fist on the table, but Duro waved her off, letting Pandora explain the deal made and then the tracking down of the Blue Daggers and subsequent taking of the Eclipse.

"And where are these elixirs?"

Pandora reached into an inner pocket and produced the vials of electric blue liquid.

"So it wasn't Razor who bombed the processing building?" asked Daraja.

"Nor killed the Razor clan member and carved a 'D' into his chest," said Pandora, which brought a nod of recognition from Brazio. "The clans were being manipulated into attacking each other."

"Are we ever going to learn who planted the bombs?" asked Daraja, clearly annoyed.

"Yes," said Pandora. "After leaving Kuma and his friends, I came straight back, intending to return to the Drops, but then I heard gunfire. I overheard discussion about an ambush and the near killing of Brazio Santos. With everything I learned from my handler, I knew finding him would be important. I managed to track him down and heal him with my opal. I'd intended to bring him back to the Machi, but then Irina found us."

"Finally," said Daraja. "What was my lieutenant up to? I assume she saw your deceit and sent you back here?"

Pandora glanced to Duro, who she guessed already suspected Irina's shattered loyalty.

"Not exactly. Irina was searching for Brazio. She's working for the same people my mother is."

"You lie, girl. Irina would never turn her back on the clan," said Daraja.

"I'm sorry, but it's true. She was promised the position of warleader for whatever new clan is forming. She knew all about the Crows' attack on Razor, and other details."

"Where is she? I want to hear what she has to say about this," said Daraja, looking around as if she expected Irina to walk in at any moment.

"She's dead."

Daraja pounded her fist on the table and glared at Brazio. "Was this you? Is this half-dead thing merely an act?"

Brazio tilted his head towards Pandora. "She killed her."

Even Duro appeared surprised by the news.

"Lies. She was three times the warrior and had more stones."

Pandora pulled out the leather pouch and upended them on the table. The four stones bounced around before coming to a rest. Duro picked out the black diamond immediately, whistling softly.

"I think we're going to need a more detailed explanation," said Duro with an eyebrow raised.

If the earlier reveals had brought anger, this story tempered it with wonder. As much as she could, Pandora left nothing out, starting with the conversation where Irina admitted her connection to the Crows and the bombing of the processing facility. A few times Brazio nodded when she searched for the right explanation, as if he were silently cheering her on. When she got to the point about the black diamond, Daraja began pacing again, a boiling anger right beneath the surface. The final moments of the fight, burying Irina alive in a cairn of rock, resulted in the leader of the Drops plopping into a leather chair.

"Where were you in all of this?" Daraja asked Duro. "You're my warleader. We've been at war it seems, but you've been doing nothing."

"I wasn't sure who to trust. I'd suspected Irina for some time but never had the proof I needed to bring it to you." He gestured to Pandora. "But she helped me see the threads. Enough I could pull on a few and unravel the plot."

"But she's the spy."

Duro furrowed his brow. "Is she?"

Daraja slammed her fist onto the table. "Have you gone soft? Or mad? She's been conspiring with our enemy, whoever they are."

Duro's gaze never left hers. He was calm and serene, which could be really good or bad for her.

"Who are you really?"

The corners of his eyes creased slightly. Did he know? Or was he fishing? It was one thing to be a spy who changed their allegiance but the more links they saw between her and them, the smaller her chances became. But if she had any hope for the Drops to truly become her family, she couldn't leave anything out. On the other hand, there should be no way that he would know anything about her relation to her mother, or the unusual aspects of her heritage. Those were secrets she could keep even if she were officially switching sides.

"I'm Pandora—"

The explanation died on her tongue. She saw it before she completed her sentence. The trip to the Lazona was a test, but not the one she might have expected. Najani. It wasn't a message from Duro to her, but a chance for the bar owner to meet and examine her. To know who she truly was.

"The handler, the one who owns the Rush. She's my mother. And there's more than that. I know who's behind the attacks, the person driving everything that's been happening in the Undercity, because he's my grandfather, and more than that, he's full-blooded maetrie."

The in-breath of surprise from Daraja was followed by a slow shake of the head, while Duro observed her quietly.

"That's why you sent me to Lazona. So Najani could meet me."

He pursed his lips in thought. "I knew something was different about you. It wasn't until I happened by her bar that it hit me what was different. Your grandmother was human?"

Pandora nodded. "I'm quarter city fae, but pass mostly as human. After my father was killed in a gang shootout, my mother took me to the Eternal City, where I spent my days training to be a spy."

Daraja surged forward, standing before Pandora with a scowl. "Who is your grandfather? Who is this maetrie that has been meddling in the Undercity?"

Pandora opened her mouth with every intention of telling them. The name was poised on her lips. Until recently, she hadn't realized that the loyalty she had for the cause had been trained into her like a dog with a shock collar. They weren't her family as much as a breeder of fighting dogs wasn't either.

"His name is—"

Her throat seized up. The name evaporated as it hit the air, right off her tongue like water on a hot stove.

"Speak, girl, or I'll have your tongue ripped out."

Pandora put a hand to her mouth and tried again. "His name is—"

The second time sent a wave of vertigo through her. They'd enchanted her somehow. Placed a geas in her mind that prevented the reveal. As she reflected on her two years in the Undercity she saw how her mind casually deflected any thoughts about him, or her experiences in the Eternal City. They hadn't wanted her to give away the game too early. They'd never trusted her.

"You'd better tell me that name."

Pandora waved at her mouth. She couldn't even tell them that she wasn't allowed to. The compulsion had taken over. She felt like a stranger in her own body. Her throat closed even more until she could no longer breathe. The world drew in around her and before she knew it, she was on the ground, clawing at her neck. The faces of three waku loomed over her. She heard shouting, felt their hands upon her, but no air was making it past. More than a geas had been placed on her. A fail-safe, which would kill her before she let slip the truth. The dots that were forming in her vision connected until she was buried beneath a blanket of darkness.

Thirty-Nine

Kuma was pushing a wheelbarrow full of bricks to close off one of the many entrances into Big Dave's Town when he heard the news about his uncle's arrival. He'd been working himself every moment, trying to keep the horrors of what happened at bay and his thoughts from centering too much on his father's capture and what would most likely come after. Kuma left the materials in the street and ran back to the house the clan used as a staging point in the town.

Brazio was seated at the table, eating noodles from a bowl with the voraciousness of a hungry tiger. A bottle of beer sat next to the bowl, and he drank from it between slurping down noodles.

"Uncle!"

He slowed his eating and stared back as if he had news. The other lieutenants were present, but they circled around him much as they used to around his father.

"Kuma, you should go," said Natsuo. "This is clan business."

Speaking past a mouthful of noodles, Brazio said, "No. He needs to stay because of his role in this."

The comment made Kuma curious, but he knew enough to keep his mouth shut. He stepped to the side, taking a position against the wall.

Brazio finished the noodles and pushed the bowl away, letting loose a belch before finishing the beer. A jagged scar on his neck made the flesh crease awkwardly, which added to the thinner nature of his uncle. He looked ten years older.

"I need to regain my strength," said Brazio as if they understood the reason.

"You were going to explain what happened at the raid," said Kazuki.

Brazio grew quiet. He stared at the table and began his tale with the reverse ambush from the Crow's hired mercenaries. The nature of his escape brought surprise, not because it happened, but how he'd managed to run inverted on the ceiling. When he awoke to Pandora's opal, a bloom of warmth filled Kuma's chest. The others had heard Kuma's tale about the Blue Daggers already, so this connected the two stories. When he got to the part about the scrap between Pandora and Instructor Irina, Kuma was certain that she would have lost, especially after the reveal of the black diamond. When he finally learned that she'd won, he found himself profoundly relieved, in addition to feeling a measure of pride that he'd beaten her the year before.

When the story moved to the Pajot in the heart of the Drops territory, Brazio took extra time to speak about the terrace gardens and the nature of their area. Admiration could be heard in his voice.

When he explained Pandora's role in the events of the Undercity, Kuma felt some betrayal, even though he'd suspected pieces of her tale. The news of her heritage, as quarter-maetrie, brought aspects of their previous interactions into focus. Then Brazio described how they'd tried to revive her when she tried to speak the name of her grandfather, a full-bloodied maetrie from the Undercity. Kuma found himself about to break in half until he heard that they managed to keep her alive, despite the spell that had triggered upon her attempted betrayal. Only the efforts of the three opals saved her, explained Brazio.

"What now?" asked Gabrielle with arms crossed.

"I do not know what they plan to do with the girl," said Brazio, glancing at Kuma.

"No, the clans?"

Brazio smiled. "Maybe I should let Kuma speak. It seems this idea was hatched between them during their meeting in the Terreno."

When all eyes turned to him, none of them kind, he exclaimed, "What?"

"It's okay, nephew. I know what you intended and without your maneuverings, we'd not be at this juncture." He rapped his knuckles on the table. His uncle had never been a cautious man, but the events that had transpired seemed to have given him a measure of it. "After the girl was safe, we had a long discussion about the fate of our clans and how we might survive together."

"An alliance?" asked Natsuo, frowning. "We'd be the lesser partner. You know it wouldn't end well."

"End well? Need I remind you that we lost over half our clan already. Their bodies probably lie in a pit somewhere off the Machi, being feasted on by critters," said Brazio, his lips pinched with anger.

"Then what was their proposal?"

"It was mine," said Brazio, hunched over the bowl. "I know I'm not the clan leader. As far as we know, my brother is still alive, though I can't imagine for long, but I had to make the offer as if I had the authority to do so."

"What did you offer?" asked Natsuo, leaning forward.

"Allegiance. That our clan pledges loyalty to the Drops and that Razor is no more."

"Are you mad?" asked Natsuo, smoothing back the wisps of hair on his balding head that had broken loose.

"I'd be mad to believe our hand was stronger than it is," said Brazio, his eyes bloodshot with pain. "If we don't then we'll be wanderers in the dark, back to the early years of our existence, but in a much more inhospitable place."

Neither Gabrielle or Kazuki made overt actions regarding the news. Each seemed to be considering it in their own way.

"If we were to do such a thing," said Kazuki lightly, as if a single word could upset the delicate state the clan was currently in, "how would it happen?"

Brazio looked to each of them. "That's the sensitive part of this. We'd have to give up control of Big Dave's Town. There's no way we'd be able to protect this space from across the Undercity. Once we leave, we'd be leaving for good. We could take the passages to the Terreno and then to the Pajot. The Crows are likely still consolidating the Machi, probably in expectation that they could be attacked. When Kuma and his friends took the Eclipse, they gave us this chance. If the alliance clans had been mobilized against the Drops, there'd be no point in remaining in the Undercity."

"We leave? Give up everything?" asked Natsuo. "What will the clan think?"

"That will be up to them. We can give everyone the option. I don't want to coerce anyone. If they wish to leave, they can return to the light or make their home wherever they please. It's what my brother would do," said Brazio.

Kuma saw the guilt in his uncle. Niran had been trying to push them towards the Drops to protect them from the coming storm, but he'd always resisted it. Now Niran was captured and Brazio was suggesting that path in his place. The mantle of leadership weighed heavily on his shoulders.

"Why not hit the Crows and take back the Machi with the Drops' help?" asked Kazuki.

Brazio pushed his bowl away. "I would like to do nothing else, but the Drops aren't interested in sacrificing their people for us. We will become Drops in all the ways that means. And it's not that we'll be safe. We can assume the alliance clans will be under our enemy's control soon. With the numbers from the Crows, our place in the Undercity will be tenuous. The way forward will not be easy. The maetrie have resources that will challenge even our best waku."

"What about us?" asked Natsuo. As the business manager, he'd spent his time in the city, working their legal establishments, brokering the transfer of illicit goods, or facilitating the laundering of the money that kept the clan solvent.

"You would each have a role in the clan. Not a lieutenant, but working with your counterpart. Their business model is different than ours, with the distribution of drugs as their main source of income. It's not ideal but it's the price of survival."

"And you?" asked Natsuo, bristling.

"Since they no longer have an Academy instructor, I would lead them, though Duro requested that he trade time with me teaching the young waku. I think we both understand that the future of our clan, should we accept their offer, is in the new generation of waku since so many were lost with the Crows' attack." He looked to Kazuki. "I'm sorry, Kaz. They don't know you. You've done an admirable job training our young waku. Look at Kuma. Without that training he could have never taken the Blue Daggers and we would not have this option. But they know me, by reputation. It was the only way."

Kazuki made a noise in the back of his throat. "I've always served at the pleasure of our clan leader. If we are to take new oaths, then I accept whatever role they offer."

"Are you agreeing with the plan?"

"It is up to each one of us?" asked Kazuki.

"It is."

"Then I accept. The Undercity is the only world I've ever known and the Drops have honor, unlike our foes. I would like to see them eat my blade in the dark," said Kazuki, thrusting his fist forward in mock attack.

Brazio turned to Gabrielle. She closed her eyes, shaking her head.

"How can we make this decision with Niran's fate in the balance?"

"If it were any other clan, there might be an opportunity to trade for him, but after hearing about our new enemies, I doubt we'll be given the chance. I hope only that he receives a quick death, preferably with a blade in his fist."

A single tear slipped from the corner of her eye. Kuma knew there'd never been anything extra between the beautiful mage and his father, but he knew in that instant that she harbored feelings for him.

"I would swear to the Drops so I might seek my revenge for him," she said, thumbing away the wetness on her cheek.

Even before Brazio turned to him, Natsuo angrily retorted, "I cannot believe you would ask this while your brother is still alive. Are we oath breakers?"

Brazio pounded on the table, snapping back with his jaw tight. "Do not speak to me like that. Or hide behind your oath in a time of upheaval. Even if Niran was here, we'd be in the same situation. We cannot hold Big Dave's Town, and I refuse to partner with those traitorous Crows. What I want is a chance to bury my blade deep in Gregor's belly and watch the lights in his eyes dim for all eternity."

Natsuo paled from the backlash. He tugged at his loose tie and looked away with crimson coloring his cheeks.

"Natsuo?" asked Brazio with the sharp voice of command.

The business manager spoke quietly without looking up. "I will swear to Daraja."

"Then we are in agreement. Gather the clan, I will speak to them. We must make this decision quickly. I want to make the journey across the Undercity before the Crows realize that we've left Big Dave's Town."

As everyone left, Brazio said, “Little Bear. Please stay. Have a seat.”

Kuma took a spot across from his uncle. He could hardly meet his gaze, because he felt the weight of the conversation that he knew they would have. It was the one he’d been avoiding in his head.

“You’ve done very well. Your father would be proud. You gave us a chance of survival.”

“The shadows do not hide,” he said, repeating the clan motto.

“The Drops’ motto would be appropriate too now. The clan is all.”

“Is this the right way?” he asked his uncle. “I feel like we’re betraying everyone that came before.”

“In a scrap, do you try to kick when your opponent’s move only offers a punch? I see your pain, Little Bear. For you, this decision is more than loyalty.”

“There’s no way to get him back?” asked Kuma as he stared into his lap.

“If there was, we’d be doing it.” Brazio leaned back in his chair, appraising Kuma. “Is there anything you need?”

“No. Why?”

“You’re like a bowstring held taut.”

Kuma tried to speak but the words wouldn’t come. He shook his head while gripping the edge of the table.

“When do I grieve? If he’s still alive? I just want to know. He spent his whole life in service to the clan. He deserved better. Not this.”

"We are at the mercy of the lives we've chosen to lead. The Undercity is an unforgiving place. His fate is no different than the Blue Daggers you killed to claim the Eclipse."

"Why would you say that?" asked Kuma angrily.

"Because you're still young. You still believe in the immortality of youth, while I'm a grizzled old warrior who's seen far too many of his friends and family die by the blade, or claw, or to the shadows themselves." Brazio ran his hand across the table. "Death waits for all of us. We do our best to keep it at bay, but it's patient. Not even the mages above can avoid it forever. It's not the manner of our deaths that others remember, but the lives we led before that ignoble end. Remember him as the leader of Razor clan. As your father, who loved you so much. As husband to Himari. Remember him as a warrior. But remember him."

Forty

"I can't fucking believe that Razor clan is coming here to swear allegiance," said Choo-Choo, standing by Pandora's side as they helped the workers put up temporary tents in one of the newer settlement caverns. "How am I supposed to call that prick, Kuma, my brother?"

"The same way—" Pandora had to pause to clear her throat. It was hard to speak after the incident. "The same way you do all of us. It's a matter of survival now, or what happened to Razor will happen to us."

Choo-Choo scowled as he drove the tent spike into the stone with a hammer. Her friends had no idea that she'd worked with Kuma to kill the Blue Daggers and had killed Instructor Irina. They only knew that she'd brought Brazio back to the Pajot after finding him near dead.

There was a good part of her that couldn't believe she was still alive. Either from the enchantment that almost killed her when she tried to speak her grandfather's name, or because she was related to their enemy. Whatever had transpired after she'd been unconscious had been enough to return her to good standing in the clan. It was possible that her near death had tipped the balance, proof that her place in the Drops had been coerced.

When she'd first come to the Undercity, she'd been completely on board with the mission, doing whatever it took to accomplish what her mother had asked her to do. But that was before she knew the Drops or really understood how much her mother had screwed her up. The years of training in the Eternal City. Training, ha! It was brainwashing. Only in retrospect could she see it. So much of that time was locked behind whatever geas they'd laid upon her before sending her into the Undercity. It spoke to how little they actually trusted her. Or maybe they hadn't trusted her mother's handling.

Pandora wondered if the woman who'd given birth to her had enough of her humanity remaining that she might ever be turned, or if she were her father's daughter. A cold-hearted maetrie with cunning to spare.

A murmur passed through the camp. News of Razor's arrival put a pause on the construction.

"Baka!" exclaimed Choo-Choo, reaching into a pocket and handing over a folded bill to Navos, who tucked it into his waistband.

"What was that?"

Navos ran a hand over his slicked-back blond hair, his grin revealing a gold tooth.

"He bet me they wouldn't make it. The Crows would take them before they got here."

Pandora gathered with the others along the edge of the tents. Daraja appeared in her ceremonial headdress, a relic of the early years of survival in the Undercity, with her Shadowmasters in tow.

Brazio Santos led the group into the cavern. She spotted Kuma and his friends in the first row behind his uncle. They looked stunned by their change in fortunes.

When Brazio reached Daraja, he snapped to attention and bent at the waist until his head nearly touched the ground. The rest of Razor matched his bow, though none as deeply as him. They stayed in their position as Daraja looked over them.

"Welcome to the darkness, the place the light forgot, where the canyons harbor terrors and the stones do not forgive. Do you renounce your former oaths, forsake your allegiances, and swear yourselves to the Drops? Do you agree to protect each other, both your old and new clanmates, with your lives? Do you agree to this with all your heart, knowing that the shadows will rise up and claim your souls should you break your oaths?"

Brazio lifted his head and spoke in a loud voice. "I agree."

The rest of his former clan lifted their heads and in a thundering collective voice said, "We agree."

"Then rise and be welcome. For the shadows do not care, but we do. We are your hearth and home, the blade that will not bend, the fist that will protect you."

A cheer went up after she finished. Pandora almost forgot to add her voice since she'd only experienced the ceremony a few times, including her own. When it was finished, Daraja slipped off the headdress and handed it to a young girl, then she moved forward and embraced Brazio. She spoke quietly in his ear before moving on to the next. As Daraja greeted each of the former Razor members, Pandora felt a tension in her chest give way.

She caught Kuma's eye briefly across the cavern. Nothing more than the spark of recognition, but then he was speaking with Daraja, leaving Pandora to mull over her feelings. She desired to reunite with him. From the moment of their first meeting, to the time they spent together in the canyon of ghosts, she'd felt his inexplicable draw, like two magnets pulling towards each other. There was too much going on for her to speak to him now, but later, once the dust had settled, they were sure to speak in the halls of the Academy.

Pandora caught Choo-Choo growling under his breath, his gaze finding the same target as her. He ground his teeth, driving the spike into the earth. The events of the last few days had brought them together under the same clan banner. She didn't know how easily the two groups would integrate, but if they could, then maybe they had a chance against her grandfather's organization. Their enemies might have the numbers and a level of financial backing that far exceeded the Drops', but they knew the shadows, they had the stones, and they knew how to use them better than anyone else. And Pandora knew their enemies better than most.

War was coming.

Forty-One

Niran was led into a room to the sounds of a knife and fork scraping against a plate and the noisy smacking of lips. He felt the sun on his back and knew he was in a high place. The elevator ride had been long.

After he was seated, the blindfold was removed, revealing Gregor enjoying a steak dinner at a long table with no one else. Niran checked behind him to see the glint of windows from the Spire, the tallest building in the city, reflecting the afternoon sun. He was somewhere in the first ward.

"I know you want to ask the question," said Gregor, greedily shoving another bite into his mouth. The plate had a small lake of pink blood that had leaked out of the near-rare steak.

"And what question is that?" asked Niran simply.

"Why I did it," said Gregor around the bloody meat in his mouth.

"It won't be a particularly interesting answer," said Niran drolly.

Gregor slammed his fist on the table, rattling the plate and his glass of red wine.

"It was your fucking arrogance," said Gregor, spittle flying from his lips. "Your fucking stones, your honor, your *waku*." He made a gesture. "You never saw me as a threat. I aimed to teach you a lesson."

Niran examined the entirety of the dining room: the exquisite cabinetry, the heavy marble table, even the height of the room in comparison to the other skyscrapers. He smoothed the coarse hairs of his white goatee that had grown messy during his transport.

"This isn't your home. This is your master's place. Don't tell me you made any decision on your own because we both know that isn't true. You're merely a servant, easily discarded when you're no longer useful."

Gregor pointed the steak knife at him. "I'll cut your fucking heart out."

A sliding door at the end of the room revealed darkness. Niran's heart grew cold even before he saw who was about to step out. It was the same feeling one got in the deepest places of the Undercity, staring into the shadows, wondering what sort of danger they were hiding.

The man—no, maetrie—that stepped into the room looked like he'd come from a corporate board meeting. He smiled, a parting of his thin lips that could wilt a flower at a hundred paces. The chalky-gray skin and gaunt cheeks gave him a haunted quality.

"Do not dare to insult my guests, Gregor," said the maetrie as he strode around the table to stand at the leader of the Crows' side. He placed a hand on his shoulder. "Apologize."

Gregor bristled, his hands squeezing to fists around his utensils until a second figure stepped into the room. A hulking maetrie in body armor. His appearance broke the standoff, leaving Gregor's chin drifting towards his chest.

"My apologies, Niran. I guess my blood still burns from the fight. I shouldn't have spoken out of turn."

"Thank you, Gregor."

The well-dressed maetrie circled the table until he took a spot next to Niran. The maetrie's dizzying presence made it hard to gather his thoughts. It wasn't the first time he'd met a city fae, but his aura was more powerful than any other.

"Niran Santos. My name is Dominion Thule."

Dominion held out his hand, which Niran shook. His skin was cool and his breath smelled like coal smoke.

"It was not my intention to reveal myself this early, but recent events have required it. As we speak, my representatives are putting the final touches on my relationship with the clans you know as the Alliance.

Soon enough those scattered allegiances will no longer exist. They will come together under a single banner. My banner. And along with the might of the Crows, we will crush the feeble resistance that is now in the hands of the Drops alone.

"Oh, yes, you're not aware, but you no longer have a clan, Niran Santos. They left everything and ran with tail tucked to pledge their oaths to Daraja. You're a man without a clan."

"I would have done the same in their place," he said.

Dominion rose and started circling the table again. He moved like a shark, without blinking, the ever-present danger evident in his smallish frame.

"You might be wondering why you're still alive. It's certainly not so Gregor has a chance to gloat for the petty slights he's endured. As you can well guess, it is my intention to take control of the Undercity and make the faez crystals the focus of my organization. These little wars you've been having. Scraps, you call them. They've interfered with the commerce of trade.

"The rest of the world is still reeling with the aftereffects of the Invasion. The Hundred Halls are coming to grips with their loss of power and the mistrust they now enjoy because of their mistakes. Replacing their head patron did nothing to assuage those fears. Rival schools are popping up across the world. They're so busy seeing the external threats they do not see the gold mine beneath their very noses."

Dominion stopped across from Niran. The city fae steepled his fingers on the table. The smirk on his lips felt like salt in a paper cut.

"What do you want from me?"

"Simply everything. Any kernel of knowledge you have in that head of yours. Which stones each of your waku wear, the locations of your mines, anything you know about the Drops. I know you, Niran Santos. You are a man of keen intelligence, of meticulous planning, and brutal execution. I've been admiring you from afar for quite some time."

"And I know nothing of you."

Dominion straightened. "This city has been my home for a long time. I see what my arrogant brethren do not. They do not think much of this world, seeing it as the failed enterprise of humans. They're blinded by their own views that the Eternal City is the pinnacle of existence and that our kind are so far above humans that it would be an insult to ourselves to even consider them a threat.

"But I see you for what you are. Opportunity. Properly molded and motivated, you can become a force unto yourself. Consolidating the Undercity under my control will be the first step."

The second maetrie, the one wearing body armor and an array of military-grade weaponry, circled around the table to take a position a few feet behind Niran.

"And if I don't?"

"Titus will cut your flesh away, bit by bit, until there's only enough left to speak the words I want to here."

Niran nodded slowly. He knew the position he was in. As leader of the clan, he wasn't surprised by this end. He'd hoped to delay it, push it back to days beyond the horizon, while getting to watch his son grow up and become the great waku he always knew he could be.

But the Undercity was unforgiving, and he'd made too many mistakes in leading the clan. He let the clan's precarious position blind him to the dangers that the Black Crows presented. From the first meeting with Gregor, he should have known that he would be betrayed. The man had no honor.

He wished there was another way. That he could see Kuma one last time before his end.

"I will tell you everything you need to know. There is no need to torture me. But I ask a small favor in return."

Dominion pursed his lips.

"You may ask."

Niran relaxed his entire body. His ruse wouldn't work if they saw even the hint of defiance. The maetrie mercenary, Titus Cabone, could likely move like a viper.

And though Niran had never wielded a stone or received the title of waku, he was a warrior. He'd trained his entire life to scrap. To make war under the most brutal of circumstances.

"I offer my absolute obedience in return for Gregor's right ear."

The proclamation brought teased chaos from the calm. Gregor released his knife, reaching for his ear as if to protect it from his maetrie master. Dominion responded, first glancing to Gregor and then, sensing what was about to happen, turning back to Niran.

The last member of Razor clan kicked out his chair, throwing himself across the table. He snatched the blade from where Gregor had dropped it, then spun it around towards his chest, driving it deep into his own heart before anyone could stop him.

"I thwart you."

The words left his lips in a whisper as the world dimmed. Shouts of alarm filled his ears, a pleasing funeral song as he slipped into the shadows of eternity.

§ § §

Continue Kuma and Pandora's adventure in Book Three of The Crystal Halls series

The Sapphire Stratagem

OTHER BOOKS BY THOMAS K. CARPENTER

The Hundred Halls Universe

SEASON ONE

THE HUNDRED HALLS

Trials of Magic

Web of Lies

Alchemy of Souls

Gathering of Shadows

City of Sorcery

THE RELUCTANT ASSASSIN

The Reluctant Assassin

The Sorcerous Spy

The Veiled Diplomat

Agent Unraveled

The Webs That Bind

GAMEMAKERS ONLINE

The Warped Forest

Gladiators of Warsong

Citadel of Broken Dreams

Enter the Daemonpits

Plane of Twilight

ANIMALIANS HALL

Wild Magic

Bane of the Hunter

Mark of the Phoenix

Arcane Mutations

Untamed Destiny

STONE SINGERS HALL

Song of Siren and Blood

House of Snake and Tome

Storm of Dragon and Stone

Sonata of Shadow and Thorn

Well of Demon and Bone

THE ORDER OF MERLIN

The Order of Merlin

Infernal Alliances

Tower of Horn and Blood

ABOUT THE AUTHOR

Thomas K. Carpenter resides in Colorado with his wife Rachel. When he's not busy writing his next book, he's hiking, skiing, and getting beat by his wife at cards. He keeps a regular blog at www.thomaskcarpenter.com and you can follow him on twitter @thomaskcarpente. If you want to learn when his next novel will be hitting the shelves and get free stories and occasional other goodies, please sign up for his mailing list by going to: http://tinyurl.com/thomaskcarpenter. Your email address will never be shared and you can unsubscribe at any time.

www.ingramcontent.com/pod-product-compliance
Lightning Source LLC
Chambersburg PA
CBHW030822310726
48980CB00006B/591/J

* 9 7 8 1 9 5 8 4 9 8 1 9 4 *